Las Vegas Crime

LESLIE WOLFE

ITALICS PUBLISHING

Italics Publishing Inc.

Cover and interior design by Sam Roman

Edited by: Joni Wilson, Susan Barnes

ISBN: 1-945302-24-0

ISBN-13: 978-1-945302-24-4

Acknowledgments

A special thank you to my New York legal eagle and friend, Mark Freyberg, who expertly guided this author through the intricacies of the judicial system.

LESLIE WOLFE

1

Silent Screams

She struggled to control her sobs but failed miserably. With every mile the man drove into the dark desert, her fear grew, panic overtaking her sense of reason, making it impossible for her to sit still and be quiet like the man had ordered.

"No, please," she whimpered, "I'll disappear. I won't say a word to anyone. I swear," she added in a high-pitched plea, her voice trembling badly.

She stared through a blur of tears at the man's intense eyes, reflected in the rearview mirror. He rarely looked at her, not even when he spoke to her, but when he did, his eyes were ice cold, feral.

She couldn't tell how long they'd been on the road, or how far away from the city they'd traveled. Far enough for darkness to engulf the dazzling lights of Las Vegas, left behind at their brightest and now gone from view. Far enough to know that no matter how loud she'd scream, no one would hear her desperate cries for help. She sat silently, petrified, unable to fight anymore, knowing what Homeboy did to those who disobeyed him.

They had entered the desolate vastness of the Mojave Desert, cold and bleak at night.

Her breath shattered as raw memories swirled in her head, repeating over and over like a broken record.

"Get rid of her," that terrible man had said, "this bitch ain't good for nothin'." The one they called Snowman had curled his lip in disgust and ran his fingers across his throat in a clear gesture, sealing her fate.

She was to be killed.

She remembered how her knees gave and she folded onto the cold, grimy floor, half-naked and barefoot, shaking, sobbing uncontrollably, while the other man, a brute she got to know only as Homeboy, smiled and licked his lips. Then he'd grabbed her arm and dragged her out of that place, mumbling, "Sure, boss, whatever you say."

She'd seen that look on Homeboy's face before.

Maybe she was better off dead than having that animal's hands on her again. Her body still ached from the hours she'd endured at his pleasure. The thought of peace soon to be found, even if in death, calmed her taut nerves. Soon she'd be free, one way or another.

No one dared defy Snowman's orders.

Her mind wandered, numb and absent for a while, as Homeboy drove fast into the night, mile after mile, without saying a word.

A slight chime came from the GPS and he braked, although there was no intersecting road crossing the highway, no available turn to take, just desert dunes, covered in shrubs and cacti, and trolled by scorpions, snakes, and coyotes.

He turned off-road and drove carefully into the desert, climbing over a hill then descending behind it. He didn't immediately stop; he kept on going, putting more and more distance between them and the road, eliminating any chances that someone could see her, could hear her screams.

She felt her heart thumping against her chest, the sound of its terrified beats deafening against the deathly silence of the desert. Fresh tears started rolling down her cheeks and her pleas were left unanswered.

She gasped when he cut the engine, bringing the SUV to a stop. Trembling, she didn't fight back when he grabbed her arm and pulled her out of the vehicle.

"Please," she mumbled, "I'll do whatever you want. Please let me go."

"Can't do that," he replied, his lips stretched in an evil smile that exposed crooked, yellow teeth. "You heard the boss man."

He let go of her arm and reached inside his pocket. Panicked, she bolted in a desperate attempt to save herself. She ran toward the highway, now hidden behind a hill, not feeling the cactus thorns tearing at her flesh, not minding the sharp edges of the desert stones bloodying the soles of her feet.

She'd run a few yards and he hadn't caught up with her yet; hope gave her wings, and she sprung uphill clawing at the stones with her bare hands, desperate to put more distance between the two of them.

She was almost at the top of the hill when his steeled grip bore into her arm, stopping her in place so abruptly that her bleeding feet sent pebbles and sand in the air. Angered, he dragged her back to the SUV and slammed her against the cold metal.

"Nice try, bitch. There's nowhere to go."

She was starting to understand that, to accept it, although every fiber in her body screamed its fear, urged her to fight, to run, to survive. She drew breath hastily and let out a blood-curdling shriek.

Homeboy laughed. "Sure, go ahead, scream. You're giving me a hard-on."

Her scream died, stifled by a sob.

He dug into his pocket and pulled out a small bottle fitted with an eyedropper. With a lewd, sickening smile, he took his time unscrewing the cap and carefully extracted two drops of the clear liquid. Then he grabbed her jaw and forced her lips open.

"No, no," she whimpered, fighting desperately to free herself.

Homeboy just smirked, ignoring her feeble kicks, and squeezed the eyedropper, releasing the liquid into her mouth. Then he held her lips sealed under his heavy hand, forcing her to swallow.

She couldn't detect any strange taste; he'd barely used a drop or two. It couldn't be too bad, she thought, gasping desperately for air as soon as he released his grip.

She felt her tongue becoming numb, then her lips. Panic opened her eyes widely and made her lungs scream for more air. She gasped, feeling an evil numbness taking over her body, reaching her extremities, weakening her knees. A strange sense of dizziness overtook her, making her reach for support, finding none until her body hit the ground. No matter how much she willed herself to move, she lay still on the cold desert dirt, feeling every stab of pain where sharp-edged rocks cut into her flesh.

Homeboy crouched near her body with a satisfied grin. He pushed aside a few locks of her hair, clearing her face, touching her frozen lips.

"You won't die," he said, while his hand fumbled with his belt buckle. "Not now, anyway. Not until I'm bored with you."

She forced her lungs to draw air and screamed, then drew another raspy breath and screamed again.

She listened but couldn't hear her own screams. The desert was completely silent, except for the brute's rhythmic grunts.

2

Gone

They sat in the unmarked Crown Vic, watching the last of the kids rush inside, after harried drivers dropped them off at the curb. It was almost eight-thirty, but some parents had a terrible sense of timing; by now, the first period had already started, and traffic should've been nonexistent in the drop-off lane.

"Let's do this," the man behind the wheel said, arranging his uniform and checking himself briefly in the rearview mirror. His name tag read, "Beasley," and the patch affixed to his uniform bore the insignia of North Las Vegas Police Department. "The job isn't going to get any easier if we wait."

"Yeah, yeah, all right, hold your skivvies, will you?" his partner, with a name tag of Greer, replied, then got out of the Crown Vic, groaning. He arranged his tactical duty belt and put his cap on, walking quickly toward the school entrance, not bothering to wait for Beasley to catch up.

They entered through the main gate, underneath a glass banner with the words, "Western Warriors" written in bold lettering. The security officer posted at the doors let them right through, but they didn't stop to ask for directions; they kept on walking.

"This place gives me the creeps, man," said Beasley. "I'd rather do serious time than go back to school. No, scratch that, I'd rather be *shot* like a rabid dog, than do one more day of school."

The two men laughed, and the resounding echo of their laughter caught the attention of a sternly dressed woman in her fifties, carrying a stack of papers and walking quickly toward one of the classrooms.

"Can I help you, officers?" she asked, forcing herself to try to smile and failing.

The two men immediately stopped laughing. Beasley cleared his throat, uncomfortable with being caught laughing, when he was about to break some bad news, and said, "We're here to pick up the daughter of one of our detectives."

The woman frowned.

"We require parental approval—"

"He's been shot in the line of duty, ma'am," Beasley replied quickly.

The woman gasped. "Oh, my goodness… I'm so sorry. Is he, um, going to be all right?"

"Yes," the second man replied, while at the same time, Beasley said, "They don't know yet; it's too soon."

The two cops glared at each other for a moment, but the woman didn't seem to notice. She kept staring into nothingness, her hand clasping her gaped mouth.

"Ma'am?" Beasley asked.

She turned toward him as in a trance. "I'm assuming you're talking about Meredith Holt, right?"

Both men nodded.

"Yes, ma'am," Beasley confirmed.

"Such a shame," the woman continued. "Detective Holt is such a nice man." She looked at them for a long moment, then said, "You'll have to sign her out at the office."

"Ma'am, with all due respect," Beasley said, "time is of the essence here. Last thing we want is for Meredith to get there too late."

She hesitated, then said, "Okay, follow me; I'll take you to her."

They walked down seemingly endless corridors filled with the smell of heated sneakers, disinfectant, and too many strange odors, while the woman never stopped talking, not for a single moment. Not even to draw breath.

"This city is falling apart, if you ask me," she said. "A nice man like Detective Holt—to be shot… that isn't right. That shouldn't happen. Where did, um, where did he get shot?"

Beasley looked at Greer before answering, "In the abdomen. It's serious." Thankfully, Greer had learned his lesson and kept his mouth shut.

After what seemed like an eternity of walking through a maze of cement-floored corridors, the woman stopped in front of a classroom and opened the door. She turned to the two men and said, "Please, wait here."

She went inside, and they heard her say, "Meredith, please come with me, dearie."

When the girl stepped outside the classroom, the men could tell she was confused and a little worried. Beasley was the one who broke the news to her. Before he could finish speaking, the girl had grabbed his forearm and begged, "Please, take me to him." She was acting brave, but her lips quivered.

They thanked the woman and left, rushing toward the school's exit. Falling a step behind, Beasley looked at the girl with a smirk on his face; she had a nice, round butt for a fifteen-year-old. She showed promise; a couple of months with the right trainers and she'd be topnotch booty. Not to mention, she was the daughter of a cop—one of the meanest, most annoying pigs he'd ever crossed paths with. He'd lost three long years of his life because that piece-of-absolute scum, waste-of-skin Jack Holt wouldn't cut him some slack when he'd caught Beasley selling a little bit of dope, just to make ends meet.

Today was payback for all the long days he'd spent caged like an animal.

He'd gladly taken the job to snatch Holt's daughter; he'd volunteered, and he didn't even think of negotiating the fee. He would've done it for free, just to put that pig's little bitch in Snowman's hands and then, when the time was right, to find Holt and laugh in his face, say something like Bruce Willis would've said. "Yippee ki-yay, motherfucker, it was me, and now we're even. You're never going to see your little girl again."

The girl stopped a few yards short of the exit and turned around so quickly that Beasley barely had time to wipe the smirk off his face.

"Where's my mom? I have to call my mom," she said, as she started digging through her backpack for her phone.

"She's already on her way to the hospital," Beasley said, frowning.

How did they not realize the kid came equipped with a cell phone and she was going to use it?

He grabbed her hand and somberly looked her in the eye. "We'll get you there in ten minutes, you'll see. We'll turn on the sirens and all. Your mom is probably already there with your dad, and they don't allow phones in hospitals, so she wouldn't get your call. You know that, right?"

The girl nodded. She wore a spiky dog collar around her neck and dark eyeliner, and her long hair, almost raven black, covered one of her eyes completely. She was trying to pass for a Goth, but she wasn't there all the way.

To see where she was going, she occasionally ran her hand through rebellious locks and tucked them behind her ear. Yeah, Beasley could see she needed some work, but her small, firm breasts and her full lips were promising, and she had fire in her eyes. Now, with her eyeliner running down her cheeks, she didn't look like much, but Beasley still felt a twitch below his belt.

When they reached the car, he held the back door open for her and refrained from putting his hand on her head to prevent her from hitting the doorframe, like he'd experienced firsthand when he'd been arrested. He'd seen that so many times in the movies he was dying to do it, to be the pig for a change, the one who got to force people's heads down. He would've loved to force that girl's head down… all the way down.

"Let me take that," he offered, extending his hand for the girl's backpack.

She hesitated a moment, then let go of the straps and watched Beasley put it in the trunk of the Crown Vic.

Beasley slammed the car door shut, making sure the girl was now locked inside, behind bars, without possibility of escape. Satisfied, he climbed behind the wheel and started the engine. Cautious, he looked left, then right, before entering traffic and they drove in silence for a while, heading north. He didn't turn on the lights nor the siren; the last thing they needed was to draw any unwanted attention.

"Hey," the girl said, sniffling and panting, grabbing the wire mesh that separated the back from the front, "where are you going? UMC Trauma Center is south of here. That's where they take all the wounded cops."

The two men looked at each other, smiling widely.

"Shut your piehole, bitch," Greer said, slamming his palm against the wire screen.

She flinched, but quickly recovered. "Hey," she shouted, "let me go!" She grabbed the wire mesh with both her hands, sliding her fingers through the holes and rattling it with all her might. "Hey!"

They laughed louder, ignoring her. When she turned sideways and started screaming for help, banging against the barred window, Beasley took out his phone and handed it to his partner.

"Here, you break the good news to the boss. Tell him we've got the cop's girl and we're coming in." He licked his lips and added, "Tell him he'll like her; she's feisty."

Stunned, Meredith stopped shouting while pallor discolored her features. She looked at the two men, slowly taking in the details she'd missed before. Their two uniforms bore different precinct insignias. There was a thick layer of dust on the car's dashboard. The driver's duty belt didn't have any gear inside its many pockets; only the gun holster wasn't empty.

Then she seemed to realize what had happened to her.

She'd been kidnapped.

3

The Call

Sunlight pierced my heavy eyelids and dissolved the lingering slumber with merciless rays making their way through a sliver of exposed window, where the two curtain panels didn't overlap. Refusing to open my eyes, I stretched lazily, remembering I had the day off, and that meant I got to sleep in for a while longer. With a smile and a satisfied groan, I tried to turn on my side but couldn't. My hair was caught under Holt's torso, and now that I'd regained some consciousness, I could sense his leg was thrown over mine, while his arm rested on my stomach.

Bollocks.

I opened my eyes, welcoming the sobering sunlight and cringed at the sight. Scattered clothing littered my bedroom floor. His tie dangled from the doorknob, and my panties put a splash of luscious red against the dark fabric of his slacks. His weapon holster hung on the back of a chair, while mine was on the carpet, next to the night table. The sweaty bedsheets were a mess, bearing statement of the heated encounter I preferred not to recall. Our naked bodies lay entangled and relaxed in unequivocal testimony of what had transpired last night.

I'd shagged my partner.

Again.

Unbelievable.

I repressed a sigh loaded with self-directed frustration and proceeded to pull my hair from underneath his body, gently, unwilling to awaken him, unable to face him yet. How was I supposed to tell him this had been a mistake and it could never ever happen again, when I'd said all that before and then last night it happened?

I wiggled away from him, feeling a pang of regret at the thought of putting distance between our two naked bodies. He'd made me feel alive again, bringing my weary, frozen heart back from the land of grief and silence. He'd made me laugh for the first time since my husband was killed. For that, I was grateful, but also a little saddened, remembering how I'd tucked Andrew's framed photo inside the sock drawer, unable to stand seeing his smiling face looking at me while another man held me in his arms, without feeling guilty and ashamed as if he were still alive and I were cheating on him.

I was badly messed up, and I kept on making mistake after bloody mistake, messing everything up a little more every bloody time.

Get a grip already, you prat, I admonished myself, finally breaking free from Holt's asleep embrace.

Tiptoeing quickly, I grabbed a bathrobe from the closet and tied the sash around my waist with a rushed gesture, then grabbed my phone, ready to leave the room. From the bedroom doorway, I stopped and looked at Holt's body one more time, enjoying the sight of him a moment longer when he didn't know what I was doing, when he couldn't see me.

Smiling, I let my eyes wander, and memories of last night came crashing in. How we'd hurried home from the restaurant, driven by an urgency we'd never felt before. How he'd slammed the door shut after we entered the house and didn't even bother to turn on the light. How we felt for each other in the dark, touching, kissing, wanting, needing.

A familiar feeling unfurled in my abdomen, bringing a rush of blood to my cheeks and warmth through my entire body. No longer eager to disappear, I weighed for a moment the option to slip back into his arms and let him wake next to me, while my eyes took in the sight of his broad shoulders and firm buttocks. Yeah, my partner had a nice, tight arse, and that was part of my problem.

What was it with women and their fascination with men's arses, anyway?

When his phone rang, I started, almost ready to run, as if I'd been caught doing something terrible. But I remained in place, steadying myself, prepared to face him and say the two words I hadn't spoken in my bedroom for almost two years.

"Good morning," I offered, while he grunted and turned on his left side to reach for the offending phone.

"Getting ready to run off on me, Baxter? So soon?" he mumbled, but then his smile disappeared when he read the name on the caller ID. He sat up on the edge of the bed and took the call with tense shoulders and a growing frown.

"Yes," he said into the phone, his voice cold, almost argumentative, but also defensive. "No, I'm fine. What happened?"

He listened to the caller intently, his body language conveying his escalating angst. He fidgeted in place, probably unwilling to pace the room naked while I was there. Curious, I stayed put, watching the exchange attentively. My partner rarely lost his cool, if ever. The person on the other end of the line must've had one hell of a grip on him.

"Don't move; don't go anywhere; don't talk to anybody; I'm on my way." He ended the call and threw the phone on the bed, then picked his clothes from the floor and started putting them on in a rush.

"What happened?" I asked, touching his arm.

He turned and looked at me; for a second, I didn't recognize him. I'd never seen fear in his eyes until that moment. Deep, all-consuming fear, the type that changes one's life forever, its memory impossible to erase.

"They got my kid, Baxter. Bastards took my kid."

There it was… a cold shower when I least needed one. Before even processing the seriousness of what had happened, before I could start thinking like a cop, I felt the sharp bite of jealousy, of my own personal brand of fear.

"You've got a kid?" I firmly propped my hands on my hips and stepped into his path, searching his eyes. "Tell me you have a wife, and I'll shoot you right where you stand."

"Ex-wife; that was her on the phone," he replied, tucking his shirt into his pants as quickly as he could.

I breathed. "What happened?"

He shook his head while snapping his holster in place. "Something happened at the school. My ex said they told my daughter that I was in the hospital. No one bothered to follow the damn protocol."

I felt a chill traveling up my spine, sending goosebumps all over my body.

"Oh, no," I whispered.

"Apparently, two cops showed up and took my daughter, saying I'd been shot on duty. People see cops in uniform and they turn into complete morons; they don't think to question anything, to make a phone call and ask."

"When did they take her?"

"Almost three hours ago."

That was really bad news. The first few, critical hours after the abduction had come and gone, wasted.

I released the bathrobe knot and untangled the sash with trembling fingers, then I let the robe fall at my feet while I put on a fresh set of clothes, moving as fast as I could. I slid my holster on the inside of my belt, then bent over to fit my ankle weapon in place, while Holt found his keys and ran downstairs, taking two steps at a time.

From the living room, he shouted, "Will you be all right?"

"Sure, I will," I replied, catching up with him, my hair undone, makeup smeared from last night. "I'm coming with you."

"No, you're not, Baxter," he said, gently pushing me aside. "I'll handle this on my own."

"Don't be an idiot, Holt," I replied, grabbing my wallet and keys. "I'm a cop and a bloody good one. Last time I checked, that's the kind of help you need in a kidnapping case."

"I want to keep this on the DL, Baxter. I can't have the entire Las Vegas Metro Police Department kicking in doors and putting my daughter's life at risk."

"And, what, I can't be trusted to keep my mouth shut? Really?"

Frustrated, he threw his arms in the air. "I didn't mean it like that, all right?"

He was distraught to the point where he didn't know what he meant anymore. He deserved some slack, and his kid deserved his focus. "I know you didn't. But you know what needs to happen, right?"

"What?" he asked from the doorway, squeezing his car keys in his hand, ready to bolt.

"We need to talk to people, look at traffic cams, interview teachers and colleagues, the whole nine yards. We need help."

I picked up my shoes and slammed the door behind me, running barefoot toward his black SUV. By the time I climbed into the passenger seat, the Ford's engine was revving angrily under his foot.

"Yeah, I know," he said in a dour tone of voice. "Buckle up."

He sped off in a cloud of burnt rubber smoke, then turned on the siren and the flashing lights the moment we hit traffic.

I looked at him, part of me still angry because he'd never mentioned he had a family. He'd grilled me for being secretive about my former life, about Andrew and my friendship with Anne St. Clair, while at the same time he'd conveniently forgotten to mention a kid and an ex-wife. I felt like saying a few things about that but realized it wasn't the time or the place. One glance at his clenched jaws and the ridges running across his forehead, at the white knuckles holding the steering wheel, and I started feeling his pain, his rage, his fear.

I reached out and touched his elbow, gently.

"We'll find her, Holt," I said quietly, wondering if he'd heard me over the blaring siren.

He turned my way briefly and nodded once, his way of thanking me.

"What's her name?" I asked.

His jaws tensed even more. "Meredith. My daughter's name is Meredith. She's fifteen years old."

4

The Ex

Four hours missing

The drive to Holt's ex-wife's house was short and tense. Holt didn't say anything else, while I kept going over scenarios in my head, something gnawing at me relentlessly. My mind stubbornly fixated on a case I'd worked on in London, the kidnapping of a superintendent's four-year-old son.

It was during my first year as a police inspector, the youngest one in London's recent history. Proud of my recent promotion, I tried my best to ignore the condescending comments that swirled around me like flurries of frozen antipathy. That I'd slept my way into the job. That I wasn't worth my salt. That I wasn't going to last long.

I knew I had to prove myself again and again before anyone could begin to trust me and I was painfully aware of what most of my colleagues said about me. That's why I was surprised to be named lead in the case of the kidnapped superintendent's child, a freckled, red-haired boy named Joshua O'Reilly. I remembered feeling both elated by the opportunity to work a high-profile case and being set up to fail, probably by some of those who didn't believe I belonged and wanted me to be unsuccessful.

It was at the height of the pedophile priests' scandal, and nowhere else did that disgrace leave a more horrifying mark than in the tight ranks of London's stiff-upper-lipped Christians, shocked with the unraveling stain of shame that had touched their very souls. Consequently, everyone looked at the missing boy's church and priest, searching for answers, harassing the clergy and the churchgoers, throwing stones at the once-revered establishment's stained-glass windows.

My gut disagreed.

Under the worried supervision of New Scotland Yard, I explored a different avenue, looking into the long list of cons, gangsters, rapists, and thieves the superintendent had locked up during his career. I strongly believed that revenge could've been the motivation behind the kidnapping.

I talked to dozens of suspects, checked countless alibis, and desperately waited for the ransom call that didn't come, while everyone's modicum of confidence in my ability to find the boy was quickly dissipating. Then, one day, not a moment too soon, I hit the jackpot. I found the kidnapper. It wasn't a felon the superintendent had locked away; it was one's mother, an old, half-crazed bat. She'd taken the boy just to make the parents suffer like she had when she lost her son to a lifelong sentence for raping and killing the teenage girl who lived next door. Thankfully, the woman had fed the child and kept him reasonably well-cared for during the five, endless days she'd had him.

But that was London, a lifetime ago; even kidnappers had morals. Now we were in a different world, one infinitely more aggressive, merciless, and crime-savvy. One where a cop didn't know what to expect, only what to hope for.

I was about to ask Holt to start looking at the people he'd put behind bars when he stopped abruptly in front of an elegant, three-car-garage home south of Charleston Boulevard and east of Jones Boulevard. The moment he pulled up at the curb, the front door swung open and a woman rushed out but froze in place when she saw me.

She'd been crying; her eyes were red and swollen. She ran her hands quickly across her face to wipe away the tears and threw me a piercing glare that I found difficult to explain under the circumstances. But maybe she wasn't thinking straight.

I pulled aside my jacket flap and exposed my badge.

"Detective Baxter," I introduced myself. "I work with—"

"You had to bring her here, Jack? To my house?" she interrupted, throwing Holt an angry glare. "You couldn't spare a moment with me, as Meredith's father, without her here?"

She made repetitive, dismissive gestures toward me while she talked but I stood firmly, waiting for her to finish unloading her anger so we could get some information and start looking for Meredith. Holt seemed to do the same, because he raised his hands in a pacifying gesture.

"Jennifer, be reasonable," he said, but she was quick to cut him off.

"Did you screw her too?" she asked bluntly, while my jaw dropped.

Exasperated, Holt ran his hands through his raven-black hair. "Come on, let's not do this now," he pleaded, but she didn't relent.

"Have the balls to admit it, at least," she added, crossing her arms at her chest.

He straightened his back and shot me a quick, apologetic glance. "Our daughter is missing, and that's the only reason I'm here. If you want to talk about that, I'll listen. If not, we're leaving. My priority is finding Meredith."

Jennifer broke into tears again, her anger gone, replaced by maternal despair. "Who took her, Jack?"

He approached her and led her inside, while I followed, bothered by an annoying question. How did she know we'd been sleeping together? Was it written on my forehead or something? I didn't care as much about her as I did about the people we worked with. Our boss, Captain Morales, would be quick to rip us apart for breaking the nonfraternization rule. The Internal Affairs bitch, Lieutenant Steenstra, was after Holt for a missing kilo of cocaine that had vanished during a bust and would love a good reason to throw me under the bus for covering for him. The other detectives in the squad weren't stupid; soon enough they'd figure things out.

We couldn't afford the tiniest wisp of gossip floating around about our private lives, Holt and I, when both our careers were hanging by a thread. He had the IAB's suspicions weighing over his head like his own personal, custom-designed storm cloud, and I had an excessive force report on my record, complete with a disciplinary reduction in pay and twelve-months' probation. I'd put a suspect in the hospital after interrogating him, and no one had given a shite that I had my reasons to lose it on him.

I closed the door gently behind me and remained standing in the hallway, giving the two former spouses some space. Holt had managed to get his ex-wife seated on the couch, while he sat in the armchair next to her, barely touching the edge of the seat.

"Walk me through what happened," he said.

"This happened," she said, pointing at a flower arrangement in a clear vase, the type that is delivered by florists with an hour's notice.

Holt walked to the dining table and picked up the card, then started reading it with a growing frown.

"Nothing is impossible. Our thoughts and prayers are with you during these trying times. We are grateful for your husband's heroism in the line of duty," Holt read quietly, rushing through the text as if it annoyed him by being too long. *"Yadda, yadda,* signed, *Western High School."* He let the card drop on the table. "And? You called them?"

The woman scoffed as if accused of being a complete idiot. "Of course, I did, right away. They told me two officers had shown up to get Meredith and take her to the hospital because you'd been shot. They told Meredith I was already with you at the hospital, that I couldn't be reached, and that you were in surgery."

"Then?"

"I called you," she replied, her voice riddled with sad, tired undertones as if telling the story had taken all her strength.

"All right," Holt said, walking toward her and crouching in front of her to meet her eyes. "We'll start talking to people, pick up her trail. Don't say a word to anyone, not even the police. Until we know who took her and what they want, that's probably the smartest way to go."

"It's probably that stupid job of yours, Jack," she pushed back. "One of the lowlifes you locked up took her to get back at you, and you're telling me you're too proud to ask the rest of the cops to look for my baby? Are you crazy?"

With every word, her voice rose a little, ending in a high-pitched scream filled with tearful resentment.

Holt plunged his hands into his pockets and sighed.

"If I may?" I intervened. "The kidnappers didn't plan for the flowers."

Both of them turned and looked at me inquisitively.

"They took her this morning, and they didn't expect either of you to become aware of her disappearance until the afternoon, correct? When school lets out?"

Holt nodded, while his ex mumbled something, avoiding my glance.

"That gives us the possibility to take them by surprise. I suggest we use that edge, and fast."

"Fine," she spat the word, "if *she*'s calling the shots and you're okay with it, I'll shut up." She stood, and Holt stood with her. She grabbed his forearm with both her hands as fresh tears flooded her eyes. "It's our little girl, Jack; don't you forget that. Find her and bring her home, you hear?"

I didn't breathe until we were back in the car. We'd wasted another twenty minutes on the former Mrs. Holt's hysterical rants, but that had been a necessary step in the process. The last thing we needed was the phone calls she could make to half the precinct and the chaos that would immediately ensue.

Despite that logic, I also believed we needed help.

5

School

Six hours missing

I thought I'd seen the worst of Holt's driving, but I'd been wrong. By the time we pulled in front of Western High School, I was happy we weren't a mangled, fiery mess of contorted metal and broken bones.

Holt didn't bother to turn off the engine; he rushed through the front doors and flashed his badge, making the security officer at the entrance nod quickly, then look sideways, probably afraid to be caught in whatever backlash the kidnapping of a cop's daughter from school could bring upon him and everyone else there.

I had to bring my stride to a run to keep up with him; he knew exactly where he was going and didn't stop until he barged unannounced into the principal's office.

Seated behind the desk and pale as a specter was a middle-aged, bald man. He wasn't aging elegantly; his beard was splotched with patches of gray hair as if only certain sections of his facial hair had received the memo that he'd recently turned fifty. His jaw was slightly swollen on the left side, probably from some dental issue in the making. He nested that section of his jaw in the palm of his hand and looked miserable.

He wasn't alone in the office. Two women sat on adjacent chairs in front of his desk, holding hands. One of them, bulky and slightly unkempt in appearance, wore an unbuttoned, white lab coat over her floral-patterned dress. *The school nurse*, I thought. The other woman, who appeared younger, had almost curled up in a ball, hugging herself and rocking back and forth, the way people do when they are severely distraught. She must've been the person who'd signed off to Holt's daughter's release from school.

The principal stood up so quickly that his chair bounced back and hit the wall with a loud bang. The woman started sobbing and turned her face away from Holt, while the nurse also stood, shoulders hunched forward and head lowered, her quivering lips a foretelling sign of barely withheld tears.

"Detective," he said in a trembling voice, "I'm so sorry. Words cannot express," he added, wringing his hands. "I'm glad you're not, um, you haven't been shot, but I'm—"

"Never mind that," Holt cut him off, reaching the desk in three large steps and stopping only a couple of feet away from the two women. "Tell me what happened, step by step."

"We assure you, Detective, that we're aware we broke—"

Holt circled the desk with feline agility and grabbed the man's lapels. "Shut the hell up," he said, inches away from the man's face. Then he let him go, and the principal fell into his chair as if his legs had given away.

Holt turned to the two women, and I noticed how he tried to control his appearance, to project calm and reason and patience, when he was nothing but a desperate parent with a badge, terrifying the people who had the information we needed.

"Which of you spoke with them?" Holt asked, sounding surprisingly calm.

His apparent composure didn't fool anyone. The younger woman tried to speak, but the first sounds she made were choked. She cleared her throat and lifted her eyes to look at him.

"I swear I didn't know," she said, speaking barely above a whisper.

"I know you didn't," Holt reassured her. "Tell me everything you can remember."

"They were cops," she mumbled, but then quickly stopped and corrected herself. "They were dressed as cops. White, thirty years of age or so, one of them younger, maybe twenty-seven." She stopped and looked at Holt, waiting.

"Go on," he encouraged her. He leaned against the desk, his back turned to the principal, and directed all his attention to the woman. "What else do you remember?"

She licked her lips nervously. "Buzz cut hair, cleanly shaven, about your height. The younger one a couple of inches shorter."

I searched for a uniformed cop photo from our precinct in my phone's photo archives and showed it to her. "Did they look like this? Their uniforms?"

"I—I think so, yes," she replied, unconvinced.

"What was different?"

"I think the younger one had a different patch, here," she pointed with a thin, slightly trembling finger to the man's shoulder.

Holt and I exchanged a quick glance. Those patches showed which police department the cops belonged to. But we already suspected Meredith had been taken by fake cops. At first, I thought the information might've been relevant; on second thought, it wasn't really that much of a surprise.

"How about name tags?" I asked, pointing at the man in the photo. All uniformed cops wore gold, metallic name tags with their last names.

The teacher stared at the ceiling for a moment, trying to remember. Her eyes kept veering up and to the left, an involuntary movement when someone accesses the memory center of their brain.

She shook her head discouragedly and clenched her hands together, squeezing tightly. I could see her knuckles turning white, and I thought I heard a whimper.

Holt started saying something, but I cut him off. "What's your name?" I asked, as gently as I could.

"Dana," she replied. "Dana Garrett."

I acknowledged her answer with a tiny smile. "Are you a teacher, Dana?"

"Yes. I teach English," she replied, then exchanged a quick glance with the nurse.

I followed her lead. "How about you?"

"Charity Arnold, school nurse," the heavyset woman replied in a hoarse voice. She must've smoked two packs a day the bulk of her adult years, if I were to draw a conclusion based on the pitch of her voice and the color of her teeth. For a health professional, she didn't look or sound healthy at all.

I looked briefly at Holt and noticed he'd crossed his arms at his chest and was fuming. As they say in police training, slow is fast. I hoped he remembered that.

"Did you see the two men, Charity?"

The woman nodded twice, her thin, bleached hair settling in wispy strands on her shoulders.

I looked at Charity, then at Dana, and asked again, "Were they wearing name tags?"

The two women looked at each other, then nodded. "Y—yes, I believe so," Dana eventually replied.

"Let's try to remember those names," I asked encouragingly.

There was a slim chance the two uniforms had been stolen and finding out who they'd been stolen from could bring us closer to finding the two men who had worn them.

"One was Beasley," Charity announced, ending a long minute of conferring with Dana. "The other one read Greer. I remember that because I thought of my old neighbor, from when I used to live in Texas."

"Excellent, that's great," I replied, feigning an excitement I wasn't feeling. "Did they touch anything, a doorknob, maybe?"

"No," she replied, shaking her head vigorously. "I remember one of them opening the door with his elbow. I didn't think of it at the time, but now…" Her voice trailed off under the weight of her hindsight understanding of what had transpired. The two men had been careful not to leave any fingerprints.

"What else did they say? Did you ask them anything?" I added, turning toward Dana.

She fidgeted in place, then reached for the water bottle she'd placed on the principal's desk but decided to refrain from drinking. Her hand settled nervously in her lap. "I asked them where you'd been shot," she said, casting a side glance at Holt then quickly lowering her eyes. "They said the abdomen, and that it was serious."

Holt pressed his lips together but didn't say a word.

"I asked if you were going to be okay," Dana added, "and one said yes, the other said that they didn't know yet, it was too soon." She looked at me with pleading eyes. "I should've known, when they disagreed like that," she added, her voice breaking. "I just thought that the younger one didn't want to tell me the truth. You know how cops are," she added.

I looked at Holt, waiting for his lead. There wasn't anything else we could learn from these three. The two men who had kidnapped Meredith had been bold and well-prepared. They'd taken advantage of the heightened emotions brought on by the shocking news they disclosed and made a clean exit without anyone making the required call to the precinct to verify their story.

"We'll need you to sit down with a sketch artist," I said, hoping Holt would let me get our artist involved. "Please wait here until he arrives."

I turned toward Holt, ready to leave, but he looked at Dana intently.

"Did my daughter seem all right leaving with them?" he asked.

Confused, the teacher furrowed her brow. "What do you mean? She was in tears, hearing you'd been shot. She wasn't all right."

"Did she seem to recognize them? Know them?"

She hesitated a little, then shook her head. "No, I don't think so."

"But she didn't react to them, as if noticing something was off about them?"

I looked at Holt, wondering what he was thinking.

"No, she didn't," Dana replied. "I'm so sorry I didn't—"

Holt walked out of the office without another word, rushing to the exit. Halfway through the corridor, I caught up with him and grabbed his sleeve.

"Holt, we need—"

"A sketch artist?" he asked, without letting me finish my sentence. "And who else do you want to tell about this? I thought we agreed—"

"We need help, Holt," I said as I climbed onto the passenger seat of his Interceptor. "We need video, street surveillance, GPS tracking on Meredith's phone," I pleaded. "We need Fletcher."

"I told you, I can't take this to the squad room. Not yet. Let me work this my way, all right? It's my kid, Baxter!"

"What are you so afraid of? Every cop who draws breath in this city would drop everything to help. We're nothing if not united when it comes to one of our own."

"Yeah… sure, we are. Morales would yank me off this case so fast, my head would be spinning for an hour, and he'd call the feds in on it just to make sure his ass was covered."

"Maybe the feds are the right approach, Holt. They have tools, a dedicated strategy, they have CARD teams. You know, it stands for Child Abduction Rapid Deployment. They might be just what we need."

He hit the brakes hard, and I felt the seatbelt cutting into my flesh. Then he turned toward me, glaring. "If you don't want to help me, fine. Get out and find a ride back home, and no hard feelings. But we'll do this my way, is that clear?" he shouted.

I felt the vibrations of his voice against my face, but I didn't flinch.

"I'm with you all the way, Holt," I replied calmly, although I wasn't feeling calm, not in the least. My heart was thumping against my chest, and I felt the urge to scream back at him despite my best judgment. He was being irrational, asinine, and a total plonker. On the flip side, considering what was at stake, I was surprised he was still keeping it together as well as he was.

One thing was certain; he needed me, more than he cared to admit. I breathed, looking at him calmly. "You can count on me," I added.

"Great," he said, turning away from me. "Then act like it." He floored the gas pedal, and the Interceptor took off abruptly, pushing me against my seat.

I rode in silence, knowing from experience it wasn't the best time to make my point with my stubborn-as-a-mule partner. In his shoes, I'd probably not have done a whole lot better.

"They might kill her if we go wide, Baxter," he said after a mile or two on the Interstate at over ninety miles an hour. "They want something, and they have to believe they could still get whatever the hell it is they want."

"What if they only want to hurt you, Jack?" I asked softly. "It's one hell of a risk you're taking."

He slammed his fist into the steering wheel. "A small one," he eventually replied. "If this were about vengeance, there would've been one abductor, not two."

"Chances are—" I started, but he cut me off.

"Yeah, exactly, chances are this is a crew on a mission, and I have to make sure they still think they can get whatever the hell they're after."

"Okay," I replied quietly. "Then let me help you your way. Let's go to Fletcher's home. I'll text him to meet us there."

"You know where he lives?" he asked, evidently surprised. "Don't tell me, you and he go way back too, or something? Another one of your damn secrets I can't be trusted with?"

"No, I just met him when I transferred in from Henderson."

"Then how?"

I gave him a long stare that he probably didn't notice, as he was focused on the thick, rush-hour traffic. "Are you sure you want to know?"

He pressed his lips together and stayed quiet.

"Look, I promise you he'll help, one hundred percent off the record."

"Do you trust him that much?" he asked, a trace of his earlier surprise still coloring his voice. I also heard a tinge of hope in his inflections and realized I had finally reached him.

"I trusted him with my life once," I replied, then added quietly, "and with yours."

6

Casey

Seven hours missing

She peered out the window, careful not to move the sheers and let anyone who could be looking know that she was home, even if there wasn't anyone out there that she could see. Feeling a chill, Casey curled up on the couch and started biting on her left index finger, grinding her teeth against the shiny, lacquered surface of her manicured nail, ripping tiny shreds of flesh from her raw cuticles.

What was going on? Had they found out?

Ever since her best friend, Meredith, got pulled out of calculus class that morning by a terrified and tearful Mrs. Garrett, her stomach had been twisted in a knot. What if the school had found out what they'd done? Worse even, what if those men got to Meredith first, and now they were coming after her?

She shifted in place, shivering, then reached out and grabbed the blanket folded neatly on the armrest and wrapped herself in it. It didn't help bring warmth to her fingers, nor did it do much to keep the monsters haunting her at bay.

That morning, when the first period had ended, and Casey was finally able to roam the hallways, she'd rushed in search of her friend. She'd started with the principal's office, the first place she'd be taken to in case they would've found out. The principal was out of the office, his door locked, and the light turned off. She probed discreetly with his secretary and found out he was having a root canal.

She asked everyone she could think of, but no one had seen Meredith since first period.

After third period, she was headed to the cafeteria for lunch, although she was nauseous and shaky. She caught a glimpse of Mrs. Garrett, sobbing violently and being escorted to the principal's office by the warlock herself. The fierce-looking and totally bitchy school nurse, who deserved a slow, painful death at the teeth of millions of hungry rats, was also crying, and that was unheard of. The warlock took pride in making others cry; no one had ever seen her shed a tear before, not even when a ninth grader had fallen to his death last year from the building rooftop.

No, the warlock never cried. Not ever. Not until that day. And the principal had returned to school after his root canal. Weird.

Something had to be terribly wrong.

She'd left dozens of messages on Meredith's phone and had heard nothing.

Casey had no reason to be in the cafeteria. The more she thought about it, the less sense it made to stay in school. She snuck out of there and raced the whole way home, not running out of breath, not feeling anything but sheer terror. If they got to her while she was at home, at least the school didn't have to know, and if the school didn't know, maybe her mom wouldn't find out either.

Yeah, right. Fat chance that was.

But if they came for her, she'd swear to them she would never tell a soul, and maybe they'd believe her. Maybe they'd let her live.

She heard her teeth chattering, and, at first, she didn't recognize the sound, as if it came from someone else. She needed a joint badly, even if that meant leaving the safety of her home and going out there by herself.

She rushed upstairs and pulled open the lowest drawer in her dresser, then reached deep inside and peeled off the small packet she'd taped to the bottom of the drawer above it. Then she dashed outside to the backyard and hid behind the tool shed, lighting up with trembling fingers.

She inhaled thirstily and held the smoke inside her lungs for a few seconds, yearning for the soothing effect it usually had. The rampant anxiety relented a little, but the facts remained the same.

Someone had found out. Meredith's father was a cop. Whether he'd found out, or the other guys had tracked the girls and now knew where they lived, it was just as bad. She and Meredith were seriously fucked, about to be grounded forever, in the odd chance they weren't both going to be killed.

Maybe Meredith was dead already.

She inhaled again and closed her eyes for a moment, imploring some peace to come to her weary mind. Instead, her stubborn brain returned a rerun of last night's events, as if she could've forgotten any of it. The man they saw, the things he said, the money he took, the look he gave them when he'd spotted the two of them huddled together, trembling, scared shitless. He'd pressed a finger to his lips in a plea for silence, and they'd nodded immediately with eyes wide open in fear. After all, the man was a cop. He could've busted them for being in a club and drinking alcohol when they weren't even sixteen yet.

But he didn't. He'd let them go with a weird, foreboding smile.

And now Casey was waiting for that man to come and tie up the loose end that she was. She'd seen it on TV so many times. Wasn't that what crooked cops did? He'd got to Meredith first, maybe because he was afraid that she'd tell her dad, but Casey was going to be next.

After a regretful last drag, she smothered the minuscule nib against the sole of her shoe, burning the tip of her fingers, then flicked it over the fence into the neighbor's yard. By now, the old lady must've had a small mound of her leftovers. Good thing they were biodegradable. Look at her, the concerned ecologist.

She headed inside with a satisfied yet tentative smile, realizing that the herb had done its part and had brought warmth to her extremities and a different perspective on life.

The moment she pulled the French door shut, she heard the doorbell ring. Her newly found serenity vanished, and she felt the urge to throw up.

Standing outside her front door, she recognized Meredith's father and another cop, a slender woman she'd never seen before.

Frozen in place, she couldn't think, couldn't react. All she could do was stare at Mr. Holt's scrunched face through the white sheers of the living room window. He was angrier than she'd ever seen him, and it was all her fault. He was going to kill her. Or throw her ass in jail, like, forever.

Holt rang the bell again, then pounded on the door with his fist. "Open the damn door, Casey, I know you're in there," he shouted.

Pale and weak at the knees, she forced herself to walk to the front door and unlock it. Then she removed the chain and opened it slowly.

"What's wrong with you?" Holt asked when he saw her. "You're white as a sheet."

"I'm sick," she managed to say, then promptly threw up right there, on the floor, sending droplets of yellowish vomit onto the man's shoes.

The woman rushed inside and helped her to the sink, holding her hair while Casey emptied her stomach. Then she helped her to the couch, while Holt paced the floor restlessly.

"Do you know where Meredith is?" Holt asked, sending a wave of renewed fear down her spine.

"N—no, I don't," Casey replied. "I thought you—"

"What?" he replied, visibly impatient to squeeze everything out of her.

Terrified, she clammed up. She couldn't think straight; she knew she couldn't tell him the truth, but where was Meredith, if he didn't know?

There was only one possible answer to that question, and it chilled her to the bone.

"I thought you or her mom came to pick her up today, during first period," she eventually said, her voice trembling badly.

She couldn't bring herself to look at the man. He'd never liked her much, and she'd always known it. He wasn't a fan of the jewelry, makeup, and short skirts she wore, of the music she loved, of the boys she dated, and he blamed her for giving Meredith wrong ideas. But they were only going to be young once, and neither girl was planning on becoming a nun. The man was a dinosaur, with all his morals and principles and rigid dress code.

Holt turned away, frustrated, cursing under his breath. Casey breathed, seeing she was about to be left alone. But did she really want that? What if the other man came by to set her straight? And where the hell was Meredith? What if she was—?

Casey couldn't finish her thought. The image of Meredith's body covered in blood and lying in a ditch formed inside her mind. Heavy tears welled in her eyes, and a sob choked her. She heaved, struggling to breathe without wailing.

The woman sat next to her on the couch, while Holt approached her again, even angrier than before.

"What the hell aren't you telling me?" Holt shouted. Casey whimpered and cowered, irrationally expecting the man to hit her across the face.

"Holt, what the hell, she's a child!" the woman reacted.

Holt stepped a few feet away, but kept his eyes fixed on her. Casey breathed again, a shattered breath of air that struggled to enter her lungs.

The woman turned her attention to her and held Casey's hand between both of hers. She had fine, long fingers and a neat manicure for a cop. Casey tensed, feeling the woman's cold hands on hers and knowing that more questions were coming her way.

"My name is Laura Baxter, by the way," the woman said in a friendly voice. "I work with Meredith's dad."

"Uh-huh," Casey replied, shooting her a brief, side glance.

"Listen, we know you're hiding something, Casey. Whatever it is, I promise you there will be no consequences. We only want to find Meredith quickly. Some very bad people have her. Please help us find your friend."

Casey fought back her tears. It was true. They'd got to her first. She turned away from the woman, wriggled her hand free of Laura's grasp and nestled her face in her hands. She sobbed like that for a long moment and eventually decided to tell them. Meredith's life was at stake; hers too.

"We went out last night," Casey finally said. "Meredith was here for a sleepover."

"Where? Where did you—?" Holt snapped, but the other cop touched his forearm, and he stopped shouting.

"At a club," Casey whispered, veering her eyes sideways to avoid Mr. Holt's glare. "At the Perdido," she added, cringing in anticipation of his reaction.

He was going to be so mad. The place was famous in Vegas for the barely legal things that went on in there, and it was recognized as a favorite hook-up place for anyone looking to get laid without having to do much dating first. Kind of like a live Tinder with music and booze.

"How the hell did you get in there?" he asked, suspiciously calm about it.

"We weren't alone," she replied hesitantly, unwilling to throw Miguel under the bus. If she did, he'd go to jail, and no one else would take her clubbing for another six long years, until she turned twenty-one. "And sometimes the bouncers look the other way."

"What happened at the club?" Holt asked.

"We danced, nothing else," she said quickly, suddenly afraid to share more. What if he forced her to testify? What if she ended up having to move to Wyoming or some other terrible place where there was absolutely no fun to be had?

"Any men paying attention to you two last night?" he asked. He seemed to be gritting his teeth, but he sounded calm on the surface.

"A few," she said, unable to contain a satisfied smile. She recalled the make-out session she'd enjoyed in the arms of a real man, a hot guy in ripped jeans and a white tee. He must've been at least twenty-five and behaved as such, sure of himself, bold, none of that high school bullshit she was sick of. But she saw no reason why she'd share that particular episode of her evening out.

"Jeez, Casey," Holt reacted. "How old are you, fifteen? You should've been home, studying, both of you. That's what you were supposed to do, right?"

"Yes, but we finished early, Mr. Holt, and we didn't think anything bad would come of it."

Holt sat across from her and stared at her intently. "Cut to the chase and tell me what the hell happened, Casey, or I swear to God—"

"Holt," the woman cut him off but then turned to Casey. "Please. This is important. What happened last night?"

Casey sniffled and looked at them for a moment. She'd already told them about the club. What was the worst that could happen?

"We drank some, uh, soda, then had to go pee," she said, staring at her hands as she wrung them mercilessly. "We weren't drunk or anything, I swear," she added quickly, seeing Mr. Holt's glare. "We really had to go, but there was a line at the ladies' room and no one in front of the men's room. I thought it was okay to go in there because you can always say you're a trannie or something, right? No one cares anymore."

Holt groaned and swore again, covering his mouth with his hand. Still, Casey heard the curses he muttered and stopped talking.

"Go on," he eventually said.

She swallowed hard, her mouth feeling dry. "Two men were in there, talking. They didn't hear us open the door at first, as we peeked in. One said something like, 'If I give you this, I expect you to make the whole thing go away,' and he gave the other man a brown envelope. Then the second man opened the envelope and pulled out some money, about this much," she added, bringing her index and thumb an inch apart to illustrate the size of the payout. "Then he said, 'Yeah, this will take care of it. No one will find that poor bastard.' Then they saw us, and they both stared at us with really mean eyes. The man who took the money told us to get the hell away, and we ran out of there."

Holt looked at his partner for a second. Casey lowered her gaze again; there was one more thing left to add to her story. She took a deep breath and raised her eyes until they met Holt's.

"The second man, the one who took the money, was a cop, Mr. Holt. He had a badge just like yours, and wore it on his belt, just like she does."

Both of them sprang to their feet before Casey could finish. They exchanged a quick glance, then the woman grabbed Casey's arm and helped her to her feet.

"You're coming with us. We're putting you in protective custody. Get ready to leave in five."

Wyoming! That wasn't happening. That just couldn't happen.

She started crying again, wailing loudly. "I didn't do anything! Leave me alone. I don't want to go anywhere. I want my mom!"

Holt turned his back to her and made a phone call, asking someone else, probably another cop, to come and pick her up. He gave the person Casey's home address, then ended the call and approached her.

"We'll sort through all this. I promise we'll keep you safe, and we'll work with you to identify the men you saw," he said, and for a moment, Casey felt grateful, hopeful that everything would end well. "But once this is over," Mr. Holt continued, "don't let me see you ever again come near my daughter."

7

Vultures

Eight hours missing

Dr. Stuart Hickman was having a disappointing day, but it wasn't all that unexpected when he'd placed unrealistically high hopes on the behavior of some feathered creatures of the sky. How were the vultures supposed to know that was the day he'd opened access to the grant people to see his systems, sharing the tracking screens for them to appreciate the value of their investment? And why would the birds care?

For months, he'd trapped and tagged the vultures of the Mojave, and that had been no easy feat. The birds were huge and robust; one flap of a wing could knock him out cold. Their sharp beaks could break a bone without much effort. Just getting them into live traps was a challenge, not to mention costly. After a while, his traps started catching birds that had been already tagged, doing little more than wasting precious time and resources.

He'd already burned through most of his grant money with the capturing and tagging. He didn't cut corners on the technology, knowing the devices would have to work for a long time. With the new tags, he could conduct nesting studies, roosting and migratory patterns mapping, everything and anything he could think of, all on the same frequency. He could even overlay a thermal map on the screen and track the birds' response to extreme weather. After all, the Mojave held the world record for the hottest temperature ever recorded, and he would've killed to have had the birds tagged on that day when the scorching heat blazed through the vast expanse of the deadly Mojave.

Now the money people were watching live, and he had nothing to show for it, but a bunch of minuscule dots scattered on a tracking screen. Some were stationary, the respective birds perched somewhere, immobile. There were a couple of committees visible, and a quick keyboard stroke overlaid the terrain layout, so he could see the group of lazy vultures killing time on the petrified branches of a long-dead tree. Other birds were in flight, but no patterns could be readily observed; their scattered flight resembled more of a study made on fruit flies. He'd hoped for a kettle or maybe a wake, which is what ornithologists and bird lovers call a group of vultures in flight or respectively feasting on a rotting carcass.

No such luck that day, and Dr. Hickman was growing weary of waiting. He'd already seen some discouraging messages from the grant board watching the demonstration of what their money had bought, and he dreaded watching a screen filled with randomly moving dots.

He pushed the laptop aside and crossed his arms on the desk's scratched surface, then lowered his head, resting his throbbing forehead on his bent elbow. That was Mother Nature playing games with him, with his life's work. And with a bitch like her, no one could reason.

He'd lost track of time when, barely audible, a light chime came from the laptop, sending Dr. Hickman into a frenzy. The system had recognized a pattern.

He jumped to his feet, pushing the chair aside, and leaned over the laptop's screen, flipping through screens at an incredible speed. He'd forgotten all about the grant people who were watching; all he cared about was the large kettle of vultures, dancing on his screen.

"Yes, yes," he muttered, running his fingers through the reddish tuft of hair that marked the top of his skull, surrounded by shiny scalp from all directions like a bunch of cattails breaking through the surface of a lake.

The kettle was a big one and growing. New vultures joined it, circling and circling, but not settling on the ground to eat. That meant their meal was still drawing breath or maybe had just drawn its last, somewhere in the heart of the desert, and he intended to witness the precise moment the kettle would land for the feast.

He grabbed the truck keys and a pair of sunglasses, then he slammed the laptop lid down, severing the internet connection with no regard for any of the people remotely watching the tagged flight who might not have given up on his birds yet. He'd have time to explain later. If he stepped on it, he could be at the site in under thirty minutes.

He drove as quickly as he dared, with a utility task vehicle in tow and his laptop on the passenger seat, its screen turned his way, so he could keep a wary eye on his finicky vultures. They whirled up in the air, still flying, still not eating. Then one of them set on the ground, turning the associated dot color from green to blue.

Dr. Hickman swore under his breath and floored it.

A few minutes later, he unloaded the UTV from the trailer and drove across the desert, leaving his truck and trailer unsecured on the side of the road. He pushed the UTV to the limit, ignoring the jolts of pain that the rugged terrain delivered to his sacroiliac joints. The laptop, open on the dashboard and secured in place with two Velcro straps, showed the majority of the birds still circling, but now four of them had landed and were ambling slowly on an intricate path leading to the location of the carcass.

Why weren't they feeding? Possibly other predators were keeping them at bay. Maybe a coyote was causing them some grief. Whatever it was, soon he'd know.

He eased the pressure on the gas pedal as soon as he could see the kettle circling, about a hundred feet above the ground. He drove a little closer, then stopped and cut the engine, afraid he'd scare the birds away. He pulled out a pair of military-grade binoculars from his duffel bag and started to examine the majestic birds. They were mostly adults, a few young ones too. The ones on the ground were large males, typically those who approached the carcass first and scared off any unwanted dinner guests.

He focused the binoculars on the object of the birds' interest. He couldn't see much; only sharp-edged desert rocks and some dirt. Then one of the vultures moved to the side, and he froze, his breath caught in his lungs. Next to the bird's claws, he thought he'd seen a woman's hand, half-buried under rocks, long, thin fingers adorned with bright, red nail polish reaching up toward the sky. But then the vulture moved a few inches, and what he'd thought he'd seen was obscured from view.

He wasn't that sure of what he'd seen. The heat rising from the desert's bedrock had the air shimmering and the light bending, creating optic illusions, the dreaded Fata Morgana of the desert, a misleading mirage playing tricks on the traveler's mind. But he had to know.

Breathing heavily, he lowered the binoculars and squinted, as if seeing with the naked eye could bring more detail than the powerful magnification of the field glasses. He couldn't see much, other than the distant kettle circling lower and lower, getting ready to set down and feed.

He had no choice.

His hand hovered for a moment above the ignition, but then he turned the key, and the engine started.

"Damn it to hell," he muttered, flooring the gas pedal and hopping over rocks and boulders as fast as the UTV could take it, getting ready to disrupt the kettle, scaring the birds into random flying patterns.

When he reached the site, three, large, turkey vultures were still on the ground, giving him evil, territorial stares and refusing to take flight. With a tinge of regret, he plugged the Bird Chase Super Sonic device into the vehicle's outlet and flipped the switch. High-frequency sounds and distressed bird calls flooded the area, and all his precious vultures dissipated within a second.

Then he saw her.

He approached the body, hand clasped tightly over his mouth.

She'd been partially buried; only her head and her hands rose above the surface. Desert winds had blown dust and dirt over her beautiful face. Strands of her long hair had fanned out around her head and were pinned in place with rocks, giving the appearance of a halo or a morbid Victorian collar. A few thin locks blew in the wind, touching her pale face, her parted lips, making her seem alive still.

She couldn't've been more than fifteen years old.

8

Visit

Nine hours missing

"I smelled pot on her, Baxter. What the hell?" he shouted angrily, turning onto the I-15 ramp with squealing tires and enough speed to make me wonder if the Ford Interceptor could flip on its side under the right conditions.

I held on to the armrest as best as I could, halfway turned toward him, a little queasy.

"You interrogated a minor without a guardian present, Holt. This could go badly in so many ways."

He shot me a frustrated glance. "The hell I did. I asked my daughter's best friend a few questions, that's all."

"You know they're going to spin it, right?" I insisted, speaking as gently as I could. "If the heat is up, they'll push back, the moment her mother hires an attorney. Then they'll turn up the heat on us again."

"Why would she get a lawyer? I didn't charge Casey with anything."

"People don't take protective custody that easily. A lawyer will be the first phone call the woman makes."

Holt didn't say a word, but I could sense he was starting to see my point. At least he wasn't pushing back against all reason anymore.

"Listen, all I'm saying is be prepared, expect that to happen, don't blow your gaskets when it does." I added, "And you should expect something else."

"What?"

"You won't be able to keep your daughter's kidnapping a secret much longer. The school knows, Meredith's best friend knows, soon Casey's mother will too, and now the federal marshals know about it. I don't know what you're trying to hide, but you're making a terrible mistake."

"Orville will keep his mouth shut," Holt said between clenched teeth, talking about the federal marshal who'd dropped everything to pick Casey up. "He and I served together. He'll keep the girl off the books for as long as I need him to."

"That was smart, by the way," I admitted with a tiny smile. "Put Casey with the feds, not the cops."

"Yeah, we don't know who she saw last night, but she described a cop on the take. Until we get some sketches, we won't know. Orville said he'll handle that for me."

Ah, the bloody male ego. Holt was asking for help and was fine receiving it, as long as no one called it help. As long as he didn't really have to ask, and other people offered. I figured it might've been the right moment to up the ante.

"Why not bring some more people into this? Not just Fletcher, but the captain, Anne, a few others we can trust?"

"No." The reply came quickly and unequivocally.

"What are you afraid of, Holt? Any parent in your place would call everyone and their mother, and wouldn't think all five thousand LVMPD officers are enough to search for their kid, even if they dropped everything else they're doing." I watched his brow furrow as I spoke, and allowed him a few seconds to mull things over, but no words came out of his tense mouth. "Tell me, what are you anticipating will happen?"

He took the exit and headed into the city, following the directions I'd put into his GPS, driving to Fletcher's home address with lights flashing and siren blaring.

"I think I know what this is about," he eventually said.

"You think?" I reacted, feeling my gut churn. "You're willing to risk your daughter's life on a hunch? What if it's whoever it was the girls saw last night in the men's restroom, and you're wasting precious time?" What the hell was he hiding, that was so important?

"If I'm right and this gets out, they'll kill her," he said, his low voice tinged with rage. "They'd have no more use for her."

"What in bloody hell are you talking about, Holt?"

He drove the rest of the way to Fletcher's place in perfect silence. I didn't insist; I could tell he wasn't ready to trust me. I'd been there myself and knew how much I'd wanted him to stop asking questions when the roles were reversed. One thing I did want to mention, if only to put the thought in his mind.

"We could at least issue an AMBER Alert."

"Too late for that," he said, cutting the engine and rushing toward the apartment building entrance, while I was only one step behind. "By the time we found out she was gone, they wouldn't still be roaming the streets with her."

He called the elevator with impatient, forceful gestures, pressing the button repeatedly as if that would've made it come faster. When it eventually arrived, he let out a long breath loaded with frustration. We walked in and I pressed the button for Fletcher's floor.

As soon as the doors closed, and the cab set in motion, he turned to face me and said, "Listen, I know what you're trying to do, and I appreciate it. But let me run point on this one, Baxter. She's *my* kid."

All the more reason why he shouldn't run point on the investigation, but I knew he wouldn't listen to reason. I already knew him well enough to recognize that once he set his mind on something, a herd of wild horses couldn't hold him back.

Surprisingly, I respected that, although under the current circumstances it drove me bloody insane.

"Okay," I replied calmly. "Just tell me what you need, and I'll do it."

"Why don't you start by telling me why Fletcher, an analyst you only met a couple of weeks ago, was willing to leave work early, rushing to help you, off the record, without any questions asked? And why does my partner know where he lives, when I've been working with the guy for years and had no idea?"

Was he jealous? I had to wonder, although it seemed wrong, being that Fletch was just a kid and that Holt had other, more important things on his mind.

"Don't worry, it was all work," I replied with a coy smile, thinking a break in the tension wouldn't hurt. "Unofficial, but still work."

"The type of work you get so secretive about?"

My smile widened. It was hard to admit, but it felt good knowing he knew about my extracurricular activities, at least in some measure, and had my back nevertheless. "Precisely," I replied. "He's the best analyst I've ever worked with, so I figured I'd want him on my team when, um, I'm working overtime."

"Yeah," Holt replied, shooting me a weird glance. "Right."

My smile lingered as I rang the doorbell but quickly vanished as the reality of what had brought us here hit me again like a punch in my solar plexus.

"It's open," we heard Fletcher shouting from inside.

I entered without hesitation, because I was familiar with the place. Nothing had changed since my last visit a week ago; his entire living room was dedicated to the pursuit of entertainment with the help of technology, and that's probably where the bulk of his paycheck went. A huge TV took up the back wall, and a gaming station with six monitors occupied a big chunk of the living space, installed on a massive desk and fitted with an ergonomic gaming chair, the kind that tilts back to deliver an immersive gaming experience. The screens displayed various scenes from *Call of Duty: Black Ops,* frozen mid-action, probably by our arrival.

I'd called him less than thirty minutes earlier, asking him to leave work early and meet me at his apartment. When did he have time to get home and start playing?

"Make yourselves at home," he shouted from the kitchen. "Wanna grab a cold one?"

"No, thanks," I replied. "We're working."

"I thought you two were off today," he said, appearing from the kitchen with a beer and two bottled waters in his hands.

He'd just come home from work but looked as if he'd barely gotten out of bed. Long, curly hair in disarray, frizzy spirals popping out in all direction as if he'd never run a comb through it. He wore a long-sleeved shirt printed with a colorful message reading, "I've gone insane. Be back soon," and a pair of track pants at least three sizes too large, hanging over his ankles as he walked, completely indifferent that he was at risk to trip and fall over the loose, frayed hems with every step he took.

"We were," I explained, "but we're still working, and this one's on the QT."

"You got it," he replied, handing me a small bottle of Perrier. "What's up?"

I looked toward Holt, waiting for him to say something, but he seemed engulfed in his grim thoughts.

"Holt's daughter's been kidnapped. We need—"

His eyebrows popped up, and his jaw slacked for a brief moment. That was his only reaction.

"Yeah, yeah, I know what you need," he cut me off while taking his seat in front of the monitors. All the gaming screens disappeared, replaced by various database windows he brought up one by one, crazy fast.

"What's her phone number?" he asked, and Holt dictated the digits quickly, pacing the space behind the desk, not taking his eyes off the monitors.

"This is the moment you wished you'd bought your kid the latest iPhone for Christmas," he said, flipping through various screens. "The phone last pinged here," he said as he pointed at a map. "A warehouse on Bruce Woodbury Beltway. Now the phone's off, so she could be anywhere."

"Can't you turn it on remotely?" Holt asked. "I remember you did that a few months ago, for that missing persons—"

"If there's power left in the battery, and if it's got coverage, at least two bars. Already trying." Fletcher scratched his head, then took a sip of beer. The bottle had left a wet circle on the desk, but he didn't seem to mind. "Why aren't the feds on this yet?"

Holt groaned, exasperated. He was probably getting sick and tired of that question. "I'd rather keep it this way for now," he replied coldly, and Fletcher raised his hands in the air.

"You're the boss," he said. "Nope, we can't turn it on remotely, but we'll know the second it's turned on by someone," he added. "We'll try street video next. When did they take her?"

"This morning, from her school. She goes to Western High."

"Got it," Fletcher replied. He started typing commands in his system, turning on various camera feeds, traffic monitors, ATMs, even some networked private security cameras from business buildings and construction sites. "Let's see," he muttered, then started whistling a familiar tune, an action movie score, if my memory wasn't playing tricks on me.

"That's them," Holt reacted, tapping his finger against one of the screens showing an older model, unmarked police cruiser pulled up at the curb in front of Western High. "Fletch, make sure there's a BOLO on that car."

"For what?" Fletcher asked. "Aren't we're keeping this quiet?"

"Aiding and abetting, impersonating law enforcement," Holt replied.

We watched in silence how the two men dressed as police officers escorted Meredith to the car. There was some back-and-forth conversation, a dialogue we couldn't hear; eventually, one of the men took her backpack and loaded it in the trunk after locking her inside the vehicle. While she appeared to have climbed into the car on her own, by the time they drove off she was pounding against the side window with both hands. Fletcher stopped the video and enhanced a particular frame. Blurry and distant, taken as the car had left the school drop-off zone and turned right, the image showed Meredith screaming, her mouth wide open and her eyes enlarged with fear.

"She already knew," Holt said, his voice tinged with rage but also with a hint of paternal pride. "She was in that car for mere seconds, and she made them."

I held my breath as Fletcher navigated from traffic cam to traffic cam, escorting the kidnappers' car as they drove away. It felt as if I were watching a horror movie in slow motion, unable to intervene, unable to stop the terror of what was happening.

"And we lose them here, on the Beltway," Fletcher announced. "It matches the location the phone pinged last. From here, that warehouse is less than five minutes due west, and there's no camera feed anywhere along that route."

"Okay, let's go," Holt said. "Thanks, Fletch."

"Wait a second," the analyst reacted. "Where do you want to go? There?" he pointed at the Google Maps image of the warehouse, shown on one of his monitors. It was a single-story, gray building that seemed abandoned or had been closed for an extended period of time. The front windows were dark, and the parking lot was completely empty. But Google Maps wasn't real time; I'd read somewhere that the images could be as much as three years old.

"Where else?" Holt replied, checking the ammo in his gun. "I need a few Glock mags. Got any?"

"Yeah," Fletcher replied, then he stood and rushed to the bedroom. He appeared within seconds carrying a couple of loaded magazines and handed them over. "This is crazy, Holt. There could be dozens of people in there. Let us help you. We can call the cavalry and safely obliterate that place. Or we could call SWAT; this is what they do for a living."

I watched the interaction between the two men, hoping that Holt would listen to Fletcher's logical arguments. But no, the determined expression on his face hadn't changed.

"I know what I'm doing," he muttered, then turned to me. "You coming?"

"Obviously," I replied.

Then we heard a familiar chime coming from the computer. That sound sent chills down my spine. I looked at Holt and saw the blood disappearing from his face.

Fletch looked over his shoulder. "New murder case just popped. But you guys are off anyway, so—"

"Where? What?" I asked, while my thoughts raced. *Please, God, don't let it be Meredith.*

He quickly clicked the mouse buttons. "They found a body in the Mojave, off the highway, a mile in." He swallowed with visible difficulty, then added. "It's a young girl, a teenager."

9

Request

Ten hours missing

Holt was frantic. His eyes, wide open, stared into thin air but appeared laser-focused, as if he were planning his next move. His black hair fell in disheveled strands on his sweaty forehead, while a sickly pallor tinted his skin. I wondered why he hadn't directed me to hell already, given that he didn't agree with anything I had to say.

I still had to try.

Knowing what to expect, I tried to stop him from leaving Fletcher's apartment, but he pushed me to the side.

"Get out of my way, Baxter," he shouted. "I have to know!"

"And you will," I replied, grabbing hold of his sleeve and delaying him a bit more. "I'll go right now. You can't just show up at a crime scene acting all crazed and not offer any explanations." I grabbed his hand and squeezed his cold fingers. "I'll go, all right? You stay here and wait for me. When I return, we'll raid the warehouse together."

For a brief moment, he stared at me with the eyes of a madman.

"Get out of my way, Baxter," he repeated, and the second time I heard a warning in his voice. There was no stopping him.

"Fine, but I'm coming with you," I insisted, and he didn't push back. He just stared at me impatiently, but I found myself hesitating, caught in a maze of questions I couldn't bring myself to voice, although one of them was causing my partner's deep angst.

What if the young girl whose body was found in the Mojave was his daughter? The thought chilled my bones. I forced myself to cling to hope, to the idea of a coincidence, although cops don't usually believe in such things. I understood how my partner must've felt, infinitely worse than I did, not knowing, wondering, terrified of what he was about to find in the desert. Before we could do anything else to try to find Meredith, we had to eliminate the paralyzing anguish that we both shared, the fear that everything was already lost, that she was gone.

"First, I have to make a quick call," I added, then speed dialed the police Dispatch line.

"Dispatch," a woman's voice announced.

"Hey, Trace, it's Baxter. Who caught the Mojave stiff?"

"No one yet, I don't have anyone here—"

"How about you give it to me? It might be correlated with another case I'm working on."

"You got it," she replied with a sigh of relief, then ended the call.

"There," I said, looking at Holt. "Now we can go."

Holt was halfway out the door when his phone rang. As if struck by lightning, he stopped, staring at the display showing an unknown caller. He turned and gestured toward Fletcher, who quickly sat at his computer and began the trace.

Holt rushed back inside the apartment, set the phone on the dining room table, and took the call on speaker.

"This is Holt," he said, his voice steady, seemingly calm.

"There's no need to attempt a trace, Detective," the caller said. The voice belonged to a younger male, possibly African American, who sounded amused, speaking slowly as if he had all the time in the world. "Please tell Mr. Fletcher to stand down."

Fletcher turned to look at Holt in disbelief.

"How did you—" Holt started to ask.

"Yes, we know where you are," the man stated, "and yes, we have your daughter." When he spoke, he sounded melodious, as if singing a half-baked tune, but the reason for his unusual intonation seemed to be his desire to convey condescension.

Holt clenched his fists until his knuckles turned white. "You took the wrong girl," he said, his voice intense, menacing. "You hear me, motherfucker? Let her go now, or I'll—"

"You'll do what exactly, Detective?" the man asked with a quick laugh. "Try to find me? Rip my chest open and take my heart out?" He laughed again, and I heard an echo, as if he were in a vast room, maybe in that warehouse. "Don't you get up in my grill. I've heard it all when it comes to threats, yet here I am, chillin', enjoying my day. Are you enjoying your day, Detective?"

"Put my daughter on the phone," Holt demanded.

"You don't set terms, Detective, I do." The man allowed a long moment of silence to go by. He didn't seem concerned at all with the call being traced, and that was a bad sign. "She's in one piece, for now, unharmed for the most part, but it's tough, you know."

"What?" Holt asked, his scrunched face turning livid.

"My crew, they're all men, and them cats got needs, vyin' for a piece of that young ass. Some of them just got out of the joint, and you know how tough life can be on the inside. Kinda dry, if you get my drift. Not sure how long I'm going to be able to hold 'em back."

I thought Holt was going to start screaming. Thick veins were pulsating on his temples as if bluish, twisted ropes had come to life underneath his skin.

"What do you want?" he asked, managing to keep his calm for another moment.

"You," the answer came right away. "Your life for hers."

I froze.

"Deal," Holt replied matter-of-factly.

He sounded almost relieved, possibly because that unusual request matched whatever scenario he'd assumed was the reason behind his daughter's abduction. He must've known who the players were and what they wanted, and yet he chose to keep it a secret from me, his partner.

"Good," the man said. "Now you wait for my next call. No cops, no feds, no SWAT or whatever other bitchin' ideas you might get, or I'll ship her overseas to please who pays the most. She's still a virgin, isn't she?"

"You son of a bitch," Holt snapped, "I swear to God—"

"Goodbye, Detective."

"Wait," Holt reacted in a much different tone of voice, desperate and subdued at the same time. "When will you call?"

The man laughed. "When I damn well please."

He hung up.

The three beeps marking the disconnected call resounded strangely in the room.

"No luck," Fletcher announced from his desk, shaking his head slowly.

"Let's go over—" I started to say, but Fletcher silenced me with a finger on his lips. Then he grabbed both our phones and examined them in detail. During all that time, I held my breath while Holt cursed a slew, going through an expansive repertoire of oaths and checking the time every five seconds.

I felt like doing the exact same thing. We were wasting so much time.

There was the slimmest of chances the kidnappers were still at that warehouse on the Beltway, maybe Meredith was there too. Holt was right to want to rush over there and put bullets in every single one of them. But the body found in the Mojave had thrown a wrench in that plan; we had to find out who that was, for Holt more than anyone else. I wished I could call the Crime Scene Unit and ask for an update, or at least a description of the victim, but the 911 call had just been posted, a minute before I'd called Dispatch. No; the quickest way to find out was to go there ourselves.

"You're clear," Fletcher announced. "He just used the GPS function in your phone."

"Did you turn it off?" I asked.

"I could do that, but there's no point. If he's hacked into your phone enough to see your location data, he'd easily turn GPS back on and laugh about it. But there's no spyware or bug that I could find. As far as I can tell, he's not listening to our conversation."

"How about the call?" Holt asked.

"It was a Skype call from overseas. Untraceable. I recorded all of it."

"Excellent," I said. "I made some notes about things I noticed during the call. The echo whenever he laughed or talked loudly. Some of his word choices; he might be former military."

"Or a gamer," Fletcher said. "Or a military movie buff. Those people would also use the phrase, 'Stand down.'"

I groaned and started out the door to catch up with Holt.

"I'm on it," Fletcher said reassuringly. "I'll pore over every nanosecond of that recording and give you everything I can find." He dragged his feet to where Holt and I stood by the elevator and grinned. "Aren't you forgetting something?" he asked, extending his hand in an inviting gesture.

I frowned, while Holt's impatience manifested in another mumbled oath.

"The hell, Fletcher? Got something to say, say it already," Holt mumbled.

"Your phones," he replied, fishing two burner flip phones out of his track pants pocket. "Leave them here, unless you want to keep that dude posted with your whereabouts, so he can see you coming a mile out. I've already forwarded your numbers to these two."

Ashamed, I handed him my phone. How could I not think of it? How could *we*? That was precisely how stupid mistakes were made, when cops stopped using their common sense in the heat of the moment. Holt's eyes met mine, as the elevator doors opened. Then we rushed inside the cab and my heart sank, overwhelmed with a persistent sense of doom.

Soon we'd know if a parent's worst fear had come true.

10

Crime Scene

Eleven hours missing

About a half mile section of Nevada State Route 160 was coned off and traffic was restricted to the left lane, pending the arrival of several backup units that were tasked with routing all the westbound commuters to the eastbound lanes. The coroner's van had pulled onto the shoulder before our arrival, and two Crime Scene Units were already in place, unloading equipment and sample kits. Several all-terrain vehicles, bearing the insignia of the Sheriff's Office, were leaving tracks up and down the dunes that blocked the crime scene from our view.

I'd expected Holt to pull over and grab an ATV. Instead, he found a place where the highway guardrail had been torn away and drove the Interceptor off-road, bouncing and tilting dangerously on the slopes covered in loose boulders and slippery sand.

Several Crime Scene technicians were already at the scene, marking the perimeter with yellow tape, working quickly and effectively without much interaction. Holt hit the brakes as close to the site as possible, sending swirls of pebbles and dust in the air, then rushed out of the SUV without even putting it in park.

I killed the engine and ran after him. As I was approaching, I watched him drop to his knees next to the body, and my heart stopped. Then he rose and turned sideways, facing away from the body, and buried his face in his hands.

Oh, no…

I touched his shoulder gently. "Holt," I whispered, struggling to find the right words.

His hands found mine and squeezed. "It's not her, Baxter," he said. "It's not my Meredith."

I breathed a long sigh of relief.

"It's a girl her age," he added. "It could've been her. You have no idea how I'd like to get my hands on the sick bastard who did this." He stared at the back of his hands as if he didn't recognize them, clenching and unclenching his fists.

Then he plunged his hands into his pockets, only the expression in his haunted eyes reflecting the turmoil of his thoughts.

"Listen," I said quietly, seeing Anne approaching us. "I know you're dying to raid that warehouse, but—"

"You do what you have to do, Baxter. I know why you took this case. But I can't be here; I have to find her."

"All I need is five minutes, all right?"

Anne and I exchanged a quick head nod and a hand wave.

"Hey," she called, "you're the lead on this?"

"Uh-huh," I replied. "What do you have?"

"Just got here, Miss Fast and Furious, give me a few."

She set her kit down near the victim's feet, while I examined her face, careful not to touch anything before the coroner had given permission.

She was stunningly beautiful, with a youthful look that glowed like the rays of the sun. She'd been partially buried under dirt and rocks, and the desert winds had blown dust over her face, making her skin appear like parchment. Her eyes were clear, although the same dust had caught in her lashes. Her lips were pale and covered with the powder that coated everything, even us, if we were to spend more than a few minutes here.

Something was off about the girl; I couldn't put my finger on what that was.

Anne approached the body, and I sought her eyes, about to ask why her lips weren't the usual bluish pale I'd grown to expect to see on a corpse, when something caught my attention, a small movement barely visible in my peripheral vision. I focused my full attention on the girl's face, studying every detail.

Then I gasped.

A fresh tear was rolling from the corner of her right eye, about to be obliterated in the dust layer settled on her face.

"Anne!" I called in a piercing, loud voice. "She's still alive!"

The coroner grabbed her kit and rushed to the girl's side. Her fingers searched for a pulse, while I watched with heartbreaking sorrow as another tear rolled down the girl's cheek, following the path left by the first one.

Two technicians brought the gurney, while others started removing the stones and dirt that covered her body.

"Gently," Anne called. "She could be bleeding under those rocks."

She took a digital thermometer out of her kit and placed it between the girl's lips. The device beeped immediately.

"She's hypothermic," Anne announced, and her assistant sprang into action. Riding the ATV like a valkyrie, she disappeared behind a dune.

"Where's she going?" I asked, removing rocks as quickly as I could.

"This isn't equipped with materials and supplies for living people," Anne replied, pointing at her kit. "It's meant for dead ones. But we have everything we need in the truck to keep her stable until the ambulance gets here." Then she turned and looked inquisitively at Holt.

My partner was pale as a sheet. "I already called it in," he said.

"Call a helo," Anne ordered. "There's no time to wait for a bus."

I heard Holt make the call, then he knelt by my side, quickly removing rocks. A few inches deep, he uncovered the edge of a tarp.

"Doc?" he called, holding the corner of the tarp with two gloved fingers. "What do I do?"

"Keep removing stones, then we'll lift the tarp without tilting it. Maybe there's evidence on it, fingerprints, DNA if we're lucky."

It took us less than a minute of feverish work to finish exposing the entire surface of the tarp. The girl's entire body had been covered with it.

"On my count," Anne said, holding on to a corner of the tarp and getting ready to lift it up. "One, two, three. Then slide over, and fold, fold again," she directed, then gestured toward one of the technicians. "Evidence bag."

The technician held the bag open while Anne carefully placed the tarp inside, sealing it quickly.

"Oh, my God," I heard her say quietly. "How much longer 'til that helo gets here?" she asked.

"Under five minutes," Holt replied.

Reluctantly, dreading what I was about to see, I looked at the girl's body, naked and crushed under the weight of the cold, desert rocks that had been her tomb, while she still drew breath. Her eyes, blue as the deep desert sky at dawn, stared into the distance, blurred with tears. Her lips remained immobile, although if I listened hard enough, I thought I heard her scream.

I couldn't begin to imagine what that young girl had been through, how it must've felt to be buried alive, in the cold, dark, desert night, and then in the scorching sun, deadly even in winter.

I willed away the shudder that had taken over my body, hoping I could get her to speak with me, to tell me anything that could help me catch the animal who had done this to her.

"Why isn't she moving?" I asked Anne. "Can she talk?"

"She's in shock. Her heartbeat is irregular and faint, and she appears paralyzed," Anne replied. "The desert gets cold this time of year, and she's been exposed out here for a while. See how the sand has settled in the folds of her exposed skin, at the roots of her hair?"

"How long?"

"I can't be sure, but at least a day and a half, maybe two. She's severely dehydrated."

"Can we move her?" I asked quietly, cringing when I realized what that meant. More pain, more blood, more silent unheard screams.

"It's risky, her heart could stop, but we have to," Anne replied. "We can't waste any more time." She pointed at the girl's legs, covered in bloodstains. "She's been bleeding for a while. Some of the dried blood is darker, almost black. That's at least twenty-two hours old. And this one," she pointed at a dark red smudge on her inner thigh, "this is fresh, under one hour. Red blood cells still hold active hemoglobin, giving them this red hue."

She beckoned two of the technicians, and they took positions around the thwarted grave. With expert hands, they eased a sheet under the girl's body, then, on Anne's count, lifted her fragile physique onto the gurney.

"Warm blankets, stat," Anne ordered, and a technician rushed to the coroner's ATV, now loaded with emergency medical supplies. "Warm saline, large bore," Anne demanded, then extended her hand without looking. Her assistant handed her a needle, waiting by her side with a bag of intravenous fluid.

In the distance, the sound of helicopter rotors spinning brought tears of relief to my eyes. The helo approached, circling low, looking for the best place to land.

"She's crashing," I heard Anne shouting. Then I watched as she straddled the gurney and started administering CPR. "Breathe," I heard her say, counting in gasping breaths, "One, one thousand, two, one thousand. Come on, breathe for me."

The technicians pushed the gurney toward the helicopter, and the noise of its blades shearing the evening air quickly covered the high pitch of Anne's vehement voice. Choked and unable to stop shaking, I studied the emergency crew from a distance as they slowed their frantic efforts, shoulders slouched forward, heads lowered.

The girl who had been buried alive in the desert was never going to name her assailant.

She was gone.

11

News

Twelve hours missing

Holt watched the team load the girl's body into the coroner's van and felt like he couldn't breathe. Against the grim visuals of the crime scene, flashbacks of his little girl growing up kept invading his mind, her crystalline voice loud as if she were there, calling him, laughing, playing in the sun.

"Daddy," she'd screamed, a screeching, high-pitched call that he couldn't ignore.

He got up from his lounge chair and abandoned his beer on the patio table, then dove into the pool to get to her.

With one quick move under the water, he got close to her, popping his head up from underneath, doing a decent imitation, at least in his opinion, of the Kraken sea monster. He snarled, mouth open wide, and made claws with both his hands, while Meredith laughed wholeheartedly, splashing him with water.

"The monster's coming," he said, but his threat didn't scare his brave little girl.

She giggled some more. "Is the monster bringing ice cream?"

He mocked a thoughtful monster, making a funny face with his claws frozen in mid-air. He felt tempted to say there were real monsters out there, who never brought ice cream to little girls; only death. But his daughter's innocence would last forever, untainted by the horrors he witnessed every day at his job. He'd make sure of that.

"What's wrong, Daddy?" Meredith's tearful voice snapped him back to reality.

He'd let his own past haunt him, and the playful face of the monster he was impersonating for his daughter's amusement had turned into a scary grimace of horror and angst. It was as if he could see into the future, a not-so-distant future when monsters he fought so hard to keep at bay would seep into his world and touch the lives he cared about, despite his best efforts.

He'd die before he'd let that happen. It wasn't a solemn oath he was taking; it was a fact he knew well.

He picked Meredith up and willed himself to laugh again. "The monster has no ice cream, Mer. What should we do?" Then he let her fall from two feet above the water, knowing her inflatable swim ring would break her fall, causing nothing but a splash.

She squealed with delight as her fall sent rainbow-colored droplets in the air.

"Let's go buy some," the girl demanded, splashing him with tiny fistfuls of water.

He picked her up again and climbed out of the pool. He dried her rebel curls and her tiny body, mixing in monster sounds and tickles, then pulled on a T-shirt and some shorts and grabbed his car keys.

"Let's go," he'd said, and Meredith had raced him to the car, squealing and laughing, feigning fear of the ice cream monster.

Holt remembered that drive to Baskin-Robbins and its 31 flavors as if it were yesterday, although ten years had since passed. He recalled how a strange chill had stayed with him that entire day and had haunted him for weeks after, as if a dark, ominous cloud was forming above his horizon. As if the real monster was watching, waiting, ready to pounce and take his little girl.

"Daddy!"

He heard the voice from his memories loud, real, as if she were there, close enough for him to touch. Frantic against all logic, he looked around and saw nothing but the usual scenery that came with his job. A new crime scene, tagged and marked, being photographed and sampled, loaded stone by stone into evidence containers, all in the hope that the killer had left a trace of himself behind.

His little girl's voice still echoed in his mind, but his partner's voice overlapped. She was standing nearby, supervising the collection of evidence from the gravesite. A man was approaching her quickly, his stride determined, uncompromising. He'd recognize that gait anywhere.

"Captain," Baxter said, "what brings you out here?"

"Not now, Baxter," Captain Morales replied, heading straight for Holt.

Oh, shit.

Holt met him halfway. "Captain," he said, his voice betraying his surprise.

"Why the hell aren't you home, waiting for that ransom call to come?"

Captain Morales was famously direct, to the point of being blunt, even offensive at times.

His words sent Holt into a tailspin of worry. How did he know? How many other people knew about Meredith's kidnapping? Maybe he'd been a desperate, first-class idiot to expect it not to get out when so many people knew about it.

Baxter had approached the two men, standing behind Morales at a polite distance and looking straight at Holt. He saw the same angst he was feeling reflected in her eyes, although she didn't know nearly as much as he did about the people who'd taken his daughter.

Holt stood quietly, at a loss for words.

"Why on God's green earth didn't you tell me your kid's missing?" the captain continued, frustration driving his pitch higher and higher.

"How did you know?" Holt asked.

"How did *I* know?" Morales reacted. "You're asking me that, instead of telling me why my best detective doesn't trust me enough to tell me his daughter's been kidnapped?"

"Captain—" Holt started to say, but his boss was too angry to give him a chance to say anything in his defense.

"Jeez, Holt, you drive me nuts sometimes," he replied. "You and Baxter are the best cops I've ever worked with, yet you both behave like reckless fools."

That statement sent Baxter's eyebrows up; she was just as surprised to hear Morales's words as he was.

"Sir, I—"

"Not another word, Holt, when I have to find out shit like this from the news."

"What news?" Holt asked.

"That nitwit teacher cried a river live on ABC News just now. As if we didn't have procedures for this scenario. She was supposed to call Dispatch and verify the information those fake cops gave her," Morales added, but then his earlier anger returned in full force. "Are you insane, Holt?"

"Sir," Baxter intervened, "if I may—"

Holt looked at his partner, urging her to shut up, to let him handle it. For a change, the most obstinate woman he'd ever met obliged. She didn't say another word.

"Captain, we're working both cases at the same time," Holt replied. "This is a new murder case, and you have no one else available. My partner and I are splitting the tasks."

"Really? Walk me through it, tell me how you're doing it."

"I have a call into traffic cams administration to trace the vehicle that took her, and I have my phone with me all the time. The people at her school are sitting down with our sketch artist."

"Is that it?" Morales said, but something in his voice made Holt frown.

"Uh-huh," he replied cautiously, wondering what had pasted the look of insulted disbelief on his supervisor's face.

Morales didn't speak at once, as if waiting for Holt to say more, to open up and be truthful. When Morales did speak, he was cold and uncompromising.

"If I ever catch you in a lie again, Holt, you're out. You already know what car took your daughter, and you have a BOLO out under a false code."

Holt lowered his head, ashamed. It wasn't as if he'd done it on purpose; he thought he had no choice, and the fact that Morales, and who knows how many others, now knew about his situation, made him fear even more for Meredith's life. The more people who knew about it, the more difficult it would be to control their actions.

He looked at Morales, attempting to apologize, but despair seeped in his tense voice. "She's my kid, sir. My daughter."

Morales shook his head and took a couple of steps in place, as if debating whether to stay or leave, then kicked a small rock with the tip of his shoe, putting a scrape on the burgundy leather covered with a fine layer of desert dust.

"Yes, she's your kid, Holt," he eventually said, raising his arms in the air, in a gesture of superlative frustration. "Go be with your wife—"

"Ex-wife," Holt interrupted. Why did everyone ignore the fact they'd been divorced for years? It pissed him off to no end, reminding him of the biggest mistake in his life. The only good thing that had come out of that marriage was Meredith.

"Whatever," Morales snapped. "Go be with your family. Let Baxter handle this murder case."

Holt shifted his weight from one foot to the other and plunged his hands into his pockets. He wanted Baxter by his side as he stormed that warehouse. If Morales held Baxter back at the scene with him, he'd have to do it alone. He'd be fine… it wasn't his first solo rodeo. He'd be better off saying, "Yes, sir," to the captain so he could leave.

"Not another word," Morales said in a threatening voice, reading him perfectly. "Go. Let the feds work the kidnapping, Holt. It's the law."

"Feds?" he reacted, the worry in his voice clear as day.

How did the Feds get involved in this already? He couldn't begin to ascertain the new dimensions of added risk their involvement could bring to what he was planning to do.

Morales gave him a long, scrutinizing stare. "Unless you already got that ransom call, and you're lying to me again?"

"No, I didn't," Holt replied, a little too quickly. He realized he hadn't convinced Morales, because the captain turned toward Baxter.

"Did he get a ransom call?"

Baxter didn't flinch, didn't bat an eyelash. "Not that I know of, Captain."

Morales shook his head slightly. "Yeah, right."

"Captain, he insists he handles this on the QT," Baxter said. "Maybe we should trust his judgment on this one. After all, it's *his* family."

Morales shrugged, but the deep ridge across his brow didn't vanish. "Too late for that, Baxter. The feds are at his house, setting up."

His heart sunk, and then started thrumming the rhythm of sheer panic. If Meredith's kidnappers were worth their salt, they had eyes on the house, watching for exactly that: the feds getting involved or too many cops asking questions on the block.

"How the hell did that happen?" Holt snapped, grabbing Morales by the lapels and shaking him as if we were one of his perps. "Who called the feds? She could be dead right now because of them!"

"Take your hands off me before I break them, Holt," Morales hissed, and Holt complied. "Be thankful I'm an understanding man under the circumstances," the captain added, straightening his jacket, "but don't push it."

Holt barely heard him; he was losing his mind. He was frantic to get out there, to find his little girl, to kill the men who took her.

Morales didn't step back; he stayed in Holt's face, looking straight at him. "There's something I'm surprised you don't know about law enforcement, regardless of agency or jurisdiction. We all tend to close ranks and pull together when one of us is shot or killed. But that's nothing compared to what happens when someone goes after a cop's family."

12

Warehouse

Thirteen hours missing

It was already dark when Holt drove away from the crime scene in the desert, heading toward the city. He floored it the entire time he drove on 160, flashing red and blue to make his way through traffic without delay. Then he cut the light show when he turned north on Rainbow Boulevard, approaching the Bruce Woodbury Beltway.

He'd seen the warehouse on Fletcher's Google Earth views, and he recognized the building; he'd driven past it a few times, not giving it a second look. In those images and his recent memory, the warehouse seemed abandoned. He didn't recall seeing a truck pulled at the loading dock or any employees' cars parked in front.

He slowed his approach on the Beltway service road, nearing the warehouse. It was larger than he remembered and completely shrouded in darkness. The lamppost in front of it had a weak, bluish bulb that barely managed to attract a few moths to swirl around its underpowered incandescence.

He cut the lights and started driving slowly toward the back of the building, his engine a quiet purr, inaudible against the sound of the heavy Beltway traffic. He was about one hundred yards from the back of the warehouse when a door opened in the distance, letting a sliver of yellowish light appear as two men stepped outside. The light vanished when the door closed, surrendering the scene to darkness.

He stopped under the low crowns of some trees and killed the engine. He watched the two men light up their smokes, chatting casually. He opened the window and listened intently, trying to catch what the two were saying.

"And she tells me, honey, I need two hundred bucks to get my hair done," one of the men was saying. The other one emitted raspy laughter that ended in a coughing spell. "And I told her, gimme that razor blade, I'll do your hair just fine, bitch!"

They both laughed, then the first one continued, "I'm telling you, the moment I get anywhere near some money, the woman smells it and wants it all.

But this time, I ain't lettin' it happen. When we get paid, this brother's haulin' ass to the Caribbean, never coming back," he said, pointing at his broad chest with his right index.

"You're smarter than you look, brah," the second man said, then coughed some more. He didn't seem to be able to control his hacks, despite the other man's slaps on his back. Still whooping and choking, he swiped a keycard and went back inside, leaving the first one by himself to finish his smoke.

It was the perfect time to move. Holt eased out of the car, careful to not make a sound, then snuck toward the back of the warehouse, keeping low and close to the hedges that surrounded the property. When he was close enough, he pulled his weapon and closed the remaining distance.

The man was heavyset and tall, his neck thick and muscular from too much weightlifting, probably assorted with steroid use. A bushy, untrimmed beard covered the lower half of his face, and several tattoos told the story of his affiliations during his stay behind bars.

When Holt was a few yards away, the man heard him approach and turned, his hand reaching behind his back.

"Don't even think about it," Holt said, training his gun on the man's chest. "Hands where I can see them," he demanded.

The man raised his hands in the air and grinned, his white teeth flickering in the dark.

Holt circled around him and grabbed the handgun he had stuck in his belt. He shoved it in his pocket.

"I'm only going to ask you once," Holt said, keeping his gun aimed at his chest and remaining at a safe distance, six feet away. "Where is she?"

The man shrugged with an exaggerated lift of his shoulders and looked sideways. "Dunno who you're talking about, brah."

He didn't believe that for a second.

"Wrong answer," Holt said, lowering his gun and pointing at the man's crotch. He pushed a switch, and a laser spot marked the target with a tiny, red dot.

The man's grin died on his lips. He swallowed hard, his eyes stuck on Holt's gun.

"Last warning, where is my daughter?"

"I swear to you, I don't know."

"What's your name?"

"D—Darrell." He stuttered severely; it could've been the fear, or maybe that wasn't really his name and he'd needed time to make one up.

"How many in there?" he asked, twitching his head toward the warehouse.

"T—two," the man said. "I'm just a temp, man, I work here. Don't know nothing about no girl."

"On your knees," Holt commanded, and Darrell hesitated, but then put one knee down, slowly, taking his time.

That moment, the door opened, and the coughing man came back out. He froze in the doorframe, taking in the scene, while Holt turned his weapon toward him. Lightning fast, the man ran back inside, shouting.

"We're blown, the five-oh is here."

Within seconds, Holt heard doors slamming on the other side of the warehouse, then a couple of cars sped away. He thought of chasing them, but he had one of the perps right here, and he could make him talk.

He turned back toward Darrell, but he was a moment too late. He felt a heavy fist blow to his shoulder, sending shards of pain along his humerus. Then another blow came right after it, knocking his gun from his hand and sending it clattering to the pavement.

Holt turned in place, facing his attacker and responding with a left punch to the man's throat. Darrell choked but wouldn't relent, throwing his entire weight against Holt's frame, looking to destabilize him and throw him to the ground. Holt took a few steps backward but then swirled again, grabbing Darrell's left arm with both his hands and sliding his body underneath the man's chest. Then he yanked with a smooth, carefully timed judo technique, and the man flew over his head, landing hard on the asphalt, air knocked out of his lungs. Without hesitation, Holt pressed his boot against the man's throat.

"Where is she?" he asked again, panting heavily from the effort.

Darrell shook his head, pushing against Holt's foot with both his hands, trying to free himself. He grumbled and groaned, but no intelligible sound came out.

Holt realized he was wasting time, precious time in which the others were vanishing in the wind. Meredith was long gone; if she were still at the warehouse, there would've been more foot soldiers guarding the premises, not just those losers. He would've been greeted with automatic weapons fire, not offered a brawl by an overly ripped ex-con on steroids.

Holt took out Darrell's weapon from his pocket, aimed it a few inches above the man's knee, then pulled the trigger.

The man's agonizing cries resounded in the night. He writhed on the ground, holding his wound with both his hands. "You can't do that, man," he cried, watching in shock how blood was seeping between his fingers. "Cops can't do that."

"Don't worry, pussycat, that's a flesh wound, through and through," Holt announced calmly, lowering his aim a little. "Next time it's the joint."

The man panted, staring at him with terrified, wide-open eyes. "N—no, I'll tell you," he stuttered, "I ain't getting paid enough to get my kneecaps blown."

"Where is she?" Holt asked again.

"I don't know," the man said, and started screaming when Holt focused his aim on his left knee. "I swear I don't. But she was here earlier. They took her away."

"Who took her?"

A moment of hesitation that Holt didn't let pass without moving his aim to the man's crotch. "Or maybe some soft tissue," he threatened.

"Snowman, he has her, I swear," the man said, spittle spraying out of his mouth as he spoke. "He'll kill me. Don't tell him how you know."

"Don't tell him you're a fucking rat?" Holt asked, kneeling near his face, thrusting the gun barrel against the man's temple. "Then tell me how I find him, and I won't drop a dime on you. I'll just double tap his head."

"It's where he's got all his girls, man, that's all I know. But we ain't allowed there. We just know the place exists, but don't know where."

Holt looked in the thug's eyes and saw he was telling the truth. Everything he knew about Snowman agreed with Darrell's spotty story. Samuel "Snowman" Klug never shared his plans with his lieutenants. He owed his nickname to his trade, pushing cocaine and other drugs onto the streets of Sin City. Word on the street said Klug was diversifying, going after all the sins, not just one. The four-million tourists Las Vegas welcomed each year were an abundant source of revenue if he was willing to cater to all their whims. And he was more than willing. There wasn't any service his organization couldn't provide.

"How about the fake cops who took her? I want their names."

The man didn't reply. Instead, he panted heavily, looking around as if searching for someone who could help him.

Holt kicked him in the wounded leg, and he screamed in pain, but then started spewing barely intelligible words mixed with ragged breaths of air.

"A couple of white guys, they're new. They're street corner dope pushers, nothing to them. One's Rudy, the other one's Foley, or something."

"What street corner?"

"On Industrial Road, behind the hotels."

"Get over there," Holt said, and the man crawled on the ground until he got close to a palm tree. Holt took out a pair of zip cuffs and had Darrell hug the tree trunk, then tied his hands together on the other side.

"I need a doctor, man, I'm dying here," he pleaded as Holt walked away.

Holt stopped for a moment to pick up his gun from where he'd dropped it during the fight, then continued his stride toward his SUV. "You'll get one," he shouted over his shoulder. "After I find my daughter."

13

Feds

Fourteen hours missing

Holt's right shoulder was throbbing with pain, rendering him a left-hand driver, but it wasn't anything an ice pack and a couple of Tylenol couldn't fix. He swore a long oath and pulled in front of his former home, now his ex-wife's residence. With one cursory look around, he spotted three vehicles that didn't belong, confirming what he'd said all along. What's the purpose of having unmarked law enforcement vehicles when they're all the same make, model, and color? Why bother? Perps saw them coming a mile away, as if they were covered in reflective decals with their grille flashers on.

Three damn cars… If Snowman's people were watching, he was getting an intriguing report. And Holt knew Snowman was watching; they had a history together, enough to suspect it had been him who took his daughter, enough to anticipate what he wanted from Holt in exchange. Not only vengeance but more. Snowman took pride in saying he never killed someone who'd done him wrong until that wrong was paid tenfold. Then he'd kill the bastard, slowly, painfully, so the entire world could hear what happened when some sorry-assed moron fucked with him.

It was Holt's turn to pay tenfold and then die.

For his daughter's safety, no price was too high.

He wasn't going to let Snowman have his way without putting up one hell of a fight. He just needed a way in.

Holt pulled in at the curb and quickly walked to the house, eager to get the whole situation with the feds sorted out. He knew their general procedure for child abduction cases, although he hadn't worked with them on a case involving an active cop's family. He suspected those were handled differently, and he wanted to make sure he understood how. The last thing he needed was a bunch of eager feds stepping on his toes when he had a job to do.

He was the only one who could do this right. He'd spent months undercover, embedded in Snowman's organization, climbing the ladder, figuring out how to dismantle his drug operations, how to find his supplier and lock him up. Then his handlers had pulled the plug, although he had nothing on Snowman yet; only on some of his lieutenants. He'd cut a few heads off the city's cocaine Hydra during the ensuing raid, but one survived, grew stronger, and now was coming after him.

He approached the house but didn't get to ring the bell. The door opened, and a stranger let him in. He had intelligent eyes with a somber expression, and a tall forehead under neatly combed over, dark hair. Medium build and slightly taller than Holt, he wore a charcoal suit with a white, starched shirt and a perfectly matched, golden tie.

"Special Agent Glover," the man introduced himself, then gestured toward the dining room where a woman sat next to Holt's ex-wife, holding her hand. "That's Special Agent Rosales. We're going to help you get your daughter back. We're with FBI CARD," the man added, probably seeing Holt's frown. "That's Child Abduction Rapid—"

"I know what it means," Holt cut him off.

When Jennifer heard his voice, she sprung from the couch and came to meet him, stomping her feet with every step of her determined stride. He'd seen her walk like that before; he breathed, swearing to himself that he was going to keep his cool no matter what.

She stopped short of running into him and propped her hands firmly on her hips.

"Great," she lashed out, "you finally came to your senses and called for some help."

"Listen, Jen, I need to—"

"Don't you Jen me, all right?" she shouted. "They told me it's about your goddamned job, some piece of crap you locked up is out to make you pay."

"We don't know that," he replied firmly, glaring at Glover. He didn't need that idiot putting ideas in Jennifer's head, to give her more reasons to scream her head off.

He'd always resented how biased she had been against his job, ever since they got married. She knew she was marrying a cop, but she'd held the secret hope she could change him, make him, "grow out of it and get a real job, one that pays the damn mortgage." When he refused, she'd turned on the heat and made him go through hell one day at a time, every day worse than the last. It took him years of enduring abuse before he walked away; not because he was still fostering some surreal hope of making things work with Jennifer, but because leaving his chronically unhappy wife meant not seeing Meredith every day. Not tucking her in at night, not reading her bedtime stories.

But Meredith had grown and was starting to be upset every time her parents argued. Soon he realized his presence in the home was doing her more harm than good. One night, after a lengthy argument that ended in a flurry of curses and slammed doors, and his daughter sobbing in her bedroom, he packed a small duffel bag and dropped it by the door, getting ready to tell Jennifer he wasn't coming back.

She was expecting it and took the news better than he'd anticipated, although she was bitterly frustrated for the loss of what she'd called, "her best years." He'd made only one mistake before leaving that night. When Jennifer had said she didn't want primary custody of Meredith, his face lit up like a kid on Christmas day. He'd tipped his hand.

Jennifer saw his reaction and immediately shifted gears. The following morning, one of the most expensive custody lawyers in Las Vegas had been retained by her using funds pulled from their joint account, and a three-year court battle ensued. Jennifer's purpose had been to squeeze every dollar she could out of him, using Meredith as leverage. If he agreed to pay a certain amount in alimony, she would let him see Meredith once a month. If he was willing to pay more, he could spend time with Meredith every other weekend.

He'd almost lost faith in the justice system when he saw his job twisted, sharpened, and wielded against him in front of a judge who fell for all of her theatrics, no objections raised by his lawyer ever sustained. "He spends his time with criminals and drug addicts," the tearful mother had declared on the stand. "His life is at risk every single day, and he might not be able to come home at night to take care of my little girl. And one day, his job will take its toll on his life… Please, Your Honor, don't let his job harm my baby," she had ended her plea, patting her eyes with a tissue for maximum effect.

One year later, Jennifer had married a dentist. Another three years down the road, the dentist was gone, leaving behind a hefty percentage of his monthly income, and his place in Jennifer's bed was then taken by a Latino restaurant owner with a dubious past. But even that one was now history, and the serial bride was on the market again from what he'd heard. He was keeping tabs on her, not because he'd had a hard time letting her go; quite the opposite. But if his daughter was forced to share her home with her mother's latest man, he'd better be Mr. Perfect Behavior Around A Child, walking the line. Or else.

"Who else could've taken my baby other than the scum you choose to work with?" she said, her voice an irritating, high pitch. Agent Rosales turned her face away from the argument she'd been watching like a tennis match, probably fed up with such family scenes.

"We'll find out, Jen," he replied as calmly as he could. "Especially if you let me do my job."

"You asshole," she screamed, then broke down into heavy sobs. "You promised me she'd be safe," she whimpered between heaving bursts of tears.

He reached out and tried to console her, but she pushed back angrily, pounding his chest with her fists. Agent Rosales intervened; she took Jennifer's arm and led her to the couch, speaking to her in a soothing voice.

Holt went to the fridge and scoured through the freezer, looking for an ice pack. He couldn't find one and chose a bag of frozen peas instead. He removed his jacket, wincing in pain when the sleeve twisted his right arm, and slapped the ice pack on his shoulder, the instant relief releasing a long, pained breath from his lungs.

"You've been busy, Detective," Agent Glover said, giving him a critical, head-to-toe look, his eyes lingering on Holt's blooming shiner. Then he approached the dining table and pulled out a chair for Holt and another one for himself. "We need to talk."

"What about?" Holt asked, still standing. He went back to the fridge, opened the door, and took out a bottle of orange juice, balancing the ice pack on his shoulder until he could put the bottle on the table.

SA Glover patted the chair invitingly. "Please, Detective."

Holt grudgingly obliged. He didn't feel like sitting when Snowman had his daughter. He needed to get going. He had a few ideas on how to find the son of a bitch; he'd learned his game once. Chances were, like with any other human being, Snowman would fall back into his old patterns of behavior and do the same things he used to do.

"Do you have any suspects in mind?" the fed asked.

Holt closed his eyes for a moment. "I've put a lot of bad people away," he said, lowering his voice so Jennifer wouldn't go ballistic on him again, screaming to let the world know she'd been right. He uncapped the juice bottle and downed it in a couple of thirsty gulps.

"Anyone in particular standing out?"

Holt rubbed his forehead, thinking what, if anything, he could tell the fed. "Not really, no."

The agent looked at him sideways. He probably saw right through Holt's lies. "How did you get that?" he asked, pointing at Holt's improvised ice pack.

Holt let out a quick, sad laugh. "Just another day in the office."

"Not something we should know about?"

He groaned, feeling his exasperation rising with every minute he was wasting talking to this man instead of going out to find his daughter. "Why don't you tell me what you guys are doing to find my daughter? You're supposed to be the experts, right?"

SA Glover stared at Holt for half a second before replying, his gaze disapproving, almost insulted. "We set up a command post at your precinct and a base here. My colleagues and I will map the sex offenders in the area, look at your caseload, former and current, coordinate any forensics, and bring in the bureau's technical assets. Here, at the house, we're set up to receive the ransom call and trace it."

"Uh-huh," Holt replied. They weren't going to do much of anything; just a bunch of database searches and stuff. They'd be busy rummaging through piles of data for at least a few hours, and that's all he needed to get to Meredith, now that he knew who'd taken her.

"Have you received a ransom call, Detective?" SA Glover asked.

He flinched imperceptibly and cursed himself in his mind. "No, I didn't. Why do you ask?"

"Routine," Glover replied, his earlier look returning. He didn't believe a single word. "You *will* tell me when that call comes in, right?"

"Right," Holt said, pushing the chair back with a loud screech of wooden legs against granite tiles. "I guess we're done here?"

The fed also stood, immediately buttoning his suit jacket.

"Can I ask, where are you going, Detective? Why the rush? Parents normally huddle up together and wait by the phone in kidnapping cases like yours."

"You've seen my ex-wife," Holt replied, lowering his voice. "I believe it's better for everyone involved if I excused myself."

He walked toward the door, then accepted Glover's help with putting on his jacket. He nodded toward Jennifer, but she turned her head away from him. Then he opened the front door and extended his left hand to the agent.

"Thanks for everything," Holt said. "Please call me as soon as you have something."

"You do the same, Detective," SA Glover replied, shaking his hand. "I know what I'd do if I were in your place. Please don't insult my intelligence; we're on the same team. Call us if you catch a lead, if you watch any relevant surveillance video, or put another BOLO on a suspect's car."

"Will do," he replied, thinking the exact opposite. He wasn't going to let these people become involved in this mess. One wrong move from any of them and Snowman would kill Meredith, just because he could, just because he wanted to teach Holt a lesson. He'd seen him do that before, cold as a snake, quick, unpredictable.

Holt was better off on his own.

Before climbing into his SUV, he looked around, taking in the details of the street: how many cars, if there was anyone killing time in any of them.

He knew what he would do in Glover's place.

Someone was about to start tailing him, and he had to lose that tail.

14

Autopsy

Twenty-four hours missing

I entered the morgue the same way I always did, holding my breath. A subconscious, albeit futile effort to keep the smell of death from invading my body a moment sooner. This time, death was delusive, because the body it had claimed had a beating heart only hours ago. I couldn't smell the stench of decay taking over the morgue, because death had not yet had the time to weave its intricate web of destruction, invisible yet unstoppable once life conceded the battle with the Grim Reaper.

I felt the need to tiptoe, as to not awaken the dead girl, no matter how ridiculous that was. She seemed peaceful, safe, at rest after enduring an unspeakable ordeal. I couldn't jeopardize that in any way, although I knew very well that she'd never be afraid again.

The cold silence of the morgue felt heavy against the distant hum of the refrigerated storage units lining the back wall. A blend of recognizable chemical smells littered the air in clouds of fumes I walked through, recognizing some but not others. Formalin, alcohol, methanol, and a sharp scent that tickled the back of my throat unpleasantly, leaving a bitter aftertaste.

Dr. Anne St. Clair was examining the victim's stomach contents under a magnifying glass mounted on a flexible arm and surrounded by powerful LED lights. I couldn't bring myself to comprehend how she could breathe normally that close to someone's digested meal, even if she did so from behind a face shield. I was standing six, maybe seven feet away, and I could smell the acrid fluids in the girl's stomach as if it were bile rising up my own throat.

I breathed through my mouth, willing my stomach to stay put instead of wanting to show off its content right next to the vic's. I managed to swallow once or twice, and the bitter taste in my mouth washed off in part.

"Hey," I said, stopping a few feet away from the table, knotting my fingers.

"Hey back at you," Anne replied, not looking up from the stomach opened for examination in a tray, under her magnifying glass.

I watched her take a tiny sample of fluid and put it on a slide, then displayed the image on a large screen mounted on the wall.

"Yeah," she said, on a long breath of air coming out of her chest, "just as I thought."

I took a tentative step closer to the autopsy table.

"What do you have?" I asked, unable to take my eyes off the marbled skin of the young girl. Only hours earlier, tears were rolling from her eyes. Buried alive, left for dead in the desert, she'd somehow managed to endure. If only she'd endured a little longer.

I turned away to hide the tears choking me, but Anne's sad smile told me she shared my feelings. "Help me nail the sick son of a bitch," I whispered.

"Gladly," she replied. "This is preliminary; I'm not done with the exam yet."

"Got it," I replied.

Anne was so thorough, so rigorous when it came to following procedure. Right now, I needed the Navy doctor Anne to speak to me, the pilot Anne who'd flown Medevac helicopters in Afghanistan under heavy fire, saving lives, fighting for every minute, every drop of blood. Screw the procedure to bloody hell. "Talk to me," I encouraged her.

She peeled off her gloves then sent them flying into a stainless-steel trash can marked with the universal biohazard symbol. Then she rolled a four-legged stool next to the table and sat, pointing at another one for me. I remained standing, too restless to sit.

"Meet Alyssa Conway, fifteen years old. The official cause of death is enforced exposure; the low temperature and dehydration weakened her body to the point where nothing could be done," she explained as if I hadn't been there to see with my own eyes her desperate efforts to save that girl's life. "She sustained blunt force trauma and crushing on large sections of her body, leading to a systemic inflammatory response."

I gritted my teeth and said nothing.

"Ever wondered why she didn't pull herself out of that grave?" Anne asked, her voice tinted with barely controlled rage.

I'd thought about that. The girl's body had been covered with a few inches of stones and dirt, but her hands and head were kept above ground, and she should've been able to dig herself out. As my overactive imagination explored the potential explanations for her immobility, a wave of nausea and dizziness took over my body. Sitting on the lab stool seemed like a great idea.

"Why?" I asked, cringing in anticipation of what promised to bring a new level of horror to an already sickening case.

"Modified tetrodotoxin, a powerful neurotoxin. You might know it as pufferfish toxin."

I strained my memory to recall where I'd heard about pufferfish. Yeah, in the news; some rich twats with a death wish risked their lives and paid $200 to eat a fish that could kill them on the spot. Yet another perfect example of how too much money transformed certain people into unredeemable plonkers.

"I thought tetrodotoxin killed you where you stood," I offered hesitantly.

"Hence the word *modified*," Anne explained.

"I'm not following."

Since when did criminals get so damn savvy? What happened to the good, old-fashioned knife or firearm? Palpable things we could track, we could find fingerprints on, bloodstains too.

"Think of cocaine, for example. Dealers buy pure cocaine from their South American sources, then they cut it here, using a variety of chemicals, some harmless, others deadly."

I frowned, shifting in my seat, more confused than before.

"Cocaine fillers could be as harmless as powdered milk. They could be mildly toxic, like boric acid, or absolutely deadly, like strychnine or dimethyl terephthalate."

"You're saying the killer diluted the pufferfish toxin with something to make it, what, less deadly?"

"Tetrodotoxin kills by paralyzing the body, by disrupting the message the brain gives the body to move, including breathing. If carefully diluted or modified, the neurotoxin can act as a long-term paralytic, effectively locking the victim inside her own body."

I felt a chill grabbing my insides and twisting them in a tight knot. "What are you saying?"

"She was conscious but unable to move. She willed her body to move, but nothing happened. Eventually, the initial dose of modified toxin would've worn off, in about eight to ten hours, and she should've been able to walk away."

Anne stopped talking, turning her face away from me.

"But?"

"He came back and fed her more poison. The bastard came back several times, refreshing the needed concentration to keep her restrained."

I stood and started pacing; I wanted to scream, or maybe I needed a stiff drink to dislodge the horror that had taken residence in my gut, sending icicles through my veins. I wanted to ask why, what possible reason could someone have to do such an evil thing, but then I understood, remembering the bloodstains, old and new, covering her thighs.

"Was she raped?" I asked in a whisper.

"Repeatedly and violently," Anne replied. "Over the past thirty-six to forty-eight hours, which is my preliminary estimate for the time she spent in the desert, she received three or four doses of poison. That corresponds to the timeline of the assaults she endured. She was raped vaginally, anally, and orally. That," she pointed toward the screen where a reddish-brown sludge was shown in a high degree of magnification, "is what's left of semen after spending several hours immersed in stomach acid."

I didn't see anything; only discolored sludge. But semen meant DNA; I knew that much.

"Does that mean we have DNA evidence?"

"We do, but not from the stomach contents; that's too broken down from the immersion in hydrochloric acid. He was careless enough to leave his mark in numerous other places where it was preserved better. The degree of decay of the semen he left behind will allow me to build a precise timeline of his visits. My report will have the entire analysis."

"Is he in CODIS?" I asked, hoping for a miracle.

"It's still running," she replied.

"All right, that's a lot to process," I replied, getting ready to leave, eager to breathe some fresh air, no matter how cold.

"I'm not done yet," Anne replied.

"Let's hear it," I said, taking a seat back on the stool.

"Alyssa Conway went missing on December nineteenth and was found almost three weeks later. During this time, she sustained frequent and varied forms of sexual assault, none as violent as what she'd gone through in the past couple of days. She was injected with powerful narcotics and hallucinogens and had this embedded under her skin," she added, handing me a small evidence jar.

It was a small, black capsule, not more than three millimeters in length.

"Is this what I think it is?" I asked.

"State-of-the-art microchip with a built-in GPS locator."

"She was tagged like a dog?"

"Precisely."

We didn't need to say anything else; it wasn't the first time the human trafficking trifecta had landed on a cold slab in Anne's morgue: GPS-enabled microchips, signs of repeated sexual abuse, and use of narcotics as a chemical restraint. Victims rarely stayed local though; when they landed on Anne's table, they were usually traced to other cities, other states. Their kidnappers knew to move them quickly, before someone they knew could recognize them in some hotel bar or parking garage on the Strip.

The computer running the CODIS search chimed, and we both rushed to the screen. A message box was popped open, reading, "No matches found."

"Bollocks," I groaned. "Bloody bollocks... I need this case closed quickly."

"Give me a sample to compare it against, and I'll run it. We'll know within minutes."

If only I could get my hands on a suspect to rip some DNA off him and hand it to Anne.

15

Bad News

Twenty-six hours missing

When I left the morgue, the sun was already high. January could be cold in Las Vegas, frigid wind lowering the nightly temperatures well into the low forties, even high thirties. Okay, maybe weather wasn't as severe as it was in other places that time of the year, but for a city that has palm trees lining its boulevards, temperatures close to freezing were unusual. Once the sun shone up high, the cold air blowing from the north lost its teeth, promising spring was not far away.

Back in my London days as a young constable, I'd learned an original way to keep my head riveted firmly on my shoulders, regardless of how terrifying the crime was that I was investigating. I'd seen one of the older inspectors do it; at first, I just copied his actions without fully understanding why.

We'd been called to a scene by a frantic neighbor who'd stumbled on a triple homicide. Someone had butchered a young mother and her two children, leaving the apartment covered in blood. The killer had dipped his fingers in the victims' blood and scribbled messages on the walls, Bible verses, mainly Leviticus verses, 19:29, 21:7, and 21:9, and a slew of profanities and curses. I never forgot those verse numbers, although I had to look them up to understand the killer's message, because he'd attempted to follow the instructions so clearly given in 21:9 and set the woman on fire but had failed. Interrupted by the neighbor who was returning a mixer, he'd fled the apartment.

That was the first homicide I was responding to, and I had pathetically faltered. I wasn't calloused enough to take in such a horrific display and not feel sick, not have the urge to chunder my lunch. Moments later, I saw the chief inspector rushing out of the apartment to look at the sky, squinting into the sun. I did the same, although not really knowing why. Just as turning on a light could dissipate a night terror and clear the mind, the bright rays of sunshine and the blue sky erased some of the emotional trauma imparted by witnessing the horrors that came with the job. The facts remained, coldly carved into my memory, and that helped me catch the killer. Emotion, on the other hand, would've stood in everyone's way.

Clear days were rare in London, but in Vegas, they're almost a given. Coming out of the morgue, I stopped on the sidewalk for a moment and looked at the sky, squinting in the bright light, and I breathed in the refreshing morning air. Then I drove to the nearest Starbucks and ordered myself a venti latte at the drive-thru window.

I pulled into the nearby parking lot and turned my face to the sun again, inviting the healing light to erase the last of the unwanted emotions I still carried after understanding what Alyssa's final days had been like. She didn't need my empathy, my tears, or my internalized nightmares; she would've wanted me to catch her killer and bring him to justice.

I breathed some more, taking small sips of the hot liquid every two or three deep breaths until my heart rate normalized and I was a rational human being again.

There was one bit of information that could help me narrow a suspect list, once I'd have one. Tetrodotoxin wasn't something that most people could pronounce, never mind understand. I'd been one of them until an hour ago. How does one go from raping women to building such an elaborate modus operandi? He had to be someone who'd learned about such toxins, maybe in his profession. I thought that was an excellent place to start.

I took another sip of coffee, pushing to the side an annoying little detail: the rapist was somehow involved with a human trafficking organization.

I called Fletcher.

"Good morning, Detective," he greeted me. His voice filled the space in my vehicle, clear and close as if he were there, riding shotgun and drinking coffee with me.

A tiny, sad smile tugged at the corners of my mouth. "Good morning, Fletch. Got a bunch of questions for you."

"And I got answers. Shoot."

"Where would someone get, um, modified tetrodotoxin these days?"

"Doc called earlier, said you might want to know that."

"Help me understand, what kind of person are we dealing with? An expert of sorts? A doctor? A chemist?"

"He doesn't have to be that sophisticated," Fletcher replied, crushing my hopes with only a few words.

"Then how? I didn't know such a thing existed until now."

"The times are changing, Detective. All he needs is an internet connection, nothing more."

"What do you mean?"

"You can go on the Dark Web and ask for a certain chemical formulation, describing the outcome you desire. He could be as clueless about fish toxins as you and me."

"You're saying he could go out there and ask specifically for what? Stuff that renders women paralyzed but doesn't kill them?"

"Yeah, like that."

I shuddered. "And then what would happen? People would bid for the gig?" I couldn't help the sarcasm that seeped in my voice.

"And he'd pay using some untraceable cryptocurrency. A few days later, he'd take delivery with instructions on how to use the product."

"This can't be legal," I blurted, although I already knew the answer. It wasn't legal; it had never been.

"It's not. We're fighting it the best we can, all law enforcement agencies do."

My thoughts wandered for a moment, forgetting I had Fletcher on the line. If we couldn't use the toxin to narrow a suspect list, what did we really have, if anything?

His DNA, for starters.

His propensity for violence; people didn't shift between phases like werewolves. If the suspect had been that brutal with Alyssa, he must've been a known violent offender or at least have a reputation for violence if he hadn't been caught yet.

The perp had visited the crime scene at several particular moments in time, and when people went somewhere, they usually took two traceable components along for the ride: their vehicles and their phones. To start my investigation on that route, I had to wait for Anne to finish her postmortem and provide me with the timeline of his visits.

I found myself smiling, anticipating the moment I'd lay eyes on that creep. Maybe there'd be no one around and he'd attempt to flee or otherwise resist arrest. In that case, my only dilemma would be Glock or Sig. I routinely carried both.

"Victim background?" Fletcher asked, snapping me out of my reverie.

There was a tension in his voice I hadn't heard before. My smile vanished.

"Sure, go ahead."

"Your vic, Alyssa Conway, disappeared on December nineteenth from her school. There's an open missing persons case for her. She's the daughter of Harold and Geraldine Conway. No juvie record, no priors for either parent. No former marriages, no disgruntlement that I could find in any of their lives. They are the typical, middle-class family. Dad's a financial advisor. Mom's a real estate agent."

"Okay, Fletch, if they're squeaky clean, then what's on your mind?"

There was a moment of silence on the call.

"Where's Holt? Is he there with you?"

That was an excellent question. I hadn't heard from him since last night. He'd ignored my calls and texts, and I'd stopped trying sometime after two in the morning, thinking I was only depleting his phone battery. All I could do was hope he was all right, making progress in finding his daughter.

I hadn't slept a wink, wondering if the kidnappers had called again with instructions, if that stubborn mule I had for a partner had surrendered himself to his daughter's kidnappers in the off chance they'd keep their word and return her safely. I wondered if I was ever going to see him again.

It was funny how, in only a few weeks, our lives had become so intertwined that I couldn't think of a future where he wouldn't play a role, even if only to drive me completely insane.

"He's not here, Fletch," I eventually replied. "I don't know where he is. Why?"

"I have some bad news, Baxter," he said, then stopped talking again.

"Spill it already," I reacted.

"Alyssa Conway was taken the exact same way as Holt's kid was. Two men, posing as cops, lifted her from volleyball practice."

No, no, no, I thought, my mind racing. I wasn't hearing that. It couldn't be true.

"How come we're just hearing about this now?"

"There are hundreds of missing persons cases still open in Vegas. We can't keep up with all of them."

"Why wasn't there a BOLO on the two suspects and their car? You'd think anyone impersonating police officers would warrant a BOLO."

"When they took Alyssa, they didn't speak with anyone. Witnesses saw them from a distance. The perps waited for her to leave practice and approached her on the sidewalk. No one had any descriptions, and there were no street cameras near that location."

He stopped talking for a moment, letting the silence set in, while my mind continued to scream. *No! Please don't let this happen.*

"Do you think it's a ser—" Fletcher started to ask.

"No," I snapped. "Don't you bloody say the words, all right? Don't make it real."

I breathed, trying to soothe my anger, my fears. I'd yelled at him for no reason. If we were to save Meredith, to catch those men, we needed to reason freely and say the words we needed to say, uncensored.

"I'm sorry, Fletch, I really am," I whispered. I wanted to say more, but words died on my lips, unwilling to come out. "Yes, we might be looking at a serial killer," I eventually said, my throat constricted and inexplicably dry. "We've only had one victim, but—"

"I'm getting the serial killer vibe," he said.

That was one way of putting it.

"Will you tell Holt?" he asked.

"Yes, I will, as soon as I can find him."

How the hell would I tell him? What words could I possibly use? The moment he heard what I had to say he'd fall apart, and for good reason.

"I don't know where he is either. His phone's off. Speaking of Holt, remember that warehouse on the Beltway?" Fletcher asked. "Were you there last night?"

"No," I replied, closing my eyes, anticipating hearing that the place had been blown sky high.

"There was an active nine-one-one call at that address this morning. They found an ex-con with a rap sheet a mile long, a little banged up, with a nine-mil hole in his leg, tied to a tree."

Holt.

"Is he talking?"

"Not a single word."

"Okay," I replied, not really thinking of what I was saying, not really able to gather my thoughts after hearing about Alyssa's abduction. "Do we have the sketches for the two men yet? Fletch, I need those men identified. Have you tried facial recognition?"

"They're running already. No hits in NCIC yet."

16

Lies

Twenty-seven hours missing

Special Agent Glover watched his colleague, SA Rosales, gently pull the bedroom door shut, after persuading Meredith's mother to lie down for a few minutes.

He didn't like Rosales much; the way she looked down on him, even though she was almost a foot shorter, brought out the worst in him. Her arrogance was so palpable, it felt as if there was a stench of something acrid in the room whenever she was present, and he wanted to wrinkle his nose in disgust. That aside, the thirty-year-old woman had some serious skills. She was the absolute best with kidnapped victims' families. Something in the way she talked to them instilled the confidence needed to calm the parents and get them out of the way, so the professionals could do their jobs. Hats off to Rosales for her diplomacy and her mannerisms, because the rest of her was insufferable.

She was smart, he'd give her that, but she was keenly aware of her superior brainpower. She wasn't the only intelligent being in the room, yet she behaved as if she were. When explaining something, the woman spoke as if, between the lines, there was a question about to be voiced: "Do I *really* have to spell it out for you?"

He sighed, seeing her approach in silent steps entirely muffled by the thick, cut-pile carpeting. She was as irritating as a bad case of anal itch on an eighteen-hour stakeout, with her slightly tilted head and her chin thrust forward.

"How is she?" Glover asked.

"She's finally asleep," Rosales replied, rolling her eyes. "I can't believe how long she lasted, pills and all."

"I can," Glover replied. "It's her kid, what would you expect? Do you have children, Rosales?"

She didn't bother to answer; she threw a side glance toward the kitchen table, where the landline phone gathered dust in complete silence, refusing to cooperate. Jennifer's cell phone, wired to a recording device and plugged into the wall for power, was also silent. Neither had rung since Meredith had been taken, except for a few concerned friends and neighbors and, for the past few hours, not once had either device disturbed the tense and tear-filled gloom of the house.

"I'd expect a ransom call," she muttered angrily. "And where's the father in all this?"

Glover scratched his chin with tobacco-stained fingers. He let his fingernails grow longer than most men, not because of some fashion statement he wanted to make, and not by much, only one or two millimeters. He was rather averse to clippers, hated scissors, and nail files made his skin crawl. The veteran agent with two honorary medals in his file, who wouldn't hesitate for a moment to jump in the line of fire to shield a child from bullets with his own body, dreaded cutting his nails. He also craved a cigarette, a real one, not the vape kind.

"He's out there looking for her, Rosales; that's what I'd do," he replied, deciding to postpone taking another smoke break for at least a half hour.

Rosales stiffened, looking straight at him. He could've sworn she stretched and stood on her toes to appear taller, even if by only an inch.

"Would you also lie to the federal agents who are there to help you find your kid? Would you be so damn stupid?"

He didn't know. Every time they landed a new case and he was faced with the tragedy of yet another family having to deal with the loss of a child, even if temporary, he silently said a prayer of thanks it wasn't him going home to an empty crib or receiving the phone call that forever changed a parent's life. He didn't know how he'd react, or what he'd do, even with all his experience with kidnapping cases. He only knew he'd stop at nothing to get his child back. He guessed that Detective Jack Holt was busy out there somewhere, doing the same thing.

"We're being played for fools, Glover," Rosales hissed. "We're watching this damn phone that's never going to ring. And do you know why?"

"No, I don't know why," he mocked her, unable to refrain himself, seeing how entitled and presumptuous she was. "Go ahead, explain it to me."

"I'm willing to bet a week's pay that Holt already got the ransom call, and he's busying himself dealing with it," Rosales said, keeping her voice low. Only a thin door separated them from the former Mrs. Holt's bedroom.

"He didn't strike me as particularly rich, to handle a ransom demand on his own," Glover replied, suspecting Rosales was right but unwilling to give her the satisfaction of admitting she might be on to something.

"Cops have their ways, you know that," she said.

Glover didn't reply; instead, he plunged his hands inside his pants pockets and paced aimlessly through the kitchen, looking at the pile of papers laid out on the table, then absent-mindedly at the laptop screen.

"He's going to screw this up badly," Rosales insisted. "He's going to get that girl killed."

Glover stopped abruptly, feeling like stomping his foot in anger. The woman was absolutely impossible with her manipulations and her twisted words. They didn't know any of that; they didn't know if Holt was screwing anything up. He would've preferred to have Holt right there in that kitchen, waiting impatiently as any other parent would do in his situation, but Holt wasn't like any other parent. He was a cop.

"What do you want to do, huh? He's an adult, a father, and he's law enforcement. He deserves some credit. Even if he doesn't, he didn't break any laws. What would you do? Chain him to the wall?"

"Yes!" she asserted excitedly. "Throw him in jail under a temporary hold, do something, only don't let him roam the streets like a madman, doing who knows what. Get him under control."

Good thing she wasn't foaming at the mouth. She was being ridiculous again; the same way she was every time he didn't immediately comply with whatever crossed her mind to do. His seniority didn't matter, nothing did. If the case went south for some reason, and that was a possibility, given no one had contacted the family in over twenty-four hours, she'd get to pontificate and tell everyone how she'd been adamant about this and that, making him look like a fool to everyone at the bureau.

Screw that... He wasn't giving in to her whims either, no matter the consequences.

Doctors hated having other doctors for patients; law enforcement wasn't any different. Working with their own kind was challenging. Glover was a stickler for procedure on any typical day, but this day was far from ordinary. Yes, ideally Holt would be compliant and let the CARD team locate the girl and bring her home. But the seasoned cop also knew the statistical odds, and those odds weren't in favor of sitting and waiting. Over thirty-two thousand missing children cases were still showing open in the federal systems, probably never to be solved. The more time passed, the lower the chances for a happy ending. And time was running out for a scared, fifteen-year-old girl who might soon be dead if they couldn't figure out a way to find her and bring her home.

"Why don't you go back to work and finish sorting through Holt's old cases? That's where I'd place my bets," Glover said, grabbing a file and starting to thumb through it quickly. "This cop must've pissed someone off really badly in his fourteen years on the force."

"How about Holt?"

"What about him?" Glover pushed back, pretending he wasn't getting it.

"Let's locate him."

"No," Glover replied coldly. "Our job is to find Meredith, and Holt didn't take her. Go back to work, Rosales."

"What if he—"

"For the last time, Rosales, drop it. Holt is a decorated Navy officer who served eight years with a Special Warfare Group. I'd say—"

"Yeah, yeah, he was a SEAL," she interrupted. "So? Don't the same rules apply to him?"

"He deserves some confidence. I'm willing to trust him."

"Never trust a word Jack Holt is saying when he's after something." Jennifer's voice startled them both.

She stood in her bedroom doorway, disheveled, pale, and red-eyed. She leaned against the doorframe, holding on to it with both hands as if it were the only thing keeping her from falling.

"Do you know something we don't?" Glover asked.

"I know the man I used to be married to. He lies like a pro," she replied. "Apparently, they taught him that in the SEALs."

Glover struggled to contain a smile. Hell hath no fury, although he couldn't understand why the woman, who had remarried twice after her divorce from Holt, still seemed so badly scorned.

"I don't believe they teach deceptive tactics in Special Warfare," he replied, "but I believe you," he added quickly, seeing her eyebrows angle dangerously.

"What should we expect from him?" Rosales asked in her charismatic, velvet voice that went a long way with heartbroken parents.

"Bodies piling up until he finds Meredith," she replied with an indifferent shrug.

She went back into the bedroom and closed the door behind her, while Glover stared after her, wondering what, if anything, was wrong with Holt's anticipated plan of attack.

He would've done the same if it was his child; have his own plan. The man deserved a break, and some real, off-the-books support from other law enforcement officers, like him and, unfortunately, Special Agent Rosales.

That might take some doing.

17

Heidi

Twenty-eight hours missing

I arrived at the Conway residence and cut the engine, then took a brief moment to summon the strength I needed to ring the doorbell and shatter the hopes of two heartbroken parents. I'd still not heard a word from Holt and wondered if he suspected there was a correlation between his daughter's kidnapping and Alyssa Conway.

Images of the crime scene invaded my mind, and unanswered questions immediately followed. But this wasn't the right time to dive into the mind of a psychopathic murderer, to try to understand his motives, his urges, his dark fantasies.

I pushed those questions aside for later and walked quickly to the house. As soon as I pressed the button, I heard rushed footfalls, and a brief moment later, Mrs. Conway opened the door.

Blood drained from her face when she saw me; without a word she stepped to the side, inviting me in. I only got as far as the granite-tiled hallway, when she broke down in tears.

"She's gone, isn't she?" Mrs. Conway asked, trying to contain her sobs with her hand pressed firmly against her gaping mouth. "My little girl is gone," she wailed, heaving, out of breath.

I wondered how she knew, then realized it wasn't that difficult to figure out. I didn't look chipper, like a bearer of good news would've seemed. I also wasn't the cop they'd been working with on their daughter's missing persons case. The badge hanging from my belt didn't leave any doubt in her mind as to who I was.

"I'm very sorry for your loss," I said, looking around for a tissue to give her. I didn't see any. I walked over to the kitchen, looking around. The house had fallen into disarray. Since their daughter had disappeared, the Conways had probably stopped caring about keeping their home in order.

I saw a roll of paper towels on the counter, littered with dirty dishes, and I grabbed it, then walked back into the living room. Mr. Conway had appeared, probably from upstairs, and was holding his wife in a tight hug, his tears getting lost in her hair. I waited, unwilling to interrupt, yet painfully aware of every passing minute.

"I'm Detective Baxter, Las Vegas Homicide," I said quietly, knowing what effect the last word would have on them.

They pulled slightly away from each other and looked at me through a veil of tears.

"I have questions about your daughter's abduction," I added gently. "I'm hoping you could—"

"Oh, *now* it's an abduction?" Mr. Conway reacted, his anger turned to bitterness under the shock of learning his daughter was gone. "We told you she didn't just leave," he continued. "But you wouldn't believe us. You said she'd run away, or maybe she was mad at us, like teenagers get sometimes, and left with some friends. You just wouldn't listen, you and your damn rules."

Feeling a bit uneasy, I lowered my gaze and stared at the floor. I'd never been a fan of the part of police procedure that doesn't take missing persons reports seriously in the first twenty-four hours. In Alyssa's case, acting immediately could've made the difference between life and death, a terrible, senseless, and horrifying death.

Alyssa had last been seen getting into an unmarked police car, with two uniformed cops. Unlike Meredith, she'd been observed from a distance, after having left the gym and crossed the street, and there were discrepancies among the witness statements. Nothing unexpected; witness accounts are often unreliable, especially when the witnesses in question were teenagers playing ball. Most of them agreed that Alyssa had climbed into the car willingly, without apparent pressure from either of the two men. Because no ransom call had been received, her disappearance had been considered a missing persons case and treated accordingly, not as a kidnapping. It was kept on the back burner for the first twenty-four hours, and by then, no new information could be found, no forensics or new witness accounts.

The absence of a ransom call further substantiated the decision to classify her as a missing person. Based on Anne's autopsy findings, Alyssa had been held in captivity and sexually assaulted repeatedly for the past three weeks, then taken into the desert for the last forty-eight hours of her ordeal. The presence of the GPS tracker microchip in her arm seemed to indicate she'd been taken by a human trafficking organization and forced into sexual slavery. The last two days of her torment pointed in the direction of an extremely sadistic serial killer.

It didn't fit. None of it did. Alyssa's story felt as if someone had pasted together two scenes from two different movies, one featuring a sex trafficking organization servicing Vegas clientele with underage girls, and the other a murderous psychopath like none she'd seen before.

But Meredith's ransom call had happened already, and Holt seemed to know what that was about, although he wouldn't share.

Bloody hell, Holt…

Then how were the two cases related? Were the two girls frequenting the same circles?

I raised my eyes and looked straight at Mr. Conway, hoping my compassion could bring even the tiniest amount of comfort.

"I understand your frustration—" I started to say, but he didn't let me finish.

"This isn't frustration," he said, gesturing at himself and his wife. "There's no word in the dictionary to describe what I—what *we* feel. You killed our daughter, you and the other cops." He pressed his lips together, as if containing his urge to scream, then took a few steps toward the door.

"Mr. Conway, please," I said, realizing he was about to kick me out. "I need some information about your daughter."

"We told everything we knew to the police, the detective who worked on Alyssa's case. If she worked on it at all. What else could you possibly want to know?"

I decided to take a different approach. "Who was your daughter's best friend?"

He sighed and pointed out the window. "The girl next door, Heidi. They've been inseparable since they were this tall," he said, lowering his palm to about knee level.

"I read in the case file that Alyssa had a boyfriend, Noel Franks," I said. "What can you tell me about him?"

"He's a kid, a seventeen-year-old kid, two years her senior," Mr. Conway replied. "We thought he might've been involved in this somehow, but after he came over here crying his eyes out every day for a week, we started thinking otherwise."

Yeah, the seventeen-year-old boyfriend didn't fit at all with the sex trafficking angle.

"We asked him many times," Mrs. Conway intervened. Her voice broke with every word, and her breathing was shallow and shattered. "He hadn't seen her leave with those cops, and he said Alyssa never told him anything that would suggest she knew who they might've been. No… she vanished one day, just like that."

"She was taken; she didn't vanish," Mr. Conway snapped. "Like we always said she was."

There was nothing more I could do but let the two parents grieve in peace.

I excused myself and walked out of there as quickly as I could, leaving their split-level house, heading for the neighbor's ranch-style, three-car garage property. By the look of those houses, the homeowners must've been successful in their professions, or they caught a good deal, because I knew I couldn't afford a house like theirs, not even if I earned twice my pay.

I rang the bell next door, and a flushed teenage girl opened immediately, wearing a smile that vanished when she realized I wasn't who she was expecting. She wore her light brown hair straight and mid-back long, with blonde highlights on the bottom. Her bra straps were visible on her shoulders underneath a white sports top, and ridiculously short, frayed Daisy Dukes left little to the imagination. Who the hell was that fifteen-year-old expecting to ring her bell?

I showed my badge and entered, after being reluctantly invited in. "Are your parents home, Heidi?"

She shook her head quickly, while her pupils dilated. "Uh-uh, no."

Bollocks… I was about to question a minor without a guardian present. Just as I recalled Holt and his interview with Casey, Meredith's best friend, I realized what the two girls had in common, Casey and Heidi. They both looked trashy, despite their young age. I wondered if that was another correlation, or it simply was the way teenage girls dressed these days.

"I have some questions about Alyssa," I started to say, but then remembered she didn't know she'd been found dead. As soon as I broke the news to her, she rushed to the bathroom and slammed the door behind her. I could hear her sobs through the door, loud at first, then more and more subsided.

I gave her a few minutes; eventually, she came out wiping her eyes and nose with a Kleenex.

"I'm really sorry for your loss," I said gently.

She walked over to one of the large, white leather armchairs and threw herself on it sideways, flinging her slender legs over the armrest.

"You have no idea," she blurted, then sniffled and wiped her nose again. "My parents are going to be so freaked out, they're going to ground me for, like, ever. Why the fuck did she have to die, huh? That isn't fair!"

I was aware my jaw had dropped and quickly controlled my appearance.

"Tell me she wasn't raped or something," she said in a frustrated tone. "That's all my mom needs to hear to dress me up like a nun for the rest of my life."

"I'm sorry to say, but yes, she was raped," I replied coldly, knowing the local news channel was going to run the story with all the sordid details for as long as it could.

"Damn perfect," she snapped, flexing her legs at the knee above the armrest and hitting the furniture with her heels in a rhythm of spoiled irritation. "Okay, so what do you want?" she turned to me and asked.

"Just some information, and then I'll let you grieve," I replied, not even attempting to disguise my sarcasm.

She didn't seem to notice it. She made an impatient gesture with her hand, inviting me to talk.

"Have any men approached you or Alyssa with, um, unusual insistence?"

She put a finger to her lips and stared at the ceiling for a moment. "Men approach us, you know," she said with a lascivious smile. "Men who aren't dead."

"Anyone standing out from the hordes of men fawning over you two?"

She shot me a side glance as if to warn me I'd taken it too far, and she wasn't an idiot. But then a sly smile bloomed on her perfectly glossed lips.

"Promise not to tell my parents?"

I made a quick cross with my fingers above my heart in a gesture I hadn't done since high school, while keeping a perfectly serious composure. "I swear."

"Alyssa sometimes liked playing games with men, you know. Make them pay?" she added, seeing I was staring at her dumbfounded.

I frowned. At fifteen, Alyssa was a call girl. Bloody fantastic. "Did your friend have a pimp?"

Heidi laughed heartily, in a resounding voice. "No, nothing like that. She wasn't a hooker."

"Then what was she doing?"

"I'll explain," she said excitedly, lowering her voice as if she was about to share a juicy secret. She shifted in the armchair, turning and sitting straight the way people normally did, back against the backrest, feet on the floor, arms folded neatly in her lap. Then she leaned forward, and I took two steps closer and crouched to her eye level. "Some guy offered us both a hundred each to let him, um, you know," she said, blushing a little.

"No, I don't know," I stated calmly, cringing in anticipation.

"To put his finger in there," she whispered. "I said 'no way'; he was gross. Sweating, bald and fat, eww. But Alyssa said yes. She needed the money. I understood that, so I kept watch while he... Um, anyway, then he was gone. Quickest hundred ever, not even five minutes." She whistled, as to express her admiration for her late friend's money-making abilities.

"Didn't you try to stop her?" I asked, feeling so nauseous I longed for a drink of water, even the stale bottle in my car.

"Nah... She needed the money pretty badly."

"What for?" I asked. The Conways seemed well-off, their house furnished with all the trimmings of a prosperous, middle-class family.

"Stuff," she replied, looping a strand of hair around her finger. "Like earrings, lingerie, you know, stuff."

I swallowed with difficulty; I was suffocated by the need to yell at the girl until I unloaded all that I had to say about her reckless behavior.

"Then what happened?" I asked calmly instead, knowing that my advice would not be well received and would represent a waste of time I couldn't afford.

"Nothing," Heidi replied, looking at her watch and frowning. "We need to wrap this up," she added. "I'm busy." She grabbed her phone and checked for messages, then sighed.

"I thought you were going to tell me something about Alyssa and how she liked to make men pay," I said, wondering where our conversation had derailed so badly.

"That's what I did," she replied, giving me a condescending stare. "You needed an example, and I gave you one. That hundred bucks was how she got started."

"Started with what?" I asked, unwilling to believe the obvious without double-checking.

She groaned and jumped to her feet, then started pacing the room, every few steps looking outside the window. "With men and money. She started to like it, the money, that she didn't have to ask her parents for it no more."

"Did she work the Strip? The hotels?" I asked, finally accepting the possibility that Alyssa had been a little more than a trashy teenager.

"No, she wasn't a whore, I told you that already," Heidi said, in an escalating tone. "Jeez... You really don't get it, do you?"

"No, I don't," I replied simply. "Was she sleeping with men?"

"Her parents would've killed her, so no. These days it's all about oral, so you don't get pregnant or caught," she said, chuckling quietly. "Then, she'd make them pay."

I stood there speechless, suddenly feeling old at thirty-six. When had the entire world gone to bloody hell?

Then I remembered what I'd wanted to ask and showed Heidi a photo of Meredith. "Do you know this girl? She goes to Western, just like you do, and she's your age. Or maybe Alyssa knew her?"

"I've seen her, yeah. I remember her... She's a poser. She's got this lame Goth thing going on, like it's halfway done. She's going for Goth but doesn't have the guts to go all the way. We don't hang out with her."

That meant Meredith might've not been as tawdry as the other girls.

"Was she, um, making men pay, by any chance?"

She laughed and dismissed my question with a wave of her hand. "Those guys like blondes. She's a brunette. If she wanted to go that way without a serious makeover, she'd starve."

A car pulled in at the curb, and a moment later, a door slammed shut. Heidi's grin widened, then turned into a scowl when she remembered I took space in her living room. Her date was there, and my time was up.

"One more question and I'll leave. Where do you girls find these men who are willing to have oral sex with teenagers and pay for it?"

18

Snitch

Twenty-nine hours missing

Holt checked his watch and cursed. He felt anguish creeping up on him, numbing his mind, paralyzing him, yet rendering him frantic. He'd been running all night, trying to find a trace, a lead, a witness, or anyone who knew anything and could point him in the right direction. His clothes were soaked with acrid sweat, but he didn't feel the chill of the windy, January day. He didn't feel the pain of his bruised shoulder, or the throbbing in his eye, swollen shut by Darrell's fist. All he felt was deepening despair for every moment his little girl spent in captivity, at the mercy of her kidnapper.

Holt knew it firsthand. When it came to mercy, Samuel "Snowman" Klug had none.

Exhausted, he leaned against the chain-link fencing that surrounded the employee parking lot of the Scala Hotel and Casino and gave Industrial Road another look.

It was relatively quiet, but it was early for the Las Vegas Strip, only 1:15 in the afternoon. Most of last night's drunks were still nursing their hangovers or getting ready for another binge session, preceded by artery-popping burgers and fries, whose smells filled the Strip joints north and south of Flamingo Road and gnawed at his empty, growling stomach. As for the local street corner pushers, they were starting to come out again, stocked up and ready for Saturday night, the best of the week by substance sales volume.

Soon the place would be crawling with kids buying and selling junk.

Holt saw a dope peddler, one he hadn't seen before, coming out of the woodwork behind the Scala with a younger kid in tow. The hotel's parking lot was undergoing renovations, and part of it was fenced off with tarp-covered, chain-link barriers. Holt crept alongside the barriers and approached the pusher without being seen.

The dealer couldn't've been more than seventeen, maybe eighteen years old, a scrawny kid who belonged in school, not selling coke behind the Strip's fanciest hotels. But his lack of experience could work in Holt's favor, and the detective was grateful for any miracle, no matter how small.

Holt left the cover of the construction fencing and approached the kid, feigning hesitation, looking left and right for any police cruiser traffic. Any legit buyer would check the street for cops; only rookie undercover law enforcement trying to set up a buy would advance on their mark straight and quick as an arrow.

The two youngsters were chatting casually, both listening to music on their earbuds and talking at the same time, almost dancing in place with hints of rhythm in their lazy, uncoordinated steps. When Holt appeared, the youngest one vanished, while the other's smile disappeared.

"Need some candy," Holt said in a low voice, after looking around again. He pulled a crisp fifty-dollar bill out of his wallet and held it out with two fingers.

"Yeah, like I need a dick up my ass," the kid replied. "What, you think I'm stupid, man? You reek of bacon. Get the hell out of here."

"Snowman sent me," Holt said, hoping he'd get the kid to cooperate. "Come on, hit me, okay?" he insisted, showing the kid his bruised knuckles, raw and bloody after an entire night's worth of pounding on anyone who could've given him any information. "I need something for the pain."

The kid looked at him with a slight head tilt, then spat on the ground. "Aren't you that cop whose kid has gone missing?"

"What do you know about that?" Holt asked, his tone different, less pleading, more threatening. He took his right hand to the side of his jacket, ready to lift the flap and pull out his service weapon.

"Nothin'," the kid replied quickly, his pitch higher, traces of discernible panic seeping into his inflections. He raised his arms in the air. "Nothin', I swear. Just some street talk, that's all."

"What street talk?"

The kid shook his head and shoved his dirty hands into the deep pockets of his baggy jeans, pulling them up an inch higher and taking a step back. By the looks of it, he was getting ready to bolt. Holt stepped toward him, forcing him to retreat against the fence where he could grab the boy the moment he made his move.

The kid looked toward the hotel, then down the street. No one was coming. He sighed and mumbled a few words, then decided it was probably better if he cooperated.

"Word's out there that some crazed-up cop whose daughter got snatched is beating on the pavement guys, trying to get them to snitch."

"Is that it?" Holt asked, a menacing look piercing the boy from underneath a furrowed brow. He removed a set of zip cuffs from his belt and grabbed the pusher's arm. "Turn around, smartass, you're going down."

"What for?" the kid reacted, trying to wriggle free from Holt's grip. "I ain't done nothin'."

"We'll figure that out," Holt said, tightening the cuffs around the kid's wrists. "I could've sworn you tried to sell me some cocaine, remember that?"

"Hey, that's a lie," he cried. "It's entrapment."

"Unless you have some information for me. Then I'd be willing to forget the whole incident."

"I ain't no snitch," the kid said, holding his head up high although his chin was quivering.

"Fine by me," Holt said, shooting another worried look at his watch.

Time was flying by with the speed of light when he wished he could make it stand still. He'd lost count of the pieces of scum he'd interrogated since last night, then let them go without charging them formally with any crime. Not because they were innocent; no. He couldn't afford the time it would've taken to call in a cruiser and turn them over to the patrols. And he couldn't make most of the charges stick in court, without being able to show any probable cause for the arrests. Most of all, he had no time to waste.

His little girl didn't have any time left.

He grabbed the boy by the collar and slammed him against the fence.

"Where's Snowman? Where can I find him?"

The kid's eyes were open wide, staring straight at Holt, filled with fear. "I— I don't know, man, I swear! It's not like we're socializin', if you know what I mean. He's up there with the fat cats, I'm down here, on the back streets."

Holt sunk his hand into one of the kid's pockets and fished out a few small plastic bags. A couple of the bags held specks of white powder; others held pills. There were enough tablets of oxy, Vicodin, ecstasy, and a few others he couldn't identify, to start a small drug store. Last in the handful were a couple of dime bags, each packing ten dollars' worth of weed.

"This bunch will earn you three hots and a cot for a few years," Holt hissed in the kid's face. "Care to try our accommodations as a guest of Nevada's prison system? Or do you want to tell me what I need to know so you can go back to poisoning people one pill at a time?"

"You're going to let me go?" the kid asked, wrinkling his forehead in surprise. "You think I'm an idiot?"

"Tell me what I want to know, and I'll keep in mind I had no probable cause for the body search," Holt replied, filled with bitterness against the legal system that tied his hands behind his back every day of the week. "Even a pro bono lawyer can get you out with no time served."

The kid stared at Holt for a long moment, biting his lip. "All I got is a rumor. He shacks out in Henderson somewhere, on a large property, so the neighbors don't hear the gunshots when he feels like shooting people. That's all I know, I swear."

"How about these two men?" he asked, showing the kid a photo of the two fake cops who'd taken Meredith.

"Uh-uh, haven't laid eyes on them," he replied.

He seemed truthful. Holt cut off the zip cuffs with a bitter sigh. "Get out of here, before I change my mind."

The kid bolted without waiting for a second invitation, and Holt hurried toward Industrial Road, where he'd parked his car. Henderson... at least he knew that much. A few years ago, after an eight-month undercover stint, Holt brought Snowman's organization tumbling down. Snowman had fallen off the radar after barely evading capture. Some voices put him in South America, others in the Dominican Republic.

Now he was here, back to the city he was addicted to, hiding under some desert rock like the venomous snake that he was.

Feeling a dull pain in his side with every step, Holt paid little attention to his surroundings, letting his mind wander. His target was in Henderson, but where? Three hundred thousand people lived in Henderson.

He needed help.

Fletcher could tell him where to look for Snowman's property, pull up satellite imagery, or whatever the hell he did to find things. And Baxter, she was resourceful and smart. He needed Baxter. For a moment, he couldn't recall why he'd left her behind and roamed the streets alone with his phone turned off.

Then he remembered. From where he was going, there was no coming back.

He was almost at the car when a middle-aged jogger, dressed in gray track pants and a sweatshirt, turned the corner and bumped into Holt. Instead of apologizing and moving on, the man stopped in front of Holt, raising his fists and getting ready to pounce.

"Yo, piece of walking pig shit, you blind or something?" he asked loudly, staring intently at Holt. Street slang intonation and pronunciation were strong in his voice, eerily familiar.

The detective thought he recognized the man but couldn't place him. He reminded him of an informant he used to work with, back in his early days as a beat cop.

He didn't have time for any of that, whatever *that* was.

"Get lost," Holt replied, but the man blocked his way, then feigned a punch to the cop's throat.

Holt pulled out his weapon and took two steps back. "All right, that does it. Hands where I can see them."

"Finally," the man muttered. "Now cuff me and haul my ass out of here."

Holt stared at the man for a moment, then nodded slightly while holstering his gun. He cuffed the man and grabbed his arm, leading him to the SUV, beginning to understand what was going on. He was dead tired, or else he would've caught on sooner to the man's intentions.

Informers couldn't be seen talking to cops; their lives depended on that, and everyone on the force knew that. A snitch's life wasn't worth more than the time it took to make one phone call and have him dealt with, quickly and violently, so that each lesson would serve as an example to anyone else who felt that cutting a deal with the police was a good idea.

Holt held the man's head down and loaded him in the back seat of his Interceptor, then drove off. For a few seconds, his passenger stayed silent, looking at Holt through the reflection in the rearview mirror.

"You don't remember me," he eventually said. "You cut me loose one time, almost ten years ago, when I was, um, allegedly pushing dope to feed my family. I owe you a big one. I would've lost my kid if I'd been locked up back then." He scratched his stubbly face and grinned, showing two rows of crooked teeth laid out in a severe underbite. "I cleaned up my act and been on the straight and narrow ever since," he added with a tinge of pride in his voice. "I cut hair for a living."

Good for him. Holt listened impatiently, driving toward the Interstate and wondering if the man had anything useful to say or was just another waste of his precious time.

"Now I'm going to help you get your kid back," the man continued.

Holt's heart swelled. "What can you tell me?"

"Not much, but I heard they're keeping her with the rest of Snowman's new girls."

"What girls?"

"You didn't know? He's into exotic escort services these days. Underage girls, rape fantasies, virgins, bondage, anything your heart desires, if you can pay for it," he added. "Once a year, he holds auctions online for the really weird shit, and he always delivers the goods. You won't believe what some people pay to get their hands on one of these poor girls."

Holt hit the brakes and brought the SUV to a sudden, screeching stop, then turned to face the man. "Are you messing with me right now? Did Snowman have you deliver a threat to me, is that it? Because if you are, they'll need dental records to put a name tag on your corpse."

"No, honest to God, no. I only want to help you get your kid back. Find where he's keeping those girls and you'll find your kid. Rumor has it he gets the new girls addicted to dope and teaches them the oldest profession in history, to cater to the rich, depraved customers."

Holt breathed heavily, letting the significance of what the man had said sink in. If his old source was telling the truth, he had even less time than he'd anticipated. The ultimate revenge for that son of a bitch, Klug, was forcing his baby girl into prostitution.

"Where does he work those girls?" Holt asked between gritted teeth, starting to drive again.

"Only the high-end hotels. He's got the bartenders and bellhops on his payroll."

19

Captive

Thirty hours missing

She crouched, leaning against the cold, looped wires, and hugged her knees, burying her face against her folded arms and letting fresh tears fall. Her sobs were quiet, subdued by fear and exhaustion. Every few minutes, she raised her head from the cradle of her arms and looked at the door, afraid of the moment it would open again.

She was cold. She'd been trembling hard with her teeth chattering the entire night, and now that the sun was high, she could feel a bit of warmth coming through the pitched roof, but not nearly enough to ease her shivers.

Most of all, she was sorry, and she missed her mom. Sorry for all the angry, cheeky words she'd spat back at her mother whenever she'd given her advice. "Don't be so slutty, Krista," she'd said, and Krista had lashed out bitterly at her mother, not because she was wrong, but because she was right. "Don't be so desperate to get a boyfriend; no one will respect you if you don't play a little hard to get. Lengthen those skirts an inch or two, and you'll have a line forming outside your door," her mother had added, then ran her warm fingers across Krista's cheeks in a caress she'd give anything to feel again. "There's time," her mother had whispered smiling, "You're so young. Trust me, there's time."

No, there wasn't. Her mother had been wrong about that, and right about everything else.

Three days ago, her biggest fear was that she was going to show up at the prom still a virgin, the last one in her group of friends to give it up. She was terrified of that as if she'd be forced to wear a sign, a scarlet letter V embroidered on the corsage of her satin gown, informing everyone of her mortal sin: no man had touched her body.

Now all she wished for were the things she had so heartily despised only a few days ago. Her mother's warm hands touching her face, her level voice giving advice. Warm clothing. A shower. A bed with clean sheets where she could sleep and feel safe.

Instead, she was half-naked, locked inside a ten-by-four chain link kennel lined up against the wall of a large garage and tucked between two other cages just like it, occupied by other girls her age. She was living a nightmare from which there was no waking up.

Krista raised her head and looked at the door, then breathed a trembling sigh of relief. She was afraid of the moment that door would open again. They would come for one of them, or they'd bring Mindy back, and she wasn't ready to face either scenario.

She looked at the neighboring cages. To her left, an empty enclosure where Mindy was usually locked up. She thought of Mindy and her heart broke. Mindy had stopped crying for a while, and barely seemed present anymore, as if she were in a different realm where nothing could touch her. Whenever the men came and pulled her out of there, she complied; she'd stopped fighting a couple of days ago.

The other girl, a feisty brunette, got on Krista's nerves. Every chance she had, the girl shouted at their captors, delivering profanities and threats without making much sense. She hadn't shared her name but kept on yelling some weird shit about her dad and how he was going to find her and kill every single one of those men. The girl paced her cage like a lanky, snarling, rabid lioness, waiting for another opportunity to irritate the crap out of their captors.

How stupid could she be? What purpose could that foul mouth of hers possibly serve?

Right then, the brunette locked eyes with Krista and held her disapproving gaze without flinching. Then Krista looked away, turning her attention toward Mindy's empty cage.

They were keeping Mindy out there for a long time. If Krista could tell the time at all, Mindy must've been gone for a few hours. If Krista held her breath and listened hard, she thought she could hear her screams in the distance, muffled by thick walls and, at times, covered by raspy bouts of laughter.

When the door opened, Krista flinched. She withdrew into the farthest corner of her cage, trembling badly, watching the opening with large, fearful eyes. Then a man came in, the huge one with the mustache. He was covered in tattoos, bizarre ones, not like what she and her friends would get. His arms, thick as tree trunks, were covered in snakes and knives and tribal tats like she'd never seen before. But the most intriguing one and the scariest, although she didn't know why, was the one on his forehead, a series of numbers below some words she couldn't make out. It must've had a meaning, if it had been deemed worthy of being inked on the man's forehead, as if it were a label identifying the man's true essence.

Behind him, Mindy barely stood, shaky, pale, hugging herself with trembling hands.

"Come on already," he snapped, turning toward her. "Move."

Krista heard a whimper as the man grabbed Mindy and shoved her into the garage, then dragged her across the dirty cement floor to her cage. He opened the door to the kennel and shoved Mindy inside, then pushed the shackle on the padlock, laughing.

"See? It wasn't that bad," he commented, talking to Mindy but giving Krista a head-to-toe, leery look that sent waves of shivers down her spine. "Soon you'll start to like it. You'll beg me for it."

"You motherfucker," the brunette shouted. "You'll be dead by the end of the day, you hear me? Dead! And I'll piss on your grave, yeah, that's what I'll do."

The man snarled and spat in her direction, then he slammed both his hands against her cage. The brunette fell silent and faltered backward until she reached the wall.

Krista started crying, and her quiet, frightened sobs stretched the man's inked lips into a lustful grin. Then he walked over to the door and left, slamming it shut behind him.

Krista stopped crying, breathed, and put her fingers through the chain links of her cage, reaching for Mindy. The girl sat on the floor crying quietly, but her fingers reached for Krista's and grabbed them, squeezing tight.

"It will be all right," Krista said, "you'll see, it will be over soon."

For a while, Mindy didn't say a word, just quietly sat on the floor, staring into thin air. Every now and then, a tear rolled down her pale cheek.

Krista continued saying comforting words in a gentle, soothing voice, wondering why she'd stopped believing in their meaning. Nothing could ever be all right again, even if they made it out alive. She thought of her mother, how desperate she must have been when she didn't come home from school, how she must be looking for her. *I'm never coming home, Mom.*

Mindy let go of Krista's fingers and withdrew a few inches, hugging herself and rocking back and forth slowly, rhythmically.

"When they come for you," Mindy said, her voice barely a trembling whisper carried forward on tear-filled breaths, "don't fight it. You won't be able to. Just let it... happen."

Krista wiped her lingering tears with a quick swipe of her hand. "What are you talking about?"

"They teach you how to please them," she whispered, turning her head away, ashamed. "If you don't do as you're told, they beat you up, then they make you do what they want anyway. That's much worse."

Krista couldn't think of anything she could say. Inside her chest, a chasm had opened, dark and filled with unspeakable horror. She looked to the right, and her eyes met the brunette's terrified gaze.

"They'll drug you," Mindy said quietly, "if you don't do what they want. They'll give you cocaine or something, I don't know, but it's bad. They drugged me the first time," she added, sniffling while she lowered her head under the burden of the humiliation she'd endured.

"Why?" the brunette asked, her voice strong, fearless. "What did you do?"

Krista wanted to slap that crazy bitch. Couldn't she show Mindy an ounce of sympathy?

"I... bit one of them, hard," Mindy replied, her eyes still avoiding Krista's. "They almost knocked my teeth out. They would've stomped all over me, but they want the faces intact, beautiful. No bruises on the skin; only where you can't see them."

In the cage next to Krista's, that crazy brunette was livid, her eyes rounded in fear, and her hand covering her mouth. She'd finally shut up.

20

Immersion

Thirty-one hours missing

A few moments earlier, eating had seemed a great idea, because I hadn't touched anything but stale water in almost twenty-four hours. I'd stopped for a drive-through at the In-N-Out Burger on East Flamingo Road and picked up a double cheeseburger with fries, knowing I was going to regret every single one of those empty calories. I took one bite, and the mouthwatering smell that had drawn me to eagerly unwrap the burger shifted into a stench I couldn't tolerate. Not because there was anything wrong with the food, other than the obvious long-term effect on my arteries; no, it was because whenever I closed my eyes all I could see was Alyssa's body, immobilized in the cold desert under a layer of dirt and rocks, buried alive.

I rewrapped the remaining burger, threw it in the paper bag it had come in, and sent it flying out the window into a trash can by the curb. I washed away the aftertaste with some cold water, and then took a long sip of bitter coffee, brewed black with two shots of espresso, the kind of stuff that injects life back into the veins of sleep-deprived, malnourished cops hunting for serial killers.

I took out my notepad and started jotting thoughts, ideas, questions. I'd been quick to paste the label of serial killer on the suspect, because of the way we found Alyssa. Carefully posed, her hair spread around her head and weighed in place with rocks, her naked body under the tarp. But was she really the victim of a serial killer? The microchip Anne had dug out of her arm pointed toward a sex trafficking organization. That very notion was incompatible with a serial killer holding and raping Alyssa for three weeks, before killing her slowly in the Mojave.

Then, if that couldn't've happened, what made sense? What scenario?

I let myself slouch a little into the driver seat, sinking a few inches lower, and took a deep breath. I steeled myself as I was about to enter a world that brought feverish chills down my spine and a dull pain to the pit of my stomach. If I wanted to catch Alyssa's killer, if I had any chance to find out what had happened to her and to Meredith Holt, I needed to understand how the killer thought. What he felt. What brought him the release he killed for.

I pushed aside the contradicting thoughts about the sex trafficking organization and focused on the killer. Later, I'd figure out how he got his hands on Alyssa, and when.

I closed my eyes and pictured him in the desert at dusk, dragging Alyssa to her early grave. Who was he? What did he look like? What did he crave?

He was strong, I knew that for sure, although the fact he had chemically restrained her seemed to point in the opposite direction. When a rapist or a killer couldn't overcome their victims with the strength of their own bodies, they employed physical or chemical restraints, ranging from a simple rope to tie their victim's hands and feet, to modified tetrodotoxin.

Yeah… precisely. A weak killer would've used cuffs, or rope, or duct tape, as seen on many occasions in the history of criminal investigations. This killer used modified tetrodotoxin, of all things. Something I didn't even know existed, after all my years on the force, catching killers and rapists on both sides of the Atlantic.

That was the key to his behavior, to understanding his urges. A toxin that rendered his victim completely inert, unable to resist or react in any way, as if she were dead. A specialty, an acquired and carefully developed taste, the deviant's equivalent of gourmet food, of molecular gastronomy.

He was a necrophile, or almost. One who was still discovering who he was. Or a smart one, who knew that preserving a dead body for extended periods of time was challenging, especially if he wanted to pay them the occasional conjugal visit.

Feeling bile rising in my throat, I opened my eyes and let the light contract my irises and mitigate the shadows of horror dancing against my eyelids. Then I immersed myself back into visualizing Alyssa's last hours.

He'd chased her, toyed with her for a while, entertained by her zest for life, her fight for survival. Anne had found deep cuts and bruises on the soles of her feet, consistent with running barefoot in the desert. Her calves were covered in numerous scratches and gashes from brushing against cactus thorns.

Then he'd caught her and forced her to ingest the poison. Based on Fletcher's research, the toxin came as a fluid, and a few drops were enough to paralyze the victims for several hours, without killing them.

Then what?

Images refused to agglutinate in my mind past the point where her body had fallen to the ground inert, able to feel pain but unable to run from it or scream for help. Capable of feeling every little thing, and he relished making her suffer. He took his time with it, savored it, carefully prolonged her agony.

Because he was a sadist. And nearly a necrophile.

That's why he hadn't killed her quickly. If he had, she'd stop feeling pain, and that would've robbed him of half his enjoyment. The other half was feeling her body completely immobile, cold as ice, subdued, and helpless under his power.

Images danced in my mind and started forming scenes as if telling a story of horror and despair. Every time he came back, he dripped more poison into her mouth and then took his time with her, raping her again, and again, and again. When he grew tired of her, he'd weigh her down under the tarp and rocks, and then go away for a while.

Where?

No idea, but something told me Fletcher was going to find out, once he finished dumping all the cellular data for the area and comparing active mobile phone numbers with the time frames Anne had estimated for his visits. There was a strong chance only one mobile number was at that precise location during those times. Others might have been driving by, but only one came and went multiple times in the past forty-eight hours, spending time in the desert with his victim.

I moved on to other unanswered questions.

Why the tarp? Was he protecting her? From what? I let my mind wander while I munched absently on a cold, greasy fry from the package I'd forgotten to throw out with the burger. No... he wasn't protecting her; he was protecting himself. The tarp made it more difficult for scorpions and other insects to hide in places where his hands or other extremities might've reached without looking, in the heat of the moment.

Because he had urges, and when an urge was upon him, he couldn't restrain himself.

With my eyes scrunched shut, I visualized him returning to the grave at dawn, running toward Alyssa, unbuckling his belt, and touching himself, driven by a relentless compulsion to take, to possess, to find release. Then grabbing the corner of the tarp and pulling it to the side, exposing her naked body with one swift move.

I breathed, realizing I'd been holding my breath for a while. With my eyes wide open, I searched for the sun and squinted, willing the images I'd conjured to form and paint the portrait of Alyssa's killer to dissipate and be gone.

Did this man have Meredith Holt?

And what in bloody hell was Holt hiding from me?

I tried his cell again and got sent to voicemail. Frustrated, I threw the phone onto the passenger seat. It was infuriating beyond belief that he knew something about who'd taken his daughter, yet he wouldn't open up to me, his so-called partner in more ways than one.

We weren't partners... we were a sad joke.

He kept his phone off, although he was expecting a follow-up call from the kidnapper with the terms of Meredith's release. That didn't make any sense, unless he had a different burner, one only the kidnapper knew to call. Had Holt been in touch with that man all this time and shut me off? Maybe he'd already traded his life for his daughter's and things went south from there.

That's typically the direction any such exchanges went, and Holt, going in by himself, showed what an idiot he really was.

I shrugged my anger away and refocused on the long list of unanswered questions. If I was going to find him and his daughter, I had to find Alyssa's killer. That was the only lead I could follow.

Meredith had been taken by two men, same as Alyssa. By all witness accounts, they probably were the same two men. Was one of them the killer? Then what was the other one's role?

There was no evidence at the gravesite of a second perpetrator and not a single trace of a second-donor DNA on the victim's body. Somewhere between the abduction and the Mojave Desert, one of the perps had vanished, leaving the other one to do his bidding.

I picked up my phone with fast-food, greasy fingers and flipped through some images Fletcher had sent, including a fuzzy screenshot taken from the school surveillance video, showing the two perps dressed as cops leaving the premises.

Neither of them looked like a serial killer.

But what did a serial killer look like? What did Ted Bundy look like? Perfectly average, normal, inconspicuous, charismatic even.

Yet my gut was telling me neither of those men was the killer.

If that was the case, who were they working for?

Serial killers are usually solitary men or women, keeping to themselves and hiding their dark nature behind a thick veil of solitude, while the MO of the kidnappings pointed to a larger group. No matter how many different ways I looked at the facts, the pieces of the puzzle didn't fit.

Frustrated, I dropped the phone in the cup holder and wiped my fingers on a tissue I pulled from the glove box, my mind stubbornly gnawing at one bothersome detail.

The same two perps had taken Alyssa and Meredith. Holt had received a ransom call, while Alyssa's family had not. What did that mean?

When I realized the answer, my jaw dropped.

It was personal. Like I'd already suspected, Meredith's kidnapping was personal, some score being settled by someone who also happened to kidnap and force girls into prostitution.

That's what Holt knew and wouldn't share. That was the sword of Damocles that the kidnapper held above Holt's head. The caller had hinted to Meredith being sold as a virgin sex slave if Holt didn't comply. At the time, I thought that was just a threat cleverly constructed to subdue the parent of a teenage girl. In retrospect, I realized Holt knew exactly who he'd been talking to on the phone.

He'd never asked the caller who he was, an instinctive question we ask of all strangers we interact with.

A tiny smile tugged at the corner of my lips. The truth could be a weird animal, sometimes poking its unwanted head out from the darkest recesses of a perp's mind. What if the caller had the possibility to make good on his threat to sell Meredith into slavery? What if he'd done it before?

That still didn't clarify where and how the serial killer fit in. If Alyssa had been taken into forced prostitution, why was she killed? To a human trafficker, girls like her were highly valuable, assets to be protected and developed, with the power to bring in serious cash. Could it be possible Alyssa had been kidnapped twice? Once from school and the second time by one of her johns? Not likely; serial killers never paid for sex; they preyed for sex.

I reached for the phone, about to call Fletcher to send him shopping for virgin sex slaves on the Dark Web, when it rang loudly. I frowned, not recognizing the number on the caller ID display, but I answered nevertheless.

"Detective Baxter," I identified myself.

"Yes, hello, Detective," a man's voice said. He sounded familiar, and I remembered who he was just as he said his name. "It's Dr. Stuart Hickman, the—"

"Ornithologist, yes, I remember," I interrupted, rushed to get to the point. "What can I do for you, Dr. Hickman?"

"My vultures are circling again," he said after a moment's hesitation. "They're not settling down to feed, just circling, but I thought I'd let you know."

My heart skipped a beat, then began pounding loudly against my chest. "Where?" I asked.

"About the same area, two miles south of there. I can send you the coordinates."

I hung up, feeling numb with angst while tears burned at the corners of my eyes. Could that be Meredith out there, fighting for her life while vultures circled above her head?

"No, no, please, God, no," I whispered, then dialed Dispatch.

Holt, you bloody fool, where the hell are you?

21

Two Cases

Thirty-two hours missing

SA Glover sifted through the pile of case files scattered on the living room table, looking for a particular one that had caught his attention. The technical analysts had run a complete search through Detective Holt's entire work history and had flagged the cases they deemed most likely to have a connection with Meredith Holt's kidnapping. A few phone calls and almost an hour later, the flagged case files littered former Mrs. Holt's furniture.

Her last name was now Sauceda; she'd kept her latest husband's name after the divorce. Glover had looked at the ex-husband's whereabouts and background as part of the initial due diligence, but the man was cleared immediately. When Meredith had been taken, he was on the East Coast attending a conference.

Meredith's mother was going through the usual stages of grief associated with a missing child that he'd seen in all his kidnapped victims' families. After the initial shock came denial, then a rage she'd targeted at Jack Holt and his job, blaming him for everything that was going wrong in her life. But that was where the similarities with other kidnapping cases stopped.

First, Mrs. Sauceda was probably right to blame her husband's job for her daughter's abduction. From what he and his partner, Special Agent Rosales, were able to derive, the unusual kidnapping had nothing to do with a ransom demand, and more to do with Detective Holt's job.

Second, the detective wasn't cooperating with the FBI CARD team. He wouldn't share his whereabouts, and he knew how to hide his tracks. Glover knew where he was; out there, pressing informants and interrogating suspects. Other cops in his precinct had been doing the exact same things all night long. In theory, there was nothing wrong with Holt's actions, but Glover preferred a more structured approach to the wake of chaos the detective and his colleagues were leaving behind.

Rosales approached with a fresh cup of coffee in her hand. Her feistiness had turned into a cranky, vile mood, probably because she was tired, had been wearing the same clothes for more than one day, and was getting sick of cold pizza.

She pulled out a chair and sat with a groan. "Any progress?" she asked, while her upper lip twitched as if she expected to see or hear something disgusting.

Glover didn't react; the woman oozed contempt and disdain through every pore. It was who she was; nothing to be done about it, although he firmly believed Rosales wasn't a good fit for the CARD team. There wasn't a single strand of team player DNA in her to complement her exceptional reasoning and communication skills. She'd probably be best suited elsewhere, in a role where she could work alone.

He pushed a few folders her way. "Take a look and tell me which ones seem likely."

They flipped through pages in silence until the last file had been reviewed. The only noises that broke the stillness of the room were the rustling of papers and the occasional slurp of coffee taken by Rosales and gulped down with the loudest sound a human could make while drinking.

"I found one," she announced, lifting one file from the pile and letting it drop in the middle of the table to underline its importance. "It's a weird case regarding a murdered cop and the thug who shot him."

"I got one too," Glover replied. "Let's hear yours first," he invited her, then leaned against the backrest and rubbed the root of his nose with his fingers, trying to stave off a migraine.

He didn't like how Meredith's case had evolved, not for a moment. He checked his watch and repressed a sigh of frustration. Thirty-two hours had passed since she was taken, and the chances to find Holt's kid alive were dropping by the minute. The absence of a ransom call was the most concerning aspect of the investigation, leading to one of two possible conclusions. Either the kidnapper wasn't intending to return the kid, or Holt had already received the call and was acting on his own. For that second scenario, Glover was running out of reasons not to charge the man with obstruction and making a false statement. Although—

"Are you listening?" Rosales said, interrupting his thoughts.

"Yeah, go ahead."

"Holt arrested TwoCent for the murder of Detective Park, but then had to let him go."

Glover frowned. "Why? Was it a bad collar?"

"No, but listen to this. Holt caught the perp with the murder weapon in plain sight in his car. He booked the thug, but then that night someone broke into the evidence locker, and the weapon went missing. They released the suspect because without the murder weapon they had no case."

"Where's this man now?"

"In jail, serving time for the shooting of Detective Park. He cut a deal."

"Why the hell did he do that?"

"Exactly," Rosales exclaimed, satisfied with herself as if she'd run the marathon in record time. "The murder weapon, presumed stolen from the evidence locker was mysteriously found under a shelf. Then, during trial, the perp felt a sudden urge to confess. I'm not buying it. Internal Affairs was involved too."

"Involved, how?" Glover asked, leaning into his elbows. The IAB involvement was an interesting correlation with the case he'd found, the first one so far.

"They reviewed the case file a few times, spoke with some of the people involved. Then nothing. Crickets."

"This perp's still locked up, right?"

"Yes, he is, but I've seen revenge orchestrated from jail before. It can happen." Rosales drank the last of her coffee and set the cup back on the table with a loud thump. "I want to talk to this guy."

"What's your theory?" Glover asked.

"That maybe Holt planted the murder weapon on him or something. If he's pissed off at Holt, he might be willing to spill."

She stood and straightened her jacket, then tucked her shirt a bit deeper into her pants.

"I'll leave now unless you have something else," she announced.

Glover pursed his lips and gestured toward the chair she'd just vacated. Rosales sat reluctantly on the edge of the seat, eager to spring to her feet and rush out of there. Then she invited him to speak with a gesture of impatience, both her hands facing upward with fingers spread as if to ask, "What are you waiting for?"

He shook his head slightly, more to himself. She was unbelievable.

"Did you know Holt was undercover for eight months, five years ago, infiltrating a drug organization, here in Vegas?"

"Uh-uh," Rosales replied, closely examining her cuticles.

"He wasn't Homicide back then; it was after that undercover stint that he was promoted," he explained. "Holt joined a distribution network with ties to the Sinaloa Cartel and was tasked to find out how it was bringing drugs from Mexico over the border and straight to the Strip. He figured it out and requested more time to get to the leader of the Vegas distribution organization, a man by the name of Samuel Klug, aka Snowman. The top brass approved his request, but then they suddenly pulled the plug on Holt's assignment and executed a poorly planned bust that went badly. Klug escaped and left no evidence of his connection to the organization. Several of his key people were busted, but some made it over the border. Seven kilos of cocaine were confiscated, but only six made it into evidence. A mess."

Rosales looked at him with an intrigued glance.

"Internal Affairs was in on this case too. We should—"

"Sounds to me the best lead is the IAB officer who handled these cases," she interrupted, taking the words out of his mouth and pissing him off to no end.

"We should question Holt about this, and yes, the local IAB."

"I told you," Rosales said, standing and pacing the floor, going in slow circles around the table. "You should've had that man followed. We knew he was up to something. What if they turned him when he was undercover? It's known to happen."

"We did follow him, if you remember. He made us in two minutes and disappeared."

"Pick him up again somewhere and this time, don't lose him," she said as if giving direction to a junior officer.

He felt he couldn't breathe, choked with anger. How did he, the senior agent on the case, end up being given direction and justifying himself to this woman? He forced himself to calm down; she'd be dealt with later after Meredith was found. Now wasn't the time for any pissing contest.

"His phone is off, he's in the wind. Finding him would take time and effort better spent looking for his child."

"Then what do you suggest we do?" she asked, crossing her arms at her chest and thrusting her chin forward.

"This is a kidnapping, Rosales, and that girl's life is hanging by a thread. Let's cut the bullshit and find Meredith Holt. You speak to your perp in jail, and I'll take the IAB."

22

Another

Thirty-three hours missing

When I arrived at the nearest point on the highway from the coordinates Dr. Hickman had sent, he was already there, unloading his utility terrain vehicle from a rusted platform trailer hooked up to his Dodge Ram truck. I pulled over behind him and rushed to help out with the vehicle. It looked like a large ATV fitted with a roll cage, with bars welded across and above it to protect the passengers in case it rolled over.

He didn't bother securing the trailer or even locking his truck. The moment the UTV had all four wheels on the Nevada dirt, he started the engine, and I hopped in the passenger seat, holding on to the crossbar above my head for balance.

He hit the gas pedal, and the UTV bolted forward, throwing dirt and pebbles in the air. Despite the loud engine noise, I thought I heard someone calling my name.

"Baxter!"

The second time he called louder, and I recognized the voice. Holt. He was still alive. I felt a rush of relief so strong, it brought tears to my eyes.

"Turn around," I told Hickman, and he immediately obliged.

As we approached Holt, I noticed the state he was in. His clothes, the same suit and shirt he'd worn yesterday, were dirty and torn. His face was bruised, and his left eye was almost shut from a direct hit. A cut marred his eyebrow, and another had split his lip.

Hickman slowed when the UTV approached Holt, but he didn't wait for it to stop. He grabbed the crossbar and jumped on, using the base of the passenger door as footing.

"Go, go," he shouted, and Hickman stepped on the pedal, setting the UTV in motion with a jerk.

I wanted to ask him where the hell he'd been all that time and many other things. I looked at him, searching his eyes, but he was staring intently at the horizon, where, in the distance, vultures were circling lower and lower.

"Can't this thing go any faster?" he asked, although the UTV was bouncing off the terrain at dangerous angles.

"That's it," Hickman replied. "Pedal to the metal."

We were getting close; I could see the birds clearly now, and I squinted in the oblique sunlight to see the object of the birds' interest. I still hoped it was a snake-bit coyote taking its last breath out there.

Without a word, Dr. Hickman reached inside a duffel bag and extracted a pair of binoculars and handed them to me.

"Thanks," I said, then started to scan the terrain ahead, although with every bounce of the UTV, the heavy rims sent shockwaves into my orbits. The glare from the setting sun was directly in my eyes, making it difficult to distinguish anything.

A gust of wind swept across the desert, lifting dust high in the air, and something else. Close to the ground, it waved and danced in the wind, as if shreds of golden silk were toyed with by the circling dust devils.

Not silk, I realized as the UTV approached.

Hair.

"Over there," I said, pointing straight ahead, right underneath the kettle of vultures. Then I grabbed Holt's arm to get his attention. "It's not her, Holt. It's not Meredith."

"How could you possibly know?" he asked, his eyes darker than I'd ever seen them.

"Her hair," I replied. "This girl is a blonde."

He shuddered. "Are you sure?"

I handed him the binoculars. Holding on to the UTV with one hand, he lifted the binoculars to his eyes with the other and scanned the area.

Then he handed the glasses to me and squeezed my shoulder gently, before grabbing on to the crossbar again.

"She's right there, by those large boulders," I said. "Where that vulture just landed."

"I see it, yes," Dr. Hickman replied.

Holt pulled out his gun and aimed at the bird.

"Please don't shoot them," Dr. Hickman pleaded. "It's not their fault."

Holt glared at him for a brief moment, then discharged the weapon in the air, sending echoes against the rocky desert hills. The vultures scattered, and Dr. Hickman reduced speed as we approached the shallow grave.

"This is close enough," I said, and he slowed to a stop.

Holt jumped off while the UTV was still moving and rushed ahead. I followed, running the remaining distance on small rocks that twisted my ankles every other step.

As I approached, I had an eerie, sickening feeling of déjà-vu. She couldn't've been more than sixteen years old. Only her head and hands were above ground; the rest of her body was covered in dirt and small rocks. Her hair had been fanned out around her head like the rays of the sun and weighed down with stones, but the wind had blown a few long strands free. She looked asleep, her beautiful face pale but untouched yet by the bluish tint of death and body decay.

Maybe there was hope. Perhaps this one would live.

I crouched next to the girl's head and felt for a pulse. Her skin was cold to the touch, and I couldn't sense a heartbeat. Then I lifted her eyelid and saw corneal cloudiness obscuring her blue irises.

We were too late. She was gone.

"Ah, bloody hell," I muttered, then I stepped away. I couldn't touch the body until Anne cleared us. I was glad I'd called Dispatch when Dr. Hickman sent me the coordinates. She wasn't far behind; in the hues of the early winter sunset, I could see red and blue flashes lighting the sky toward the highway. Within moments, the Crime Scene techs would be taking over the scene.

It was as good a time as any to talk to my so-called partner. I walked over to him and got in his face. "Where the hell have you been all this time, Holt?"

He stood silently, avoiding my gaze. Deep ridges marked his forehead, and his knuckles were raw and swollen. He'd been in fights, probably in desperate attempts to get people to talk.

"How did you know to come here?" I asked, thinking he might consider answering a more straightforward question.

He looked at me briefly, then looked away. "I heard the Dispatch call on the radio," he eventually said.

Across the dunes, we could see two ATVs approaching at high speed. Anne was driving one of them; I recognized her buzz-cut hair and thin frame from afar.

"Why are you here, Holt?" I asked, then realized how stupid my question sounded. "I understand why you needed to see for yourself," I added, gesturing toward the girl's body, "but why are you still here?"

He stared at me without saying a word, his eyes dark and almost menacing.

"It's bad enough you won't let me help you find your daughter," I said, "but you're—"

"Yeah, that," he said with a long, pained sigh.

He wasn't making any sense. He must've been completely exhausted; he probably hadn't had anything to eat or drink since his daughter's ordeal had started. I rushed over to Dr. Hickman's UTV, looking for a bottle of water.

"My partner isn't exactly there for me," Holt said, following me and speaking in a low, sad voice.

I froze in place. "What do you mean?"

He ran his dirty hand over his mouth in a downward gesture, clasping his chin. "You couldn't find someone else to take this case off your hands?"

"And do what? Wait for you to turn on your damn phone? You ran away from me, Holt, not the other way around. I called and called." I stopped talking, waiting to hear what he had to say, but nothing came from him. "I have a job to do, the same as you do, and not long ago you used to care about all that."

I opened Dr. Hickman's duffel bag and found a bottle of water and a Snickers bar. Embarrassed to be going through a man's possessions without permission and yet satisfied with the findings, I grabbed both items and turned to Holt. I extended my hand with my offering, but he wouldn't take them from me.

"Don't be ridiculous," I said, but he still wouldn't take the water from my hand. He made me angry as hell, while at the same time my heart broke to see him so damaged, so desperate. "Come on, Holt," I pleaded, "you need your strength."

He grabbed the bottle, unscrewed the cap and downed it all in a few thirsty gulps.

"Yes, we need to catch this sick son of a bitch," he said, "but pardon me for thinking of my kid first."

"But that's exactly what—" I blurted, then immediately clammed up, as soon as I realized what I was about to say. He'd been off the grid for so long, he probably didn't know about Alyssa's kidnapping yet.

He walked closer to me, and grabbed my arm.

"What the hell aren't you telling me, Baxter? Come on, spill it."

I hesitated a little, thinking of the shock he was about to experience.

"I have a right to know, damn it," he shouted, and a few CS techs raised their heads from the work they were doing and looked at us.

"Alyssa, the girl we found yesterday," I said, choosing my words carefully, "was abducted the same way Meredith was, apparently by the same two men."

I'd expected him to falter, keel over, curse, or throw a fit. I had not expected the look he gave me, a cold stare, the kind I'd seen before when he put two and two together on cases we'd worked on previously.

"I see," he said calmly. "I have to go."

I grabbed his sleeve. "You're not going anywhere, Holt. Not without me. Not this time."

He looked at me, the intensity in his eyes scary, a bad omen I couldn't understand. But I didn't lower my gaze, I didn't look away.

"Please, tell me who this man is," I asked. "You know who took your daughter, don't you?"

That moment his burner phone rang. He took the flip phone out of his pocket and answered the call on speaker without checking the display.

"Yes," he said, "it's Holt."

"Hello, Detective," a man said, with laughter in his voice. I recognized the voice I'd heard before, at Fletcher's place, when he'd called the first time. "It's time to meet."

"Say when and where," Holt replied, the urgency in his voice unmistakable.

"There's a gas station at the corner of East Windmill Parkway and Bermuda Road, a 7-Eleven. Two AM. Come alone or face the consequences." The laughter in the man's voice was gone.

"I'll be there," Holt replied.

"Don't get any crazy ideas," the man insisted. "You called in the feds after I told you no cops. The entire city is looking for your kid. That's not what you promised me, Detective. I feel tempted to make her pay for your sins."

"No," he shouted, "please, don't. I didn't call anyone. The feds saw that teacher spill it on TV."

"I'll believe you this time, Detective, for old times' sake. See you tonight."

"Wait," Holt said. "I want to speak with my daughter first."

"You're not setting terms, Detective."

Holt clenched his fists and swallowed hard. "Either I speak with her or no deal."

I heard muffled talk as if the caller had covered the mouthpiece of his phone and was speaking with someone else.

"You know you'll have to pay for your attitude, for real," the man said.

"I just want to speak with my girl," Holt insisted calmly.

There was some chatter, the sound of open and shut doors, then a girl's tearful voice came across the air.

"Daddy?"

"Mer," Holt said, "are you okay?"

The girl sniffled and whimpered, then took a deep breath and blurted, "Large garage, five men, tattoos—" Then there was a loud noise; she screamed, while the phone clattered to the floor.

"Mer?" Holt shouted. "Meredith?"

"Your girl is a piece of work, Detective," the man from earlier said. "I'm itching to teach her a lesson."

"If you touch her—"

"Windmill and Bermuda, two AM, alone," he said, then hung up.

23

Lessons

Thirty-four hours missing

He yanked Meredith's arm brutally. She whimpered, but he didn't care. He busted the door open and shoved her into the garage, then grabbed her arm again twisting it hard behind her back, until she fell to her knees.

"You think you're so smart," he said, then slapped her across the face with his other hand. "Think again, bitch."

She saw stars, and tears started rolling from her eyes, although she despised herself for crying in front of that animal, for showing weakness and fear.

He let go of her arm and spat on the floor. She looked straight at him, her teary eyes filled with hatred and contempt. She stood hesitantly, her head throbbing from the shock and the pain, not taking her eyes off of his.

"He's going to kill you first," she hissed, then grinned while wiping her face with the back of her hand.

The second blow came immediately, without warning, sending her tumbling across the floor. He reached her in two steps and grabbed her hair, dragged her to the cage, then shoved her inside and locked it.

"Not before I teach you some manners," he said, glaring at her, then at the other two girls. "I'm going to enjoy breaking you in."

Krista stood against the back wall, shivering and whimpering, while Mindy sat on the floor, her eyes hollow, her face immobile. When the man left the garage, slamming the door shut behind him, Meredith breathed, then started sobbing quietly, hugging herself. She dropped to the floor, feeling too weak to keep on standing.

"What the hell is wrong with you?" Krista asked, her voice reeking of hatred. "Do you want to get us all killed?"

Meredith looked at her, then lowered her eyes. "It's not about you. They only want me."

"Oh, so you're so damn special, huh? Then what are we doing here? Keeping you company?"

"No," she whispered. "You're right, we're all in hell."

"Then stop making these crazy threats. Keep your filthy mouth shut," Krista commanded, punctuating her request with a slam of her hand against the wire wall of her adjoining cage.

"Do you know where we are?" Meredith asked, looking at Krista first, then at Mindy.

"Like we'd tell you if we knew," Krista replied. "Who knows what stupid shit you might try to pull off. Do you know what they do to punish girls like us here?"

"Look, my dad is a cop, and he—"

"Yeah, yeah, we've heard it all before," Krista replied. "They'd kill us all before they let a cop in here, that much I can tell you. And they'd probably start with your scrawny ass."

Meredith scratched the site of the microchip implant they'd shot in her arm on the first day of her captivity. It wasn't hurting her, but just knowing it was there made her want to tear her flesh off to get to it, yank it out, and stomp it under her feet.

"There are others?" she asked quietly.

"What did you expect?" Krista scoffed. "Yeah, there are others, smart girls who learned their lessons, and now sleep in real beds, take showers, eat real food." She paced her cage slowly, the look of bitterness on her face inexplicable.

"Then why are you in here, if you have all the answers?" Meredith asked quietly.

Krista stared at the back wall, then at the ceiling. "I—I'm afraid," she eventually said. "Of those men, you know. When they took me, I was so scared I threw up all over them." She slid her fingers through the wire loops and rattled the cage wall. "Now I know my lesson; next time I'll do better. I'll do whatever they want, just to get out of here." She crouched to the floor, grabbing her lower abdomen with both her hands.

"Did they hurt you?" Meredith asked.

Krista nodded, tears pooling in her eyes. "It hurts inside, down there." She sniffled and squeezed her eyes shut. "They gave me a shot; it made me dizzy and nauseous. But it doesn't matter; I have to behave next time, I have to."

"Why?" Meredith asked, although she thought she knew the answer.

Krista's rage returned in full force. "Because they keep the misfits in here, the ones they're going to kill if they don't believe we can make money for them. If they don't think we can be trusted."

"How do you know this?" Meredith asked. "Who did you talk to?"

"They let me use the bathroom," she replied. "Another girl was there. She was dressed in silk, not rags, and wore real jewelry. She said she started like us, only a month ago. She seemed happy."

"Happy, my ass," Meredith replied. "You must be a total moron if you think—"

"Henderson," Mindy said. "We're in Henderson. I recognized the sound the tires made when crossing the overpass at 215 and 515. Then we drove only a few more minutes after that interchange."

"Thanks," Meredith said.

"Great," Krista intervened. "Now how are you going to tell your daddy that valuable piece of information? Are you telepathic?"

Meredith stared at Krista but didn't say a word.

"Then we're still screwed," Krista whispered. "I'll have to learn to do what they want."

"They'll teach you," Mindy said, speaking softly, her voice weighed down by immense sadness. "Just give them a couple of days."

"How about you?" Meredith asked. Her head was spinning, the earlier pain subsiding, leaving room for petrifying fear.

Mindy chuckled sadly. "They're going to kill me soon. I'm not a fit."

"Why?" Krista asked.

"I have a strong gag reflex. I can't do what they want me to do."

24

Cocaine

Thirty-four hours missing

Holt folded the phone and let it slip into his half-ripped jacket pocket, then turned to me and stared, his jaws clenched tightly, his teeth gritting.

"Are you coming?" he asked and climbed behind the wheel of Dr. Hickman's UTV.

"One second," I replied, as I beckoned the ornithologist to come over quickly.

He rushed, his gait crooked and clumsy as if he'd never run a yard in his entire life.

"Dr. Hickman," I asked, as soon as he was within earshot, "what would cause your vultures not to eat? This girl was already dead, and still, they didn't touch her."

He rubbed his chin and tugged at his overgrown mustache. "They're smart birds," he said hesitantly as if speaking before he'd finished thinking things through. "There must be something wrong with her, something they could only smell up close. Otherwise they wouldn't even circle."

"How do these birds choose where to circle?"

"They're attracted by any form of life that is still for a while. In the desert, that's all it takes to become carrion. Although they strongly prefer herbivorous animals, not omnivores, like humans are."

"Baxter, for crying out loud," Holt shouted. "We need to go. Now."

"Have your vultures circled like this in the past? In this area?" I asked, climbing in his UTV.

"We just finished tagging the birds, and before the kettles were smaller, more dispersed—"

"Yes or no, doctor, please," I interrupted, aware of the passing of every second.

"Yes," he replied, staring at the sky for a brief moment. "Geez... I hope there aren't any other girls buried alive out here. I didn't think of that," he added, sounding ashamed. "When I get back to the lab, I'll pull the locations from the computer history and send you the coordinates."

"Thanks," I shouted over my shoulder because Holt had already set the UTV in motion. "Someone will bring this vehicle back."

"He didn't hear you, Baxter," Holt said grimly.

"No, but you did, when I asked if you knew who took Meredith. Talk to me, Holt."

He pressed his lips together as if the words fought to come out but a part of him wouldn't let them.

"I told you I worked undercover a few years back; that's when I got addicted to cocaine," he said. "The organization I infiltrated was led by a man named Samuel Klug, known on the streets as Snowman. Back then, he only dealt in snow; that's street for cocaine."

"Yeah, I know what it means. Is he the one who took her?"

"Yes," he replied. "I recognized his voice the first time he called. He's got it out for me for bringing his organization down five years ago. He managed to escape back then, and there was no direct evidence against him to justify an extended manhunt. He'd always been the man behind the curtain, pulling strings, calling the shots."

He stopped talking, and I didn't interrupt his thoughts for a while, although I wanted to scold him for not sharing that piece of information earlier. But moments passed by, and he didn't continue.

"Then what happened?"

"He got away. Most of his people didn't. That day, when the bust went down, he lost a lot of dope in the ensuing seizure." He clenched his right fist and slammed it against the UTV's steering wheel. "I didn't think he'd be back. I was a reckless fool, thinking he'd just go away and leave me, us, this city, alone for good. I believed he'd steer clear of the cop who had almost locked him up. No; for him it's payback time, and I should've seen him coming."

"Could he be the serial killer who's done this?" I asked, gesturing toward the desert we were leaving behind at full speed.

"No," Holt replied quickly. "He's a killer, a psychopath, and deserves to be shot on sight. But he's no serial killer, Baxter."

"Are you sure? How else would you explain—"

"He's a straight shooter, vindictive and evil; not a pervert who rapes dying girls, keeps souvenirs, and what not. He's got an entire organization of hookers—"

"Rape isn't about sex, it's about power, about control. And this Snowman seems to be a power freak, based on what you're telling me."

"And I'm telling you, he didn't do this. It doesn't fit. No, he took Meredith because he has a rule. If someone did him wrong, first they must make him whole again, repay the debt somehow, then be punished, most likely killed."

We reached the highway, and Holt stopped the UTV next to the railing, then ran to his Interceptor. As soon as I jumped in and closed the door, he pulled a U-turn and headed back into the city at full speed, lights on and siren blaring.

"Okay, but the same two men kidnapped your daughter *and* the victim of a serial killer. How do you explain that? Is Snowman one of the two men who took Meredith?"

"No, he's not. Snowman is African-American, thirty years old, no priors. No one's ever managed to land his ass behind bars. I came close, but the brass pulled the plug early, and he skated."

"Then what do you think happened? What's the correlation between Meredith and Alyssa?" I choked as I said Alyssa's name, remembering her paralyzed body, buried alive, defenseless, waiting for the predator to come calling again.

"Two different sources told me Snowman is into human trafficking and enforced prostitution these days, to supplement his drug trafficking income. Maybe Alyssa was one of the girls he kidnapped for that reason. He must've used the same two knuckleheads to grab Meredith."

"You're on to something," I said, feeling a wave of frustration rile me up. "If you'd kept your damn phone turned on, you'd know that Anne found an embedded tracker in Alyssa's arm. That supports your theory about forced prostitution. That, and the fact that the poor girl had been repeatedly raped over the past three weeks since she'd been taken."

"A tracker?"

"Yes, a GPS-enabled microchip, pretty high end. Fletcher is tracking the source, hoping to get to the buyer."

"I need to speak with him," he said.

I dialed Fletcher and connected the call to the car's media system.

Fletcher picked up immediately.

"It's Baxter and Holt," I said. "We need—"

"Oh, you found him," he reacted. "We were both worried about you, Holt," Fletcher said. "What do you need?"

"Pull everything you have on Samuel "Snowman" Klug. Figure out what property he owns or occupies in Henderson. It should have a large garage."

"That's it? Find a Henderson property with a large garage? Three hundred thousand people live in Henderson, and there are over ninety thousand detached homes with a garage. You have to give me more than that."

"There isn't anything more," Holt snapped. "Find known associates of Klug's; focus on white people, not black."

"Wait, maybe there is more," I intervened. "That house could have five active mobile phones pinging the towers, and one of those signals could be the one who visited the Mojave crime scene."

"Got it. What else?"

"Any news on the mobile phone users who visited the desert site?"

"Not yet. I have to look at all carriers, all subscribers, then filter out. It will take a while."

A wave of disappointment washed over me like a cold shower. I'd hoped he could correlate the signal to identify the property, but not if he didn't have the phones identified yet.

"How about those microchips?" I asked.

"Detectives Nieblas and Croker are pulling in the vendor now. We'll find out who he sold that particular one to."

"I know who he sold it to, and that doesn't do anything for me," Holt said. "Can you hack into them? See the location of the chips?"

"Not sure I follow," Fletcher said. "What chips? We only have one. I'd need the serial numbers and identifiers to visualize the locations of any other chips."

"Press that vendor," Holt replied. "My gut tells me he sold Alyssa's chip as part of a bulk order. Localize them all, see if we can find more than one in a certain location. If that location is in Henderson and it comes with a garage, that's the jackpot."

"You're looking for a place where he might keep the girls, I get it," he replied.

"Thanks, Fletch," I said, after looking at Holt and seeing he didn't have any other questions. "I might call you later, okay?"

"Yeah, but don't hang up just yet. About the crooked cop your daughter and her friend surprised in the men's room, I have the composite based on Casey's description running; so far, no matches. I'm running it against the LVMPD employee database, with special approval from the sheriff himself."

"How did you pull that off?" I asked.

"Everyone's pitching in," he replied. "No LVMPD employee is willing to go off duty until we find Meredith."

"Thanks, let us know."

"Will do," he replied, then ended the call.

Three beeps marked the beginning of uneasy silence. I struggled to find the right words to say. What could I possibly tell Holt that could make him reconsider what he was about to do? It seemed crazy; I couldn't think of a single, possible scenario in which Snowman would keep his word and promptly release the girl the moment Holt gave himself up. He was a fool for even considering it. Either that, or he was bloody lying to me again.

Holt turned right, and I recognized the street he lived on. I decided to give him yet another chance to come clean.

"What are you planning to do?" I asked. "Turn yourself in?"

He pulled to a stop on his driveway. "What else can I do but go?"

"Uh-uh," I reacted, surprised by the intensity of the fear and anguish I felt at the thought of losing him. "You can't do that; I won't let you."

We walked to the house, and he unlocked the front door. We entered a typical bachelor's living room, littered with sports magazines and scattered clothing. A few books were stacked on the end table; James Patterson, Tom Clancy, and a couple of others I didn't recognize. Beer remnants at the bottom of a bottle of Bud Light generated a stale smell with a tinge of brewer's yeast in the air. I frowned when I saw the bottle; one of the rules of the twelve-step program was to stay sober and away from all intoxicants, not just the one that brought the addict into the program.

"Not your choice to make, Baxter," he said while slowly taking his jacket off, protecting a hurt shoulder by the looks of it.

I propped my hands on my hips and got in his path. "You're stepping into a trap, Holt. He's going to kill you, and there's no guarantee he'll keep his word and let your daughter go."

"I know that," he replied grimly, as he pushed me gently to the side and opened the kitchen pantry. He bent over and dug through a toolbox, extracting a sledgehammer.

"Okay," I said, trying to breathe deeply but failing. "I'll give you six hours, and if you're not out of there, I'm bringing the entire department in on this."

"I won't last six hours," he replied, and then slammed the hammer into the wall, right next to a painting. "Not unless he's got other plans with me."

At first, I thought he was taking his anger out on the wall, but soon I realized I was wrong. As the hole in the wall expanded, and pieces of drywall fell to the floor, I was able to see the object hidden in there. It was a small package, the size of a book, wrapped in aluminum foil and then vacuum sealed in plastic.

When he was able, he reached into the hole, extracted it, and ripped the plastic open. The package drew air with a hiss, and I smelled the familiar odor of gunpowder.

"What the hell is that?" I asked.

"A bargaining chip," Holt replied calmly, continuing to unwrap the contents from the layered packaging.

"Cocaine?" I reacted, my voice a high, screechy pitch brimming with frustration. "Is this the missing kilo of dope from that bust last month?"

He shot me a long, tired look. "Yes," he admitted. I heard sadness in his voice and a trace of guilt.

"You lied to me," I reacted, starting to pace the room angrily, trying to refrain from doing something physical as an outlet for my anger. "You bloody lied to me, Holt!"

"Yes," he replied, lowering his gaze. Then he looked up again. "I needed to do this."

"The IAB is after you for it," I said, gesturing at the brick of dope lying on his coffee table on a stretch of wrinkled aluminum foil sprinkled with gunpowder.

"I know," he replied, rubbing his forehead and shifting in place. "Listen, we have to—"

"No, you listen," I replied. "I lied to them for you, putting my career and my entire life on the line. They had me investigate you, and I swore you didn't take that coke. I covered for you against all logic, because I knew an addict will always do anything in his power to get his hands on more dope. Tell me you're not using!" I urged him, at the same time holding my breath and hoping he'd somehow manage to win me over again, to prove to me that what we'd had together wasn't a complete lie.

"I'm not using, Baxter, I swear. You can test me once this is over."

"Okay, fine," I replied, unconvinced. If he believed Snowman was going to kill him in the next few hours, what was that commitment really worth?

"Why didn't you tell me about the IAB investigation?" he asked. "Who's the bigger liar, partner?"

My shoulders fell under the weight of my arms as I let them drop from my hips. Why did I, really, keep it from him?

"Because I couldn't bring myself to believe you could've done this. Why, Holt? Why did you steal the cocaine?"

"Damn it, Baxter, I don't have time for this now!" he shouted. "Grill me some other time, turn me into the IAB if you damn well please, but lay the hell off me already."

I watched him splash some water on his face at the kitchen sink, then strip off his clothes and put on clean ones. His ribs were bruised badly, and his left shoulder hung lower than the other, a sign of trauma. Yet he didn't care; he was about to turn himself into the hands of a psychopathic killer with a grudge, in less than five hours.

And he was going to die.

Unless we could find Meredith before then.

I excused myself and went straight to the bathroom. As soon as I locked the door, I took out my phone and texted Fletcher.

"Do something," I wrote. "Send patrols to knock on every door in Henderson that doesn't belong to a middle-class family with an impeccable record and three kids. Find those cell phone users. Find that house." I hesitated for a moment, my fingers lingering above the screen, then added. "I need everything there is to know about Snowman Klug and the show he's running on the Strip."

I flushed the toilet and washed my hands, then heard a chime. "On it," was the reply I got from Fletcher. I steadied myself, thinking through what I was about to do, step by step. Was I making a mistake? Probably, but I was desperate.

He'd lied to me, more than once, but I wasn't going to let him die for it.

I took a deep breath and got out of the bathroom and walked over to Holt. He'd finished loading a small duffel bag with enough guns and ammo to start a neighborhood war and had extracted a wad of cash from an empty coffee tin.

I gave him a long, sideways stare and said, "We're going to my place next."

25

Resources

Thirty-five hours missing

Fletcher sat behind his desk, slurping loudly the remnants of soda from a can with the help of a thick, green straw. When he started sucking more air than fluid, he tossed the can into the trash and popped open another one he took from his drawer. Satisfied, he gulped thirstily about a third of the fizzy liquid and burped discreetly into his hand.

He didn't take his eyes off the screen the entire time, mulling in his mind the best course of action under the circumstances. He usually would've called Holt and dumped his findings in the detective's charge, but with his daughter missing, he wasn't really a viable resource. Baxter was out there with Holt, helping him. That left Fletcher by himself to deal with a potentially homicidal, crooked cop.

He had no idea what he should do. If he took the case to his captain, a slew of questions would arise, items best left unanswered, at least for a while. The alternative, however, was to let a crooked cop go about his business undisturbed, a couple of days after being paid off to make someone disappear. Maybe it wasn't too late for that someone.

He shouldn't've let himself get drawn into this off-the-books mess. Good intentions paved the road to the unemployment line, possibly the yellow line, the one behind twelve-foot fences, ornately decorated with rolls of barbed wire. He'd never been so scared in his life. What if he made the wrong judgment call and people would die?

Fletcher scratched the roots of his curly hair right above his right ear and whistled, pushing his anxiety away, happy for a brief moment that the precinct was almost deserted. It was after 7:00 PM, and every cop in the city was out there looking for Holt's daughter, asking questions, pressing informants, banging on doors. At least he could think in peace.

When he least expected, the composite sketch of the cop who Meredith and Casey had seen conducting business in the men's room of the Perdido Club had returned a match. A sergeant from Sector A by the name of Pete Mincey.

He had twelve years with the force; this was going to get ugly.

He stared at Mincey's photo, displayed on his main screen in a view from the LVMPD employee database that he'd accessed with special approval from the sheriff. He could try to speak to the sheriff about it, but what would he do other than delegate the case to Captain Morales? And the captain would have questions, more questions than the sheriff had asked, starting with why he'd gone over his head straight to the top honcho for approval.

"Argh… crap," he muttered, "this is going to get ugly."

"What's going to get ugly, Fletcher?"

He jumped out of his skin and turned around so quickly he almost fell off his chair. A quick tap on the keyboard made Sergeant Mincey's service photo disappear from his screen, but it was too late.

"Um, Captain, n—nothing, really," he replied, flustered, stuttering badly. He breathed and counted to three in his mind, invoking whatever form of zen he could think of. The man standing next to the captain was the scariest of the two because he was the unknown. A tall, well-built, black suit, white shirt, and gray tie in his early fifties, with an uncompromising look on his face rounded off with a disappointed smirk barely visible in the twitch of his upper lip. "What can I do for you, Captain?" he managed to ask in a casual voice.

"How about start talking, Fletcher?" the captain replied, pulling out a chair and straddling it.

He wasn't going anywhere… the bulldog was there to stay, with an appetite for his rear end.

"I'm not sure what you're talking about," Fletcher replied, feeling the urge to set his hair in order. He fumbled with some loose curls that were getting in his face, but he couldn't do much. They were too short to tuck behind his ears, yet too long to keep out of his eyes.

The captain groaned and exchanged a brief look with the man in black. "Why don't we start with the two fake cops who kidnapped Meredith Holt, shall we?"

"Yes, what about them?"

"The BOLO on them and their car came from your system ID, Fletcher, and that was before anyone knew Holt's kid was missing."

He stared at the ceiling for a brief moment, thinking hard what to say not to dig his hole any deeper than it already was. Then he stared at the carpet for another moment, but the stained surface offered no answers either.

"I sometimes do that," he managed to reply. "I put BOLOs into the system for the detectives I work with."

"From home, after leaving early because of health problems, son?"

He lowered his head. There was no point; the captain wasn't an idiot. But the secrets he was keeping weren't his to share.

"We're on the same team here, Fletch," Morales said. "We all want the same thing: Holt's daughter returned safely and the people who took her locked up behind bars."

Fletcher shot the man in the black suit a side glance. "Who is this?" he asked the captain. Before he could share anything, he needed to know.

The man took a step forward and extended a hand. "Special Agent Glover, FBI CARD team, assigned to Holt's case."

He swallowed hard. "What can I do for you?" he asked, hoping they'd stop with the questions and just ask him to trace a phone number or something.

"We need to know what Detective Holt is up to, where he is, what he's keeping from us. We believe," Glover shot the captain a quick glance, "that the detective has been in contact with the kidnappers all this time."

Fletcher stood and raised his hands in the air, lowering his head at the same time. "Listen, I don't want to cause any—"

"Sit down," the captain ordered, and he complied. The tone of his boss's voice didn't leave any room for negotiations.

"Let's start over," Glover said. "Do you know where Detective Holt is?"

He shook his head. He really didn't know, and he felt grateful he didn't have to lie.

"What are they having you work on?"

He bit his lip; there was no escape from the two men, no way he could talk them into giving it up and going away.

"Are we on the same team, Fletch?" the captain asked, menacing undertones seeping into his voice.

He nodded, then cleared his throat and said, "Henderson. Holt has a lead about a large property with a garage, somewhere in Henderson. I started to narrow it down, but so far I couldn't identify it."

Glover signaled Captain Morales, who left his chair and approached him. Then Glover whispered in his ear, "If Holt trusts this kid, let's work through him. Let him be the interface. We'll give him resources, everything he needs."

Fletcher pretended he hadn't heard a word from the two men's whispered conversation, and looked away, waiting, refraining from biting his fingernails. Those resources the fed had mentioned sounded awfully good. His systems didn't have anywhere near the horsepower of federal databases and facial recognition applications. The carrier-integrated tools they used to locate mobile phone users and triangulate their positions at various times were second to none. Maybe cooperating with them wasn't such a bad idea, and he probably could keep his job if he did.

"Do you have a way to communicate with Baxter and Holt?" Glover asked.

He stared at the man, still weighing his choices, then looked at the captain quickly.

Morales nodded impatiently.

"Y—yes, I think so."

"They carry burner phones now?" Glover asked.

"Yes."

"Okay," Glover said with a quick, pained sigh. "Call this number," he added, offering a Post-It note with numbers scribbled on it. "Karyn is our technical analyst, the best in the entire field office."

"Now?" he hesitated, not knowing what they expected him to do.

"Yes, now, she's standing by."

A moment later, he was talking to a sharp analyst with a nasal, drawn-out, Texas drawl who ran searches faster than he'd ever seen before. It took her under two minutes to identify the two men who had taken Meredith, once he'd shared with her the best image he could get from the surveillance video.

"Okay," Karyn said after a chime was heard on the open line. "I give you Rudy Huber, posing as Officer Beasley, and Jeremiah Foley, impersonating Officer Greer. A long list of priors for both model citizens, mostly drug-related. Huber has a couple of B&Es and a battery charge too. BOLOs out. Oh, you might want to know that Holt was Huber's arresting officer."

"How did you get them so fast? My search has been running since yesterday," he blurted, completely forgetting about the captain and SA Glover. "My system couldn't get more than four facial match points; the images were too grainy."

"Our system extrapolates and cleans it first, then assumes a certain degree of facial symmetry, and constructs the points you're otherwise missing. What else do you need?"

Fletcher looked at the captain with the excitement that kids have when they unwrap a new and fantastic toy. Then he stared for a moment at the desk phone, wondering how far he could take this newfound collaboration.

"There's a GPS tracking chip, high-end tech, I can send you the specifics. I need to track and hack into all the chips in the batch it was sold with. We need to locate the ones currently in use."

"Send the serial number over," Karyn replied.

He emailed her the info in a message devoid of subject or any other content except the serial number she needed. When he looked away from his screen, the two men were frowning at him.

"Spill it, Fletcher," the captain said. "What's with the chip now? Wasn't this evidence found on the Mojave body? A totally different case?"

"Ah, you don't know about the correlation," he muttered. The captain scowled at him, probably to remind him whose fault that was. He cleared his constricted throat and explained. "Meredith Holt and Alyssa Conway, the Mojave victim, were both taken by those two," he said, pointing at the screen where the mug shots of the two fake cops were displayed. "These cases are related; if we find Alyssa's killer, we'll find Meredith."

SA Glover glared at Fletcher, then at Morales. "Unbelievable," he groaned. "Why didn't you tell us sooner? This entire team should be charged with obstruction."

The open phone connection crackled with some static when Karyn came back.

"Okay, so typically these GPS chips are manufactured and wholesale-released in batches. Retailers buy a batch or a part of a batch, then split it up and sell the individual units," Karyn said. "I'm willing to bet a bucket full of cold beer on ice the perps bought the exact same batch the manufacturer released. No one blows up and repackages batches of product just for fun."

"Then, can you hack into the batch this one came from?" Fletcher asked. "I need all those dots lighting up nicely on a map."

"Sure can, but it will take a while. I'll be in touch." She ended the call without saying goodbye, just as Fletcher wanted to ask for help in tracking the mobile phone users who'd strolled through the Mojave. As soon as the captain and the fed were out of his hair, he'd call her back.

Glover pressed his lips together and shifted his weight from one foot to the other, giving him a menacing look. "What else do you know about this case, Mr. Fletcher? Who was that cop on your screen earlier? And how the hell did you get access to search the employee database?"

26

Gear

Thirty-five hours missing

Holt drove fast on Flamingo Road, heading for my place, after I'd pleaded with him for at least one full minute without repeating anything. He didn't cave until I twisted his arm and said, "If you want my help with this, we're going. You're not the only one who needs to pack up some gear." Then I used the tiny fraction of influence I still had on my partner to force two candy bars down his throat and a venti cup of extremely strong coffee. Where he was going, Snowman wasn't exactly going to greet him with a set table and a comfy bed.

I shuddered when I remembered where he was going. I had confidence in my abilities and even more in his. He was a former Navy SEAL, who didn't need much help from anyone on any given day, and that included me. However, he was going to face a motivated enemy who had enjoyed more than five years of revenge planning time. So many things could go wrong.

I pushed the thought aside and forced some optimism into my voice. "What was with the gunpowder?"

"Huh?"

"That cocaine brick was packed in gunpowder and vacuum sealed. I can understand vacuum; no particles make it out of the package if there's no air to carry them, but why the gunpowder?"

"It throws off drug-sniffing dogs' noses, or so I've heard."

"Were you expecting a raid at your place?"

"You never know," he replied grimly. "Never know what to expect."

We rode in silence for a while, a thought gnawing at my mind and leaving bleeding wounds behind it.

"Why did you turn off your phone, Holt? Fletcher and I were the only ones who had that number."

Tense muscles danced under his cheeks. "You would've found me and stopped me," he eventually said.

"From what?"

"From trying to find her."

The man was behaving like a complete idiot. That was the only possible conclusion. Because the alternative, that he didn't trust me worth a damn, was too painful to consider.

"No, you twat, I would've helped you, like I'm doing now."

He didn't reply; he kept his eyes on the road but reached out and squeezed my hand. My eyes moistened.

"If that bloody phone of yours were on," I continued as if nothing had happened, "you would've learned we'd made some progress. The composites came back from your friend, the federal marshal, and Fletcher is running a search for that son of a bitch. Then I heard Mrs. Hardin, Casey's mom, was raising hell at the precinct with an expensive lawyer in tow, screaming you detained her daughter illegally. Which, by the way, you kind of did."

He shrugged.

"The captain told her off, I heard, then she had the misfortune of running into Anne on her way out. You want to know what happened?"

Another shrug. "Yeah."

"Rumor has it that Anne dragged Mrs. Hardin into the morgue and made her take a look at Alyssa's body, then told her if she wanted Casey to take the next available slab, she'd be happy to call you and ask you to release her kid."

Holt's lips fluttered, stretched into a smile that defied the tension on his face. "She's really something, your friend, Anne."

"Yeah, she is."

"You never told me, what's the story with you two? You seem to have a special connection that goes beyond cop and coroner."

I felt saddened for a moment. He'd always pried into my past, into my relationship with Anne, and wouldn't let go. That spoke volumes about his cop nose, his talent as an investigator, but considering the pile of lies he'd poured on me lately I felt irritated by his question.

I breathed and looked at him for a moment. He needed to know that trust was possible between two partners. Maybe then he'd reciprocate and wouldn't lock me out anymore.

"Anne flew helicopters in Afghanistan," I said, my voice sounding frail, trembling. "Two people were the top helo pilots in their unit; one was Anne, the other was my husband, Andrew."

"Oh," he said, shooting me a quick glance. There was a dark intensity in his eyes I'd seen before, but not since his daughter had been taken.

"We were close, the three of us. Anne and Andrew shared the camaraderie of having served together. Anne and I shared the passion for justice, for setting things right no matter the cost, and Andrew and I... we used to share a life."

He turned on to my street and pulled in the driveway. "Thank you," he said quietly before getting out of the car.

"Let's move," I replied, forcing the emotion away from my chest. There would be a moment for it later. "We don't have time to waste."

I asked him to wait for me in the living room and get himself something to eat or drink while I packed a few items. His eyebrows shot up while he watched me rushing up the stairs.

Once in my bedroom, I didn't hesitate. I'd rehearsed what I had to do in my mind over and over and knew every step I had to take to get ready for that night.

I stripped into my bra and panties and pulled out a small wheelie from the closet. I packed two different sets of clothing. A dark blue, Anne Klein pantsuit with a Miu Miu white blouse and Jimmy Choo heels to match, and a pair of stretch jeans and a UNLV sweatshirt paired with sneakers. I gave it a moment's more thought and threw in an Altuzarra, one-shoulder, black, stretch dress with generous side slits and added assorted heeled sandals. I quickly went through my jewelry drawers and picked a few long, thin necklaces in gold, then pushed the open suitcase out of the way.

Still in my undies, I pushed the racked clothing items to the side and exposed the back wall. I pressed the button on the far edge of the shelf, and the wall shifted to the side, released from its locks, revealing a second closet.

"Whoa," I heard Holt's voice behind me. It gave me a start and filled me with instant rage.

"Don't you ever do as you're asked? What the hell is wrong with you?"

He completely ignored my questions, inviting himself to look into my second walk-in closet. "Are you CIA or something?" he asked, then whistled when he laid eyes on my gun collection.

"Or something," I replied. "Now, because you're here, sit your ass down and shush."

He threw one more appreciative look at my hidden treasures, then sat on the edge of the bed. "Make it quick, Baxter, we ain't got all night."

I opened a small drawer and extracted a subdermal GPS tracker, then fitted it inside the implantation syringe, while Holt stared at me with disbelief. I approached him and said, "Drop your pants. We're going to put this where they won't be checking."

"Where the hell is that?" he asked, eyeing the needle as if it were a twelve-inch blade.

"Inner thigh," I replied.

"Is it an RFID microchip?"

"No," I replied, getting ready to poke him. "Radio frequency identification is reactive; it sets off alarms a mile out. This is a silicone-coated GPS tracker. I'll have your location on my cell phone."

"How long will the battery last? Can't be much time."

"Not that long, six hours, tops."

"That's some serious tech, Baxter. It's hundreds of dollars apiece."

I plunged the needle in, and he flinched. "I only had this one. You owe me dinner at a really fancy place, so better not get killed tonight. Now pull up your pants and sit back down."

I needed eyes and ears on him too, not just a locator. I opened a small, plastic box and pulled out a tiny camera and its receiver. I flicked the switch and tested it with an app I had installed on my phone. It was low resolution, but it got the job done. I turned to look at him, in search of a place to put it.

There was a lot I didn't know about what he expected.

"What do you think is going to happen, once they pick you up tonight?"

He shrugged again. It was becoming an annoying habit. "Probably beat the shit out of me and then kill me," he said calmly. "Unless I can find my daughter and get the hell out of there first."

"You don't have an action plan figured out?"

"Based on what? There's not nearly enough information to build a tactical plan. He has my daughter and is looking for revenge. That's all I have, all I know."

"And you just said yes to Snowman's request to meet," I stated the obvious, still in disbelief.

"'Never say no to the hostage taker'. You know the rule. For the rest, I'll think of something on the fly."

"Yeah, okay, but why not bust through the doors with a bunch of SWAT and be done with it? Why play his game?"

"The Snowman I know wouldn't keep Meredith where he's meeting me. He's smarter than that. If I don't follow the rules, he'll have her killed just to see me scream."

He had a point. We had no way of knowing where Snowman was going to take Holt after he picked him up or where he kept Meredith. Even if I followed Holt after the 2:00 AM meet, I couldn't be sure I'd have the girl's location.

"They might tie you to a chair and beat you up," I said, my voice slightly trembling. "That would make the shirt collar a bad choice for this thing. One drop of blood and it's out of commission. How about here," I said, then pinned the tiny camera onto the hem of his left pants leg. "If you can, lift your trousers when you sit, so the hem will point up."

"Uh-huh," he replied, studying it curiously.

I grabbed his left hand and slid a silver wedding band on it, a simple one without any design. "If anyone asks, you're engaged. This is an encrypted frequency reactive device that will only respond to the paired emitter. In case the GPS malfunctions or runs out of juice, and we lose you. But this ring requires us to be in close proximity."

"How close?"

"Under twenty-five yards," I replied, worry seeping in my voice.

"This is Fletcher's paradise, and he doesn't even know about it," he commented as he tucked in his shirt. "Or does he?"

"No, he doesn't," I replied with a nervous smile. "Let's keep it like that."

I went back into the closet and opened the gun cabinet. I pulled out a bra holster and put it on, then inserted a Sig 365 in condition one, ready to use. I picked up a fresh pair of slacks and a clean shirt and got dressed.

"Where do we go from here? Henderson?"

"No," he replied grimly. "The Strip. I'm willing to pay big bucks for an underage, high-end escort who's into kinky stuff. She might have a thing or two to share."

I took one look at him and groaned. No one in their right mind would send him a high-end escort, the way he looked tonight. Raw knuckles on both fists, a bruised jaw, a cut eyebrow, and a monumental shiner.

I took off the shirt I'd almost finished buttoning and folded it, put it in the wheelie, and fished out the little black dress instead. The slacks went into the suitcase, while the black sandals came out. In went the pants belt with my service weapon and two full mags, out came a thigh holster with a Sig 938 in condition two.

Holt watched me change clothes without saying much, eager to get going.

"One more thing," I said. "You need a new set of fingerprints." I pulled what I needed from the closet, then slid the wall back in its place and rearranged the clothes on their hangers. I led the way downstairs, carrying the fingerprint kit, two new burner phones, a prepaid satellite phone, a military-grade monocular, and two radios, just in case we needed them.

"Real fakes or smudged?" I asked, offering him a choice between two, tiny, plastic containers.

"What the hell is this?" Holt asked, staring at me as if he'd never seen me before.

"I'm giving you fake—"

"I know what you're giving me, but who the hell are you?"

At first, I thought he was joking, but he was dead serious. Apparently, there was a limit to Holt's tolerance for the unexpected, and I'd exceeded that limit.

I started applying adhesive to my fingertips, then pasted on a set of fake prints. Within seconds, the adhesive had congealed, and the silicone prints were in place, ready to use.

"Why don't we discuss that after we get your daughter back?"

He looked straight at me, and I sustained that piercing gaze without batting an eyelash. After all, he'd just dug out a cocaine brick from his wall. Who was he to judge me?

"Real or smudged?" I asked again, impassive.

"Smudged," he replied. "Where do you get the real ones?"

I smiled, proud of my craft. "Terminal patients in a clinic in Sichuan, China. I get the molds sent over, the rest is up to me."

I applied the adhesive to his fingers and noticed the slight tremor in his hands. "Tired?"

He gave me a sad version of the lopsided grin I knew so well. "What do you think?"

"I think you'll get her back, Holt, that's what I think. I know you will."

As he waited for the adhesive to set, I texted Fletcher with the IMEIs and SIMs for the new burner phones and the subdermal GPS tracker frequency. He was the only one who knew where we were and where we were going.

Then I touched up my makeup and accessorized generously, aiming for the high-end escort look myself. A tiny, envelope-flap, clutch handbag in black leather ornate with Swarovski crystals completed the attire.

I was ready.

27

Fear Factor

Thirty-seven hours missing

We approached the vast lobby of the Scala Hotel and Casino from the adjacent parking structure, walking along endless, lavishly decorated hallways and riding down on wide escalators. I watched the huge, digital displays rotating through adverts for shows, restaurants, and concerts, and, for a brief moment, I let my focus slip away, wishing Holt and I were there for a real vacation, set to enjoy Gordon Ramsay's gourmet cuisine, or watch Elton John live in concert.

We reached the lobby and had to stop for a minute; Blue Man Group was doing its preshow parade, filling the space with rhythm, sound, and color. As soon as the actors cleared the way, we scurried across the marble floor toward the check-in counter. As discussed, Holt waited some fifty yards away, near the elevator bank, watching for anyone who would've paid too much attention to either of us.

I dazzled the receptionist with my megawatt smile; he was a thin, young man with a bleached mullet, about twenty-two, yet he checked me out shamelessly.

"I have the penthouse for the night," I whispered and extended a matte black American Express card without a name on it.

His brash smile froze as he mumbled, "Yes, ma'am," and started typing on his keyboard.

I held my breath, hoping Fletcher had managed to tap into the Scala systems on time and snatch that reservation. I relaxed a little when he generated a magnetic keycard bearing the Scala logo and extended it to me.

"Two, please," I replied calmly.

He obliged, then finalized my check-in quickly, and I was able to join Holt near the elevators. A few moments later, we entered the forty-fifth floor Scala penthouse, among the best Las Vegas hotels have to offer to those willing to fork out over two thousand dollars per night.

The living room was extensive and lushly decorated with modern furniture. Leather armchairs, a couch facing the breathtaking view of the distant mountains, a fireplace burning happily, and two sets of French doors leading to the terrace. That outdoor oasis of luxury was a wonder in itself, something I'd never seen before. White cushioned lounge chairs were scattered around the marbled space, surrounding on three sides a private infinity pool overseeing the city's million lights below. I could've spent a lifetime enjoying that place.

Instead, I shot Holt a look, and we rushed downstairs. We had work to do.

My first stop was at the bar, where I sat on a plush, burgundy sofa, leaning against gold, silk-fringed pillows and crossed my legs, showing a lot of skin. The bartender took less than a minute to notice me and appeared by my side.

"What will it be tonight?"

I patted the seat cushion next to me. He hesitated a little, stared at my bare legs for a split second, then sat on the edge of the couch. His nervous smile revealed crooked teeth and a tiny bit of lettuce stuck between his upper incisors.

"I think you could help a girl in need," I whispered, leaning toward him provocatively.

"Uh-huh," he replied, nodding a couple of times. "Anything."

"I need some… company, if you know what I mean," I said, tugging playfully at my necklace, twirling my fingers around the fringe medallion, and looking at him sideways.

"You mean, um, me?" his voice climbed, conveying his disbelief.

I touched his cheek with the tips of my fingers. "Not so fast, handsome, I have different tastes. I like girls," I added, then licked my lips and batted my eyelashes for added effect. "Sometimes I want men like you to join the party, but the girl has to be special."

He swallowed hard and tugged at his tie knot, releasing it a little bit. I saw tiny beads of sweat forming at the roots of his brown hair and on his tan forehead. "What kind of special would you like?" he asked slightly stuttering, then swallowed again.

"Young, really young and innocent," I murmured. "I love to open their eyes to the pleasures of the flesh. Will you make that happen for me? Then, maybe the two of us could share a virile man like you."

His hands were trembling so badly he would've said yes to delivering me a date with a crown prince, then would've died trying to make that happen. He nodded spasmodically, and I squeezed his knee, sending a noticeable shiver through his entire body.

"I'm in the penthouse," I said, running my finger across the edge of his lower lip. "Send her up, wait a couple of hours, then join us."

"Y—yes," he replied.

I stood and sashayed away, swaying my hips with every step. When I turned toward the elevator, I caught a glimpse of him slamming the tray and the order book on the counter and rushing toward the back.

Good.

Soon, Holt and I would have someone we could talk to.

I'd just stepped into the elevator when a chime alerted me that I had a message. As I read it, my gut twisted into a knot, as if a terrifying creature was unfurling in there. Dr. Hickman, the ornithologist, had sent a list of other locations, dates, and times when the vultures had circled in similar patterns.

Five locations. Five dates, roughly one week apart. Five possible girls who'd been buried alive, endlessly raped and tortured until death finally found the mercy to release them from their hell.

I dialed the number for my boss, Captain Morales, and steeled myself, anticipating the myriad questions he was going to ask. Where was I, and what was I doing? Did I know where Holt was? When was I coming in? What news did I have about Meredith and the search for her kidnappers? How about the case I was assigned to, the murders of Alyssa Conway and Elizabeth Lovato, the two girls found in the desert? Anne had probably shared with him the identity of the second girl, Elizabeth, and the fact that she'd died immediately after being given the modified tetrodotoxin; her asthma an unforeseen complication that had left her killer frustrated and likely to take another girl out there soon.

As I waited for Morales to pick up, I swiped my keycard to unlock the door and signaled Holt to stay quiet, then put the phone on speaker.

"This is Morales," he said, almost startling me.

"It's Laura Baxter, Captain. My apologies for the late-night call, but I need your assistance with the case I'm working on."

"Shoot," he replied quickly, and I thought I heard someone else talking around him, a male voice I didn't recognize. It was almost ten in the evening; the man presumably had a life.

"I have a list of five possible crime scenes out in the Mojave, and I believe it's time we bring in dogs and thermal-sensor helicopters, in case the sick bastard has another victim buried alive out there."

I expected him to ask me why he had to do my job for me and dispatch all those units, and I had a well-rehearsed lie ready to serve.

"Consider it done. We'll start our search tonight."

"Thank you, sir," I replied, then hesitated, unsure if he had anything else to ask or say.

"Good luck, Baxter. Catch that bastard." Then he hung up, leaving me slack-jawed in disbelief.

"What just happened?" Holt asked. "Does Morales know what we're up to?"

I shook my head. "Not that I know of; there's no way. Maybe he was just busy, distracted, or who knows. Tomorrow he'll have our hides nailed to his office door, like any other morning."

That moment, I heard a timid knock on the door. I signaled Holt, and he disappeared into the bedroom, leaving the door ajar.

I removed the chain and opened the door, smiling, then gave the young girl an encouraging nod. She walked inside, looking around with round, fearful eyes, checking out every corner of the room. The excessive makeup she'd applied on her eyelids made her appear cheap; her foundation was caked, her inexperience probably a factor. Where her skin was left uncovered by cosmetics, it was pale. She looked unhealthy, thin, and weak, unstable wearing the four-inch heels she didn't know how to walk in.

"Come in, take a seat, my dear," I said, showing her to one of the armchairs.

She sat, seemingly a little relieved. I sat across from her and offered her a cold can of Coke. She smiled, then popped the cap and drank a few gulps.

She was yet to say a single word.

"What's your name?" I asked.

"Chloe," she replied in a tiny voice, shooting me a squirrelly look.

"We need your help, Chloe," I said, all the seduction from my voice gone, replaced with a friendly tone. "We're looking for a missing girl your age."

That moment, Holt stepped into the living room, and she jumped to her feet.

"I—I don't… I can't, no, sorry," she said, rushing to the door.

Out of options, I grabbed her thin arm and stopped her. She yelped.

"We're not going to hurt you, I swear," I said, speaking as soothingly as I could. "We're looking for Meredith, have you seen her?"

Holt showed her a photo of his daughter, but she barely looked at it and shook her head so violently her long, bleached hair came undone from the updo, sending a hairpin to the floor.

I grabbed her left wrist and held her forearm under the light, then touched the spot where someone had injected the tracking chip. She whimpered and wriggled, trying to break herself free from my grip.

"Where are the people who gave you this, Chloe?"

"No, no, please," she pleaded, starting to sob. "I can't."

"You'll be safe, I promise. You'll be able to return home to your family, and we'll put these people behind bars," Holt said, showing her his badge.

At the sight of his ID, the girl's knees gave, and she let herself fall to the ground in a heap of inconsolable wails.

"No, no," she pleaded between heaving sobs, "you don't know what they'll do. Not to me, to everyone."

"What do you mean?" I asked, feeling a chill down my spine, because I suspected what she meant.

"They'll beat all of us," she whimpered. "If one of us does something wrong, if a customer complains, or if we talk to anyone, all of us are punished."

"Punished how?"

"They hurt us badly," she said, shielding her face from us, ashamed.

I looked at her body, searching for visible signs of abuse. I saw none.

"Where it doesn't show," she whispered, her face flushed, her eyes lowered to the ground. "Please, let me go."

Holt crouched next to her, and she pushed herself away, trying to distance herself from him.

"It's my daughter," he pleaded. "Please help me find her."

She shook her head slowly, as tears rolled from her eyes, running mascara-tinted streams of moisture into her caked foundation. "I don't know who she is. I can't help you."

I looked at Holt, asking him silently to let me talk to her some more. I offered her a hand, and she followed me to the couch. Then, obediently, she drank another sip or two from the can of Coke.

She shivered badly, trembling from her entire fragile being, and I offered her one of the plush bathrobes that came with the penthouse. She wrapped it around her body, all the time continuing to cry softly.

"Please, let me go. I'll tell them something to explain why I don't have the money. Please."

"We'll give you—" I started to say, but Holt cut me off.

"You're not going back there, you hear me?" he shouted. "What kind of man do you think I am, to let you go back to those monsters?"

She stared at him with hollow, round eyes, her tears gone. Then she nodded slowly, accepting her fate.

"I can't... There's seventeen of us," she whispered as if begging us to consider the harm that her cooperation with us would do to all those girls.

"We will get them all, and you're going to help us," Holt stated firmly, turning his back to her to talk to me. Obscured by Holt's broad shoulders, she slipped out of my view for one brief moment.

"We need to get a radio car out here, to pick her up," Holt said. "Have Fletcher wait for her with a medical team. He should look at the chip she has in her arm."

The gust of fresh, cold air swept the room, and my heart stopped upon realizing what had happened. Chloe had run out on the terrace and climbed over the glass guardrail, ready to let go.

"Chloe! No!" I shouted and rushed to the terrace. Holt ran faster than me, but still couldn't catch her arm before she released her grip.

The white bathrobe fluttered quietly as her body fell forty-five stories to the ground.

28

Lust

Thirty-nine hours missing

He liked to come into the garage and look at them. Seeing how they trembled when he stepped inside, how they retreated until they hit the back wall with nowhere left to go made him twitch with the promise of a massive erection. He actually came into the garage every chance he got, just to run his hand against the cage walls, to hear them whimper, to smell their fear.

The one in the far kennel didn't know him yet, not as well as and as personally as the other two did. She didn't lower her gaze when he stared at her; instead, she glared right back at him, muttering oaths, her nostrils flaring, her fists clenched. One hour with him and all that feistiness would be erased from her being for the rest of her ridiculous existence. One hour was all he needed.

But he couldn't touch that one yet; Snowman would kill him.

The boss had been furious after he'd seen the newscast about Alyssa Conway and had made it very clear: when he told his men to get rid of a girl, he expected that girl to disappear forever, never to be found again. One more mistake, and he'd put a bullet into each of his security men's skulls, just to teach everyone a lesson.

He stood there in front of the boss, taking the scolding with his eyes lowered to the ground, hating every minute of it, feeling the flush of humiliation light up his face. Someone like him, to be degraded like that in front of everyone else, was unacceptable, and since it had happened, all he could think of for a while was how to kill Snowman, slowly, painfully, making him beg for mercy.

Then his thoughts rushed back to the girls, the ones in the garage and the ones in the desert. How the fuck did the cops find Alyssa? He'd been careful. He'd driven at least two miles from the highway before stopping and setting up her resting bed. He'd chosen the location thoughtfully, considering the terrain and the direct line of sight from the highway. No one should've ever found her body, yet they had before he had the chance to be done with her.

He gritted his teeth in frustration and kicked the cage where that swine's daughter awaited her turn. She barely flinched, and he bared his teeth and cussed at her. The girl in the next cage whimpered and crouched to the floor, hugging her knees. Krista was the girl's name, not that he cared, but when Snowman gave an order, he had to know which girl he was talking about.

His mind didn't linger on Krista's smooth skin and perfect curves; he'd tapped that more than once and found it mediocre. His eyes moved on to Mindy, who sat on the floor leaning against the wall, her eyes lowered, absentminded, almost indifferent. Perfectly still... almost ready.

Soon, Snowman would give the order; he probably wanted to give Mindy one more chance. Killing her was a waste of a fantastic, little body and a tight ass that would've raked in cash like no one else. Natural blondes always scored high with the customers, regardless of what turned them on.

He was itching to take Mindy for a drive in the desert. He'd have to move farther south and drive inland at least five miles this time, to make sure the cops wouldn't find her body. But he was eager to go, frustrated by the way his last affair ended, too soon, so soon he barely had time to indulge once.

That girl had died quickly, within moments of getting there. He'd dripped the two drops between her lips, and she was gone. He'd counted carefully and was sure he didn't screw it up. No, it had to have been that bitch's fault, dying on him like that for no reason. He'd barely had the time to take her once, her body cold and perfectly still, subdued to perfection under his hands.

He remembered what she felt like and stared at Mindy with a growing urge to break her out of that cage and take her to the Mojave now, today. His body screamed for the delayed release, clouding his mind, making his entire being ache with need.

But Snowman wasn't the kind of man to mess with. He'd seen his boss kill people for far less, for a beer not chilled enough or for a door left open. Taking one of his girls before he was done with her was not a good idea.

He put his hand below his belt and rearranged things down there, grinning when Krista whimpered. Then he crouched on the side of Mindy's cage and whispered, "Soon, baby, soon."

The girl didn't react in any way; she just sat there, inert. She was the one who could make him happier than anyone he'd had before. She had it in her blood to be serene, obedient. That's how he liked his women, still, not squirming endlessly, focused only on their pleasure, not his. That was the problem with all those sluts; either they writhed and screamed to escape from his grasp, or they fidgeted senselessly looking for their own release, not caring for a moment about his. Two drops of the elixir, and all that was gone, leaving them able to feel, to see, and to hear without robbing him of his own moment of bliss.

He knew he should take Mindy into the desert and put a quick bullet in her head, then leave her there for the vultures and coyotes to prey on, scattering her bones across the expanse, never to be found again. He also knew that once Snowman gave the order, he'd take her to a place like no other, deep into the barren lands, and share with her moments he'd never forget, for days in a row, for as long as he could keep her alive.

No one could rob him of that pleasure.

29

Exchange

Forty-two hours missing

Holt drove his unmarked Interceptor to the Windmill and Bermuda gas station and parked it on the side, as instructed. Then he started ambling back and forth in front of the pumps, killing time, waiting for Klug's men. It was two in the morning; there was almost no traffic whatsoever, and my white Toyota stood out like a sore thumb.

Behind the gas station, there was a small strip mall with a Wells Fargo bank. I parked there and pretended to be on a phone call while keeping my eyes on Holt. It was dark and difficult to see that far, but nothing else was moving in that entire area except him.

A dark blue Ford Transit approached on Windmill, coming from I-15; it slowed and entered the gas station. The sliding door opened when it was passing near Holt, and two men grabbed and pulled him inside the van. The door slid shut and the van sped away, without having completely stopped.

I refrained from flooring it and chasing the van; I had Holt's GPS tracker showing up nicely on my phone. I let the van gain a good lead and followed from a distance, keeping it in sight but far enough to not draw any attention at that time of night, when the absence of traffic posed an issue.

The van continued on Windmill Parkway for a while, then turned right on Green Valley Parkway and passed the Legacy Golf Club. The driver used the maze of residential streets off Wigwam Avenue to check if he was being followed, making turn after turn and slowing down. I didn't fall for it; I stayed well behind, giving him time to regain confidence and drive to their final destination. After a while, he exited the neighborhood via Timberbrook Circle, then turned left on Wigwam, then left again on Green Valley, resuming his original course.

He slowed after the overpass at I-215 and turned into the deserted mall. Then, after another few minutes of navigating between stores and restaurants, the van pulled up at the loading dock of a large store. The sign, now dark, read, "Wholesale Plumbing Supplies and Tools."

I didn't need to read the sign to know where I was. Any cop who'd worked in Las Vegas had heard of that place. It was believed to be a front for the local drug trafficking business, was even raided a couple of times, but nothing could be proven. A few, more seasoned cops insisted the company was the money laundering arm of the prosperous narcotics pushing trade, but again, nothing was documented, so no charges were filed. By day, the place buzzed with activity, its reputation also being an excellent supply store, where plumbers and contractors could find any fitting, washer, or tool kit they could think of.

The loading dock backed into an open area, forcing me to keep my distance. A few hundred yards away, there were some newly developed houses, and I pulled in front of one and killed the lights. Then I extracted the monocular from my bag and searched for the van in the viewfinder.

Two large men held my partner by the arms. A fourth man slid the van side door shut, and the driver peeled off, turning the corner and heading toward the main road. The men dragged Holt inside the store and immediately closed the loading door. Within moments, the place seemed just as deserted and as quiet as it had been before they arrived.

Against all reason, I waited for Meredith Holt to walk out of there, although I knew men like Samuel Klug never kept their word. Not even Holt expected the encounter to be a fair exchange; he knew Snowman better than that. Waiting, listening intently, my mind wandered, going over what little I really knew about Klug.

Until my partner had first mentioned him, I'd barely heard his name. I never worked Narcotics or Vice. I was a Homicide cop, part of the Homicide Bureau within the Las Vegas Metro Police Department. As far as I knew, Klug's involvement with sex crimes was relatively new, and to that day, he'd never made my radar for any homicide either. My only participation with the substance trafficking world had been my endless search for my husband's killer, until one day when I found him staring me in the face with his odd eyes from across the interrogation room table. But even in those days, I'd never heard Klug's name.

How did someone like him keep so clean?

I needed to learn more about him and quickly, if I were to be of any use to my partner.

I waited, watching and listening to the camera feed from Holt's pants hem. I didn't see much, only a grainy, dark view of a shopping aisle, and almost no movement as if he were standing somewhere, immobile. I couldn't hear a sound either, except for his heavy breathing.

I needed to get inside that place. But how? What could I possibly invent to justify my presence on the premises? How could I bang on that door and not get shot, not put Holt's life in danger and his daughter's too?

I started playing several scenarios in my mind, living through them as if they were real, and seeing how they all ended in blood baths with nothing achieved. It reminded me of playing a strategy game on the computer, where I chose to do different things each time yet lose just as badly.

Then I heard sounds coming from my phone. The video feed was still grainy, but there was movement and increasing light, the image choppy, something I had expected considering I had attached the camera to the leg of Holt's pants. It was bouncing with every step he made, swinging violently, the noise of his footsteps on cement louder than the voices in the background.

Then the image stopped, centered on a large, leather armchair occupied by an African American male in his thirties. He wore a gray suit, from what I could tell, and a white shirt, all but the two lowest buttons undone to show his hairy chest and a thick, gold chain with a cross pendant. He slumped on the armchair with his legs spread out and his elbows splayed on the armrests, and stared dead ahead, probably at Holt.

"Well, if it isn't the mighty Detective Jack Holt, coming into my house again, this time invited," the man said.

"Hello, Klug," I heard Holt's voice. "Or do you prefer Snowman?"

"I prefer you to shut that yapper before I tape it for you."

Holt didn't respond.

Snowman shifted in his seat, slouching a little lower. "I'm surprised you had the balls to show up," he said. "You know you're not getting out of here alive, right?"

"Right," Holt replied calmly. "Where's my daughter?"

The man laughed heartily, patting his stomach with a ring-studded hand. "Someplace safe, keepin' my homies some company."

I cringed.

"You son of a bitch," Holt said, and the image on my screen moved erratically, as if he were trying to run but couldn't. "That was the deal, my life for hers."

Snowman made a dismissive gesture with his hand. "Yeah, yeah, that was the deal, and I didn't pop her. You get to die, she gets to live, a life of luxury among my best-producing girls on the Strip."

I heard Holt shout, "You lying piece of—" but then someone hit him hard because his words were cut mid-phrase. Another blow came right after that, the sound of knuckles punching bones was unmistakable, as were Holt's groans of pain.

For a long moment, all I could hear were Holt's raspy breaths.

"That's what you had in mind for me?" Holt asked, still panting. "Four, white ex-cons with tats beating the shit out of me? That's lame, Snowman. That's fucking lame."

Another blow came, and then another. The last one knocked Holt to the ground and the image on my screen tilted sideways. They picked him up, while I jotted some notes. Four Caucasian males with prison tats. It was a start.

The beating continued; I could barely stand it. I wanted to barge in through that door, gun drawn, and raise hell, but I was afraid for Meredith's life, afraid what a psychopath like Snowman could do in only seconds.

When they stopped pounding on Holt, I heard his raspy breaths again, the only sound captured by the tiny camera for a few seconds. Then he cleared his throat, spat on the floor, and asked, "What the hell do you want, Klug?"

The man smiled widely, showing bright white teeth and a sparkling tooth jewel. It must've been a diamond because even in that faint, grainy video, I could see its bright flickers of reflected light. He leaned forward, resting his elbows on his knees.

"It's payday, motherfucker. Today you get to bleed."

I winced, expecting some more blows to rain down on my partner. Instead, I heard his voice, a little raspy, but strong, undefeated.

"I know you, Klug, you always want something."

He laughed again, his cackles sending echoes against the high ceiling of the store. "Not before your meat is tenderized to taste."

The blows started pouring mercilessly. After a few more, the image tilted again, and I could see Holt had been thrown to the ground, and two men were kicking him hard.

Then the image disappeared. I heard a crackling noise, and the sound was gone too.

I was in the dark.

30

Collaboration

Forty-three hours missing

Fletcher looked over his shoulder every few minutes, fearing that Captain Morales and the fed would return to grill him some more. He'd managed to disclose only some of the things he knew, but he was getting anxious, afraid he'd forget what he'd said to whom and when. He was good at keeping secrets, if no one threatened him. He was not secret agent material, not that he'd ever claimed he were or wished he'd be. No 007 in his future; he was destined to remain a nerd forever, albeit one with a cum laude degree from MIT and a solid influx of job offers hitting his inbox every week.

When Fletcher's desk phone rang, he smiled widely and rushed to pick it up.

"Yeah, this is Fletcher," he said, although he knew who the caller was and couldn't hide the smile in his voice. Not many callers would hit his office line at three in the morning. Karyn was probably the first.

"Hey," Karyn said, her voice chipper, filled with excitement. "I finished running the cell towers."

"All carriers?"

"All of them," she replied calmly.

"Wow," Fletcher whispered. The feds must've had some real processing power to pull that off in only a few hours. Connections with the carriers too, to open access so damn quickly.

"I went back for the last two weeks," Karyn announced. "I pulled tower ping history and looked for commonalities, for patterns in usage. The good news is, not many phones became stationary in the Mojave, at the far edge of a tower's reach. Only one of them did, actually."

"And the bad news?" Fletcher asked, knowing how the symmetry of good and bad news usually worked in a technical investigation.

"It's a different one each day. All burners, no GPS enabled."

"Argh... That means all locations are approximate."

"Yeah, because all we have to work with is triangulation, not satellite positioning. For the latest two crime scenes, we don't even have three towers to work off of; only the two along the state route, one east and one west of the crime scenes."

"Resulting in a swath of terrain where he could've actually been, not an actual point. The intersection of two circles, not three," Fletcher completed her thought. "Do those swaths include the crime scene locations?"

"Yes, they do. But, again, it's a different phone each day."

"Smart son of a bitch," Fletcher muttered, thinking. Maybe the perp's daily habit to get a new burner phone had a benefit after all, something the perp might've not considered. "What if we mapped where these phones have been, the days they were active? Can you see if they all, or at least some, visited a residential address in Henderson?"

"I got you," Karyn said, typing quickly. "Your coroner's estimations of the killer's timeline in the desert were a great help narrowing down the cellular traffic in the area. Otherwise, we'd still be crunching."

She typed some more, grumbled something unintelligible to herself, while Fletcher muted the line to slurp loudly from his freshly opened can of pop. He was intrigued by the FBI analyst; it was rare to find someone who was an intellectual match to his data and analysis abilities. Then he wondered how old she could be; was she more like his age? Or pushing fifty, overweight, and wearing bottle-bottom glasses?

Nah... her voice sounded youthful.

"Okay, so, let's see. Between his visits to the crime scene, he went back and forth to a Henderson address about eighty percent of the time."

"Not sure I follow," Fletcher said, wanting to kick himself for becoming distracted trying to picture Karyn in his mind.

"I'll explain. I looked at the days when there was any stationary cell phone traffic in the desert, pinging off of one of those towers. By stationary, I defined the parameter as someone not moving out of that tower's range for at least thirty minutes. That eliminated all the highway traffic passing by, even folks who might've stopped to take a leak at the side of the road. With me so far?"

"Uh-huh," Fletcher replied.

"That returned a number of eight days out of the past fourteen, and eight different burner phones. During each day, the perp's phone of the day pinged at that tower at least once, twice, sometimes three times. And in about eighty percent of the visits, he went back to a Henderson residential area afterwards or came from a Henderson location. Always the same area."

"Bingo," Fletcher reacted, excited at first, but immediately deflated. "You don't have an address, because it was triangulation, not GPS, I get it."

"Tell me about this address you're looking for," Karyn said. "You have no idea what I can do."

"I'm starting to imagine," Fletcher replied. "I don't have much; only that it has a large garage, and that it should be relatively isolated. An informant mentioned Klug shooting people there without concern for neighbors' nine-one-one calls."

"Keep it coming," Karyn said, typing quickly.

"I don't have anything else. Oh, just one thing: Holt said to exclude the homeowners who are family people with kids and gainfully employed. Can you do that in a query? If not, I'll weed them out by hand."

"We don't do anything by hand here, except make coffee," Karyn laughed. "Sending you the list of possible addresses now."

"How many?"

"Seven."

Fletcher jumped off his chair with excitement. Seven! He could work with seven. He could look at them via satellite, have detectives do drive-bys and get a feel for those places, and look at prior history of activity or any red flags on any of them.

"Karyn, you're awesome!"

"Not really, but thanks. I still owe you the mapping of GPS trackers coming from the same batch as your victims."

"Any issues with that?"

"They're mapped, here you go," she said, pushing a screenshot of her system to Fletcher via the messenger interface. "But you can't spot a pattern; I think I know why. It's three AM. The girls are still working, scattered all over the city."

He studied the map for a moment. Tiny blue dots marked the location of each girl, and Fletcher counted fifteen. Each dot was in a different location, sometimes two in the same place or close vicinity. Most of the dots lined the Strip, and one was a little south of the city, on a highway, probably in transit when the screenshot was taken.

Another one was in Henderson.

"Does this dot in Henderson coincide with one of the seven addresses?" he asked, holding his breath.

"Damn," Karyn muttered, "why didn't I think of that?" She fell quiet for a second, then shouted, "Yes. You have your address, Fletch. Can I go to bed now?"

"Nah," he laughed. "What's the fun in that?" He was delaying the moment he'd have to say thanks and hang up. "Um, maybe we can have a cup of coffee together? You and me?" he asked, his voice tentative.

There was a long moment of silence, and he almost withdrew his invitation.

"That could be a terrible idea," Karyn said, the smile in her voice clear as day. "Yeah, sure, why not?"

She ended the call, leaving Fletcher smiling until he realized he could've googled her, instead of obsessing over how Karyn looked like.

"I've turned into a complete idiot," he admonished himself quietly, running a search with her name. Then, happy with the results of the image he found, he sent a high-priority, flagged message to Captain Morales.

"Have a highly likely address for Meredith Holt's location. Requesting warrant now."

31

Territories

Forty-four hours missing

I'd been sitting in my car in the same place, my eyes scanning the loading dock's door every few seconds, waiting. Nothing had happened in almost two endless hours. Not another sound or image from the camera attached to Holt's pants. No one came, and no one left the plumbing store during the time I'd been watching it.

I put all that time to good use. Fletcher had sent me everything he could get his hands on from our colleagues in Narcotics, and I started studying Snowman's business. I had very little time to learn every aspect, every player, every influence in the Vegas underground trade.

I kept Fletcher on an open line while reading the materials he'd put together for me, and I asked the occasional question. I remembered what Holt had shared a couple of weeks ago about his undercover mission in Klug's organization. He'd been deployed to identify how the drugs made it across the border from Mexico straight to the Strip without detection. He'd done his job; he found out they were shipping the powder in meat carcasses, the pouches slid under the ribs of the frozen animals. The dogs didn't sense them, and even if they did, the presence of the meat discredited the dogs in the eyes of their handlers. X-ray didn't reveal anything either, because the structure of the carcasses, flesh and bones, rendered blurry, intricate-pattern images on the screens, against which the packets were difficult to distinguish. Brilliant.

But that transport method had dried out after Holt plugged that hole in the system. The hundreds of meat trucks crossing the border every day from Mexico were now inspected with a different, more powerful type of X-ray machine and software that recognized geometrical shapes against all backgrounds.

And yet, white death poured in from the south, unabated.

I moved on to the next report, skimmed it, then read it again. It went in detail over the distribution of power in the Las Vegas drug trade.

Snowman reigned over the richest territory in the city that never sleeps and had direct access to its four million annual tourists because he owned the Strip.

His kingdom encompassed the entire east side of the city to I-15, the Interstate dividing the city in half, north to south. The two halves weren't equal in surface; the west side was broader, but tourists rarely visited that part of town. That area belonged to another slime bag, a Latino with an impressive rap sheet by the name of Carlos "Dry Bones" Juarez. Dry Bones had earned his street name once his pushers learned that he liked to take snitches and thieves into the desert, shoot them, and let the sun dry their bones.

There it was, the desert again. I didn't regard that as an unusual coincidence though; with its proximity to the city and its extreme, deadly climate, anyone who was in the killing business used the desert as a dump site.

I remembered most of what I read from the days I used to troll the streets hunting for my husband's killer. I knew Dry Bones really well, personally, because I'd interviewed him a couple of times in prison, where he was about to finish serving his nickel. Then he was back conducting business as if nothing had changed, beating the streets in his black Cadillac SUV with chrome wheels and ridiculously raised suspension. I also knew Bones's right hand and best bud, Pedro "El Maricon" Reyes, doing time alongside his boss for a while, because I'd put him there after sending him to the emergency room for a little visit.

I flipped back through the digital pages, making sure I understood everything clearly. Every square inch of territory east of the Interstate belonged to Snowman, the affluent customers, the junkies who lurked around the casinos, the crazed-up tourists, the irresponsible youngsters who really believed that what happened in our city had a real chance of staying there. Snowman's product was first class, cut with clean, decent fillers and priced accordingly. The product was so good, rumor had it that his network had many business clients who snorted a little coke to keep up with the demands of a high-intensity workload without fear of nasty side effects during quarterly meetings.

But the moment one crossed the Interstate to the west side where less coin hit the streets, the coke was cheaper, the clients poorer, and the boulevards not so glamorous. The price of a well-dressed hooker dropped by 50 percent, and a hit of cocaine dropped by at least 25. The sleazy, east-side clients were in Dry Bones's territory, where heroin was nasty, meth was downright lethal, and coke was cut with low-grade fillers, likely to land first-time users in the hospital.

I frowned, looking and not finding a way into Snowman's game. I didn't see anything I could use, any name I recognized, any piece of information that could open the door into Klug's organization.

I checked the plumbing store door one more time; everything was shrouded in darkness and silence. I closed my eyes for a fraction of a second, thinking. Where was all this coke coming from, and how?

Most important, what did drug dealers fear the most? The loss of a customer? Not that much; a new sucker was born every minute, and dope dealers were skilled at pushing free product in schools and clubs to get people hooked. But the thought of losing one's supply, that was scary. After Holt had strangled the incoming flow of cocaine from Mexico, the entire organization Klug controlled had fallen into disarray for months. Dealers killed one another, ratted on one another, each desperate to be the first to get their hands on some product and keep the cash coming in. It took Klug a while to patch things up.

Who held supply in their hands, held power over the organization?

That was my way in.

"Hey, Fletch?" I asked, waiting for him to acknowledge. He'd been on mute for a long time.

"Yeah, go ahead," he replied. I heard him munching on something crunchy and realized how hungry I was.

"Do you have any intel on the supplier? Who's sending the stuff?"

"It's the Sinaloa Cartel," he replied quickly. "Same as before."

"For Snowman, I get it. How about Dry Bones? Where's he getting the poison?"

"Sinaloa," he repeated, taking another bite of whatever that was.

"What? Both of them have the same source?" I asked, feeling refreshed at the possibilities unfolding before my mind's eye. "How positive are you?"

"One hundred percent," he replied. "The DEA gave us the name of their contact: Anado 'The Don' Cardenas. He's pretty high up in the Sinaloa, this Don. A few years ago, the DEA had him confirmed as *lugarteniente*, a lieutenant, the second highest rank in the cartel. He could be a drug lord by now, or close enough."

"How come he's still drawing breath and pushing product into Vegas if we know who he is?"

"Eh, you know how it goes," Fletcher replied. "DEA suspects, but can't prove anything. Just like us, they need someone undercover to help them intercept a major shipment or put two or more of the top players in the same room talking business. Without that, we have nothing, and the perps continue pushing the dope across."

"Get me anything you can about this Don, Fletch. I need to know how to get to him: phone number, location, everything you can get from your friends in the DEA. How would Snowman interact with him? How would our pal, Dry Bones?"

"I don't have any friends in the DEA, Baxter," he said, sounding deflated.

"Well, then, make some."

32

Internal

Forty-five hours missing

Special Agent Glover stood in the dark, looking at the quiet street from behind the living room window sheers. Mrs. Sauceda was in the bedroom, and his colleague, Special Agent Rosales, kept her company. At times, wails and whimpers came through the closed door. As the hours rushed by, Meredith's mother grew increasingly desperate, afraid she'd never see her daughter again, losing every shred of hope she had left.

Per procedure, they set up a base in the home of the victim, making it easy to intercept any incoming ransom call. After almost two days had passed without a call coming through, he'd given up all hope that the kidnapper was after ransom, or that a call was going to come in at all. He suspected Holt of keeping many critical details to himself, including that call.

He'd invited Internal Affairs Bureau Lieutenant Steenstra for a chat, because her notes were present in both case files he'd shortlisted as most likely to be related to Meredith's abduction. He called her shortly after four in the morning, and the lieutenant promised she'd be there in thirty minutes. In anticipation of her arrival, Glover had disabled the doorbell, not wanting Steenstra's arrival to disturb Mrs. Sauceda.

The street lit up as Steenstra's headlights appeared. The lieutenant parked alongside the curb and walked briskly to the door but didn't get a chance to knock.

Glover held the door open for her, inviting her in. They shook hands, as Glover observed how perfectly professional Steenstra appeared, although it was still dark outside and less than an hour ago, he supposed she had been sleeping in her bed. She wore a metallic blue pantsuit tightly adjusted to accentuate her thin waist, and a white shirt with a raised collar that underlined her long neck and proud stance.

She took a seat where Glover indicated, at the dining room table, where two thick files were stacked and, on a coaster, an almost empty coffee cup.

"Some coffee, Lieutenant?" he asked, keeping the pot in one hand, and reaching for a clean cup with the other.

"Sure, why not?" Steenstra replied, eyeing the two files.

She took the cup from his hand with both of hers and nodded in lieu of thanks. "Why am I here, Agent Glover?"

He pushed the two files her way. "These two have your notes. We believe the detective's daughter's kidnapping is related to one of them."

She opened the first file, looked at the name, then closed it and opened the second one, reading from it just as briefly. "I see. What do you want to know?"

"What's your history with the detective? What's your impression of him?"

"Detective Jack Holt is extremely independent and holds little respect for the procedure manual," she said, weighing her words carefully. Glover could tell she was holding back. "He has a strong sense of right and wrong, thankfully, because he'll stop at nothing to get his man. He's not in the slightest way a political player or elbowing for advancement. He's driven by the need to rid the city of people who break the law."

"You're describing the perfect cop, aren't you, Lieutenant?"

"Not in the least," she replied, leaning against the backrest of her chair and folding her arms at her chest. "The procedure manual is critically important for the system's ability to prosecute the cases effectively and to bring criminals to justice the right way. Las Vegas Metro Police aren't the OK Corral, but Detective Holt doesn't seem to care."

"Ah, I see," Glover reacted. "So, is it possible he used the wrong approach or bent the rules in the apprehension of certain perpetrators? I'm asking from the perspective of his daughter's abduction, which is what I'm here to assist with."

Steenstra sipped carefully from her steaming cup. "Yes, it's possible. I'm surprised you narrowed it to only two cases."

"Let's talk about this one," Glover said, pointing at the thickest of the two files. "In our experience, a long and successful undercover stint is likely to earn a cop a lot of enemies, people who feel betrayed—and were, for that matter—and will relentlessly seek to exact revenge."

She sat calmly, her hands folded neatly in her lap.

"You see, Lieutenant, Holt is out there by himself, trying to track down the people who took his daughter. I'd like to be able to anticipate his next move, the people he might interrogate next, actions he might be willing to take, so we could be out there helping him, instead of waiting for a call that doesn't seem likely to come."

She pointed an index finger at the ceiling, then at Glover. "See, that's where you're wrong, Special Agent. You think he's out there by himself, and I'm telling you Baxter's right out there with him, whether we know it or not."

"Really? How can you be so sure?"

"They share an unusually strong bond, these two. They only met four weeks ago, but they'd do absolutely anything for each other."

"Tell me about Baxter," Glover asked.

"She's a top-notch detective. She came to us from the United Kingdom, when she married an American Navy pilot and moved here. She's been trained by New Scotland Yard, an expert in interrogation and deception techniques, and one of London's youngest police inspectors, if I'm not mistaken."

Glover whistled. He would've liked an asset with Baxter's background on his team.

"But," Steenstra continued, and by the tone of her voice, she was about to list Baxter's less popular traits, "she's been on my radar since she beat a suspect to a pulp and scored a disciplinary transfer to our precinct, a reduction in pay, and a suspension, followed by twelve months' probation. That's when she was teamed up with Holt. Two mavericks teamed up... I honestly don't know what the deputy chief was thinking when he approved that."

"You said there's nothing these two wouldn't do for each other. How do you know that, Lieutenant?" he asked, scratching his chin thoughtfully.

"This is one of those situations when it's better to take the word of another cop at face value and leave it like that. Believe me, I know."

"And that means what, exactly?" he insisted, wondering what Steenstra was hiding.

"That means she's out there with him, searching for Meredith, doing whatever it is they see fit to do to find her. And bodies are piling up."

"Bodies?"

"Only one death so far, a young girl who committed suicide from a Scala hotel penthouse that was coincidentally occupied by someone whose name doesn't ring a bell but shares a striking physical resemblance with Detective Laura Baxter."

"Ah," he reacted.

"Yeah," Steenstra said. "That girl happened to have a tracking microchip embedded under her skin, just like the two victims found in the Mojave Desert, a case assigned to Detective Baxter."

"Then, she's working the case, I'd think," Glover replied, frowning a little. Those IAB people always saw conspiracies where there weren't any. He also remembered what that kid, Fletcher, had said. The serial killer case that Baxter was working and Meredith's abduction were connected.

"Yeah, right, working the case... In disguise, booking two-thousand-dollar hotel rooms with her own money?" Steenstra asked serenely.

He couldn't think of anything to say. The lieutenant was probably right. But she didn't seem like the type to exaggerate things. "You said, *bodies* are piling up. But, there's only one?"

"One dead, two in critical condition at the hospital after having been interrogated by someone resembling Holt, and five more severely injured, including one suspect who was shot in the leg, probably for information."

"Oh, I see," Glover replied and turned his head to hide a chuckle from the lieutenant. It was probably what he would've done. "They all had priors, I presume?"

"Irrelevant," Steenstra reacted, raising her voice. "We have procedures for a reason. We can't uphold the law when we feel like it, and then break it when it's about our own families."

Wait 'til it's your family staring at the wrong end of a gun, Glover thought, irritated by the lieutenant's pompous self-righteousness, although he knew she was right.

"What about the missing cocaine that's showing on Holt's file?" Glover asked. "Is that in any way related to this case?" he tapped the cover of the Snowman file.

"Yes, but indirectly," she replied. "Holt went undercover in Samuel Klug's organization five years ago. The missing cocaine is from a recent bust, a couple of months or so. It so happens that the recent bust involved people in Klug's territory."

"Do you believe Holt took the cocaine?"

"I absolutely do, but I wasn't able to prove it."

"You think the abduction is about revenge?"

"For a kilo of coke? I doubt it," Steenstra replied. "We seized the entire stash that day, but one kilo never made it to the evidence locker. The perps don't know Holt stole it."

"*If* he even stole it," Glover replied. She was quick to pass judgment in the absence of evidence, that woman. If it wasn't for the significant differences in physical features, she could've been Rosales's sister.

"Like I said, Special Agent Glover," she replied calmly, "I believe he took it, and it's one of those cases when you should take another cop's word for it."

"So, you don't think Samuel Klug is out to get revenge?"

"Not for that kilo of coke, no. Klug could be after Holt for the losses he incurred five years ago, for all his people we locked up, for the two who got killed in the shootout, for being forced into exile for a few years."

Glover stared at the landline phone on the nearby counter, wired into complicated recording and tracking equipment.

"That means it's possible a ransom call will never come," he said.

"If I were a betting woman," Steenstra said, "I'd say the call had already come, to Holt personally, and things are already in motion. He won't share; the man's a maverick, a cowboy."

Glover interlaced his fingers behind his head and stretched. Exactly what he'd suspected from the first moment he'd seen Holt lying to his face. Exactly what he'd feared, seeing that young analyst, Fletcher, trembling, about to shit his pants, but not betraying the detective's secrets. Precisely what he'd figured out, listening to Baxter's call to Dispatch, asking to be assigned the Mojave victim's case, Alyssa Conway.

Apparently, there was still some shred of hope to find Meredith Holt and return her to her family, but he was cut off from the real investigation. The lack of trust Holt displayed toward him and the CARD team, despite their proven record of accomplishment, pissed him off to no end. But at the end of the day, Holt was the parent. A federal agent could only recommend things like the ransom being paid, or who could take part in an exchange, but the parents had the final say because it was their child.

Glover smiled, thinking of his family, of his little boy sleeping soundly at that early morning hour, the darkest before the light. It was Holt's darkest hour; no one had seen or heard from the detective in a while, nor from his partner. Whatever they were out there doing, Glover could only hope they'd get to Meredith in time.

He turned toward Steenstra, pretending not to see the quizzical look on her face and trying not to feel offended by her contempt for the likes of Wyatt Earp. After all, he came from a long line of Arizona cowboys and marshals.

"Why don't you walk me through both these cases in detail, Lieutenant?"

33

Inmate

Forty-seven hours missing

I hesitated a little before leaving the stakeout position behind Wholesale Plumbing Supplies and Tools. I had a plan, but in all fairness, it was half-baked and included a few Hail Mary passes. It also meant I had to lock eyes again with the man who'd killed my husband, and not for the reason I'd been dreaming of, like putting him in jail for the rest of his life with a murder conviction or wrapping my hands around his neck and squeezing harder and harder until his last breath left an agonizing, thrashing body.

The wanker was in jail all right, doing a dime for drug trafficking. We couldn't build a case for Andrew's death; there wasn't enough evidence. The murder weapon was gone, no witnesses stepped forward, and I had nothing pointing in his direction other than my husband's dying testimony, "Eyes like Grandma."

Andrew's grandmother had heterochromia. Her left eye was green, while her right one was blue. When he whispered those words to me from the emergency room bed at the University Medical Center, I assumed he was talking about the man who shot him, but I couldn't be sure. I was too frantic to ask him more questions; I just kept calling his name and begging him not to leave me.

I went back to work immediately after he was gone because work meant access to police systems and resources, and I had a killer to catch. I looked everywhere... pulled countless names out of databases, searched for known offenders with heterochromia, tried everything I could think of to find the man who'd pulled the trigger on an innocent bystander and destroyed my life.

Then I started roaming the streets at night, after my day shift was over, looking for that man everywhere. Somewhere, on some dark alley, there was an odd-eyed man dealing dope and carrying an unregistered weapon, and I was about to find him. The official investigation into Andrew's death had concluded that my husband had stumbled upon a drug deal in progress and the dealer, spooked, fired his weapon and ran. So, I started looking at drug dealers everywhere and hating everything that had to do with that terrible vice.

More than a year later, uniformed officers collared a perp wanted for a separate issue and landed him in my interrogation room because of a correlation with a case I was working. I entered the room and looked at him, then froze. Staring at me with unspeakable contempt, the perp's eyes, one green, one blue. Then he said things to me that confirmed he knew who I was. Indirectly, he confessed, or at least admitted knowledge of my husband's murder, when he asked, "Your nights lonely these days, *chota chica?*" I looked into his mismatched eyes and saw my husband's killer, laughing at me.

And I lost it.

I came down on him badly, pummeling him with both fists and not stopping until they dragged me off his fallen body that I'd kept kicking and pounding into a pulp. It took the doctors a while to render him able to leave the hospital and head straight to arraignment.

But I couldn't prove he was my husband's killer. After that incident, they didn't let me near him to get a confession. Instead, they suspended me and gave me a rip and a disciplinary transfer. I was lucky I still had a job, even if it came with probation and mandatory counseling.

Just remembering all that made me sick to my stomach, a vile bitterness climbing up my throat and burning everything in its path.

And now I had to look into those odd eyes again and ask Pedro "El Maricon" Reyes for a favor.

That was my bloody plan.

I steeled myself as I approached the prison. It was early, not even seven in the morning, and there were no other visiting vehicles lined up at the main gate. When the sentry approached, I flashed my badge and he lifted the barrier.

I went through the routine of showing ID, leaving my service weapon with the main desk, then being escorted to an interrogation room, where I waited for a few tense minutes. Then I lost my patience and walked out of there, searching for the officer who was supposed to bring Reyes. I found him chatting with another CO, and that lack of urgency sent a wave of rage throughout my body.

"What the hell are you doing?" I asked. "And where is bloody Reyes?"

"It's still early, Detective," the corrections officer replied unfazed, a tentative smile fluttering on his lips. "The shift is just—"

"I don't care who you have to wake up, you hear me? Just get Reyes down here, right this minute!"

The smile wilted, and he rushed toward the holding cells. A minute later, Reyes was being hauled into the interrogation room, his hands and feet in chains.

I felt my heart beating quickly against my chest, and I breathed fast and shallow, raspy pants of air that didn't fill my lungs with anything but an unreleased scream of pain, of longing. I willed all those whirling emotions away and forced myself to appear calm, composed, indifferent. Andrew was gone; nothing I did to that piece of shite, Reyes, could bring my husband back. Hopefully, Jack Holt was still alive, and so was his daughter. Maybe those two could still be saved.

I steeled myself and looked into the mismatched eyes of the man I could easily kill with my bare hands.

"Hello, Reyes," I said calmly. "I see prison life agrees with you."

He looked around panicked, but the corrections officer was already gone and the door behind him locked.

"What do you want, *chota puta?*" he hissed, shooting side glances left and right as if someone was going to emerge from the cinderblock walls and rescue him. "Came back for more blood?"

I studied his face for a moment. His nose was crooked, and so was his left brow ridge, the signs of the fierce beating that I'd delivered a few months ago.

"I'll be attending your parole hearing soon," I said. "Time flies, doesn't it?"

He frowned and lowered his head to run his chained hands against his nose in a quick gesture. He was scared.

"If you help me, I'll vouch for you and say how you've been completely reformed, as if you were the recipient of a successful brain transplant," I spoke coldly, barely able to keep my apprehension under control.

"You must be crazy, bitch. I ain't up for parole for another four years."

"Not if I have the sentence commuted to simple possession," I replied, looking at him calmly, not showing any sign of deceit.

I didn't have the authority to offer that kind of deal, but he didn't know it. I was counting on that.

"Think about it, you could be out of here in four, five months, tops."

He wiped his nose again, this time against the sleeve of his orange jumpsuit. "What do you want? To beat me up again? That gets you off, bitch?"

I shrugged, feigning indifference, and allowed a twitch of contempt to curl my upper lip.

"If you're not going to help me, I will bring the weight of the world against you in that hearing, and make sure you never see the light of day for as long as you draw breath," I replied coldly, looking at him straight, without blinking. "You think you only have five more years to serve, but things happen in prisons, you know. An inmate gets shivved, two others swear it was you, and ta-da! You're in for life. One more such slip-up and they'll gladly give you the needle."

That also wasn't true, but I was on a roll, encouraged by his increasing pupil size and the slight tremble in his chin.

"Okay, okay, I get it. What do you want?" he asked, barely a whisper.

"That's easy," I said and handed him a burn phone. "Vouch for me, and I'll vouch for you. Betray me, and I will definitely fry you."

He took the phone, extending both his cuffed hands to grab it from my frozen fingers. "Who do I call?"

"Make sure your boss, Dry Bones, vouches for me too, or he'll get picked up tonight on something or other, and do at least another dime. All on me," I added with a charming smile as if I were offering him dinner at a fancy restaurant.

Out of the blue, he sent the phone flying across the room and lunged at me, screaming his rage. The phone hit the wall and came down on the floor in pieces, while I didn't even flinch.

"Is this how it's going to be, wiseass?" I asked calmly, feeling the urge to rip him to shreds, to close those odd eyes forever. All I could hear in my mind were Andrew's dying words, and it seared me inside as if a red-hot blade was slicing through my heart.

He pounded both his clenched fists against the table. "No way you're making me snitch, *puta*! If you think you're going to get away with this, just wait 'til my homies pay you a late-night visit," he added, his odd eyes glinting with rage and his lips curled, exposing his teeth. "I can get things to happen from inside. Just wait."

"That's all you have to say?" I asked, standing slowly, taking my time.

"I ain't no rat," he replied.

"I'm not asking you to be."

"Then what?"

"You'd be doing your boss a favor. I'm going after his competitor, Snowman. All you have to do is tell whoever asks you that the Don sent me to look at Snowman's affairs and tell Bones to say the same. He'll get whatever territory Snowman loses."

His face started to straighten up as the rage that had crunched it before was wearing off.

"That ain't so bad," he said, looking at the broken phone with regret. "Got another one?"

I pulled another burn phone from my pocket and handed it over. "On speaker."

He started dialing a number, then stopped before hitting the call button. "What's your name, again?"

"Olivia Gaines," I replied. That used to be my stage name in London. How appropriate.

He called Bones, and they talked for a while in a mix of Spanish and English I was able to decipher without any problem. As expected, Bones saw the value in having his competitor destabilized and found himself entertained at the thought of making that happen.

Reyes flipped the phone shut and handed it to me politely, no brash gestures. "When can I get out of here?"

"I'll get things set up in the next few days. If everything goes well with Snowman's crew and no one suspects a thing, I'd say that by April you should be walking down the sunny side of the Strip again."

He grinned, bobbing his head like a complete idiot.

"One more thing," I asked. "What's the newest territory your crew has moved into?"

"Northeast metro, why?"

"Just because Don's envoy would know that," I replied, then I winked and pounded twice against the scratched, yellow door. A CO quickly unlocked it and escorted me out. I looked over my shoulder at Reyes, noticing the cocky grin on his lips and his brazen gaze, and I cringed at the thought of seeing him out there enjoying his freedom, getting away with putting my husband into the ground.

It seemed unfair.

I was never going to let that happen.

34

Building Olivia

Forty-nine hours missing

The early morning shift from the local Walgreens was a bit reluctant to accommodate my request to block the ladies' room with a mop bucket on wheels and a "Closed for Maintenance," yellow sign, but they did it anyway. I dragged my wheelie in there and locked the door behind me, then dialed Fletcher's number and put it on speaker, placing the phone on the counter between the sinks.

"Hey, Fletch," I said, as soon as I heard his voice. He sounded tired, like everyone else for that matter. Tired, and something else I couldn't put my finger on. "Hey, I've lost the camera feed. Holt's gone in—"

"I'd rather not know, Baxter," he replied in a heavy breath of air. "I'm sorry."

I frowned at myself in the full mirror. I'd expected the brass to start leaning on him; I didn't think it would be so soon.

"They're asking questions?" I inquired in a gentle voice.

"Yeah," he replied, sounding almost ashamed.

"What do they know?"

I held my breath, hoping no irreparable damage had been done, hoping they didn't know Holt's current location. Fletcher had the serial number for Holt's GPS microchip and could've tracked my partner's position. A SWAT team barging through the plumbing store doors sounded like a terrible idea, one that was guaranteed to get people killed.

"They know the two cases are correlated, and they know how," he said, speaking slowly. I could picture him with his head lowered, shoulders hunched forward, eyes riveted to the floor. "They also know the address in Henderson that Detective Holt was looking for."

"Oh, you got that?" I asked, feeling a wave of excitement. "How?"

"The feds offered their help. They have this incredible analyst," he blurted. "She's awesome!"

I breathed deeply once, then again, thinking. If the feds worked with Fletch and offered their help, that meant they had him in their crosshairs, watching his every move. He probably didn't know it and telling him would only freak him out. But I couldn't make my plan a reality without his help, with or without the risk of having the feds find out what I was doing. It was safe to assume Fletcher's phone was monitored, listening devices were in place around his desk, maybe even video.

I breathed again, deeply, calming my stretched nerves.

"That's wonderful," I told Fletcher, "one hell of a job finding that address. Did you tell the captain?"

"Y—yes," he replied. "And Karyn, the analyst I was telling you about, got the two kidnappers identified; I'll send you the specifics."

"Excellent," I replied. "Okay, now, I need your help," I added, letting a smile seep in my voice. "You're an artist, you know that, right?"

"Uh-huh," he replied, suspiciousness coloring his voice.

"Good. Then let's build a character from an action movie, a powerful and intimidating businesswoman named Olivia Gaines. Let's bring her to life."

He hesitated a moment, the silence complete, not only void of his words, but also of the sound of his fingers dancing over the keyboard. Then he started typing.

"Full background? How solid?"

"Bulletproof, Fletch. They will check."

"Age?"

"Um, thirty-four," I replied, shaving two years off my real age. A girl can never look too young.

He started working, asking me quick questions here and there, while I changed clothes. I took off the black dress and high-heeled sandals and put on the blue pantsuit and matching jacket. I replaced the thigh holster with an ankle one and snuck a Sig 365 in a belt holster worn on the inside. Then I put on the black pumps, a pair of kitty heels built on a metallic frame, in case I needed the heels to do more than support my weight.

Then I moved on to my makeup. I wiped and rinsed off my evening makeup and applied carefully a day-time, business-formal layout with just a tiny bit of eye shadow and an illusion of blush.

"Holy crap," I heard Fletcher's flustered voice. "Wait a second, okay? I got to look into something," he added, then muted the call and silence overtook the open line.

My hand trembled slightly with the lip gloss stick, and I glared at my betraying fingers. Was I afraid? Maybe just a little. For the most part, I was tense and anxious, eager to go back to the plumbing store and get to Holt. Why would they keep his daughter alive for so long, and why would they keep him? If this was about revenge, they should've been dead by now.

"I'm back," he suddenly said, panting a little.

"Is everything okay?"

"Absolutely," he replied. "They brought in the dirty cop, Officer Pete Mincey, remember him? The one who took the bribe in the Perdido Club's restroom?'"

"Ah, yes," I reacted, wishing I were there to grill him, although I knew now his pursuits weren't related to Meredith Holt's kidnapping.

"Who's talking to him?"

"The big man himself, Sheriff McGoldrick. I didn't know he still did interrogations."

"He's a cop, Fletch; of course, he does."

He muttered, and then I heard him unwrap something and there was a crunching sound as he took a bite. That young man had the metabolism of a rocket; it burned everything he ate, and he still looked skinny, even if half the time he was munching on a snack or slurping five hundred calorie drinks.

"I'll pull your ten card from the system and attach it, okay?"

I squeezed my eyes shut. This was about to get interesting. "Nope. I'll send you the prints. If I take photos of my fingers, can you extract?"

"Sure, I can, but aren't those the same prints as your ten card? We have them in the employee database."

"No, they're not."

A moment of silence ensued, then he whistled. "Wow," he eventually said. "Will you tell me how you pulled that off, sometime soon?"

"Sometime soon," I replied, then took photos of my hands and sent them to him via the messenger app.

"Okay, I got it," he confirmed. "Nicely done, Detective. They look perfect, whoever those might belong to."

Ah, Fletcher, shut up about the bloody fingerprints already, I felt like screaming. If the feds were listening to the call, that issue was going to pose some problems when I found myself in an interrogation room across from a pissed-off fed or, even worse, my boss. Good luck explaining fake prints to any of them.

"I'll give you a record," Fletcher said, "say, five years for—"

"Olivia Gaines never did time," I replied, rehearsing the intonations I was planning to use. "Only dumb people do time," I added, infusing the right amount of arrogance in my words.

Moment by moment, I was entering the part I was about to play. As I'd learned in my days performing on London theatre stages, the key was becoming Olivia. Not acting Olivia or pretending to be Olivia but becoming her.

She was powerful; she traveled on private jets and held the fate of entire organizations in her hand. She was impatient and a stone-cold killer. You crossed her, you died. No questions asked, no excuses. Everyone knew she pulled her gun and double-tapped a rat in under three seconds. She was Don's trusted associate, charged with inspecting his distribution organizations and making sure their businesses were tight and the associated risk managed to a minimum. She had the power to cut off the supply to a network just because someone talked to the cops about the weather. She was fierce.

She was also beautiful and knew it. She held her head up high, and wore her long, wavy hair loose on one shoulder. At night, she liked to eat at fancy restaurants and speed in her sports car, turning heads wherever she went. But she was all business, even when she was pretending to play. No one had touched her and lived to tell the story.

Satisfied with the Olivia I had constructed in my mind, I finished arranging my hair, accessorized quickly with a pair of diamond earrings and an expensive bracelet, then gave myself a thorough look in the mirror. Olivia Gaines looked back at me, impatient and fiery, ready to face Snowman.

"You were saying?" I asked Fletcher.

"What would you like me to put on her record? She can't be squeaky clean; they won't buy it."

"She's suspected of drug trafficking in the UK," I said, "because whatever I do, I still sound like a Brit. That won't go away with makeup and fake prints." The moment I said it, I wanted to kick myself. In case the feds hadn't caught that detail the first five times, I had to say it again and now they knew for sure. The hell with it. "She's wanted by Interpol. Carries British and Colombian passports."

"Known associates?"

"Amado 'The Don' Cardenas, Carlos 'Dry Bones' Juarez, several high-ranking pushers in Bones's organization, and add a few more names from the Sinaloa Cartel."

His fingers stopped tapping on the keyboard. "Baxter?"

"Yeah?"

"Be careful, all right? These people will kill you on the spot if they smell you're a cop."

I grinned nervously. "I know that, Fletch. Make that background stick; bury it under a layer of fake identities and associations like only you can do. It just has to work for a day; that's all I need."

"Consider it done," he replied, sounding satisfied with himself.

"I need two other things," I said, starting to pack the suitcase and makeup kit. "First, I need to officially arrive in Vegas. Book me on an inbound flight from Colombia on a private jet, complete with a flight plan and customs declarations, and reserve the most expensive Mercedes convertible you can find in this entire city. I need that set of wheels to wait for me at McCarran International in twenty minutes."

"You got it. What else?"

"Now this one's going to hurt. Remember that recording you got from the NSA with Don's voice? Who did that voice remind you of?"

"Um, vaguely, maybe Detective Nieblas?"

"Exactly," I replied. "You have precisely thirty minutes to coach Nieblas how to speak like Don, including accent, word usage, the works. See if the DEA has any recordings of Snowman talking with Don. Apply pitch correction filters on the phone that Nieblas is going to use, and some static and background noise for authenticity and camouflage."

"He's going to kill me, Baxter," Fletcher reacted. "You know Nieblas, he's not that friendly, and he hates Holt."

"All cops pull together when another cop's family is under attack, right?"

"Right."

"If needed, remind him of that. If that won't work, threaten, bribe, or blackmail him, I don't care. But when anyone in Snowman's organization dials Don Cardenas's phone, that call will be rerouted by you straight into the detective's hands. All he needs to do is sell Olivia Gaines as Don's personal envoy with the power to dry up the well. Got it?"

"Yeah, I got it," he replied, his voice hesitant and a bit sad. "At which point do I call this in? What if we don't hear from you?"

If the feds were listening in, that was the moment they needed to hear my message.

"You *do not* call this in, Fletch, you read me? Never. No matter what happens... promise me you'll wait for my call."

"Geez, Baxter, you're batshit crazy," he replied.

I laughed quietly while locking my wheelie. "No, Fletch, I'm just that desperate."

35

The Meet

Fifty hours missing

I didn't belong in that place, and it was obvious even from the parking lot, where my black Mercedes S-Class Cabriolet stood out among contractor trucks and beat-up vans like a princess among pirates. Fletcher had outdone himself, grabbing that impressive piece of German engineering from an exotic car rental under a fake name he'd constructed as an alias, just as Olivia would've done.

I ignored the appreciative looks my silhouette was eliciting from the predominantly male patronage and entered the store walking briskly, clacking my heels and holding my head high. In passing, I smiled when I noticed several customers crouched or leaning to look at items located on lower shelves, all of them proudly displaying the infamous view of the hairy butt crack that usually accompanied the notion of a plumber at work. That tiny bit of amusement did nothing for the anxiety gripping my gut in an iron fist.

Was Holt still alive?

The thought of being too late sent shivers down my spine.

Many things could go wrong with my plan. Nieblas could do a poor job posing as Don Cardenas. My cover background could have a crack, or that piece of slime, Pedro Reyes, could find a way to leak my identity to Snowman's organization, just to get even for his crooked nose. But none of those scenarios scared me as much as the thought of being too late for Holt, for his daughter.

I walked toward the back of the store searching for a way in, seeing two men hanging around a door leading to an employee-only area. I recognized one of them immediately, from Fletcher's video surveillance screen grabs, and later, the man's rap sheet texted to my phone. It was Rudy Huber, the man who'd kidnapped Meredith Holt wearing a cop's uniform with the name tag, "Beasley."

The second man looked entirely unfamiliar; he wasn't someone I'd seen before. I pretended to check my phone for messages and snapped a quick photo of the man and sent it to Fletcher. I approached the two men with a tight-lipped smile.

As I drew closer, they started shifting in place, looking at each other, then at me with increasing uneasiness. Huber unbuttoned his jacket, probably to make sure he had easy access to the weapon bulging at his side.

"Tell Samuel Klug I'm here," I said coldly.

"Is he expecting you?"

I let my smile stretch a corner of my mouth. "If he's smart, he's expecting me. Why don't you go ask him?"

"Your name?" Huber asked, giving me a look from head to toe.

"Olivia Gaines," I replied calmly. "Tell him Don Cardenas sent me."

The mention of Don's name had the effect of a double shot of espresso served intravenously to both men. Huber rushed through the restricted access door, while the other man, a white male with a traditional goatee, the chin-only version without the mustache, kept his eyes on me as if I were a ticking chunk of C4. He followed the same characteristics and probably shared a similar background with the rest of Snowman's lieutenants we'd been able to track. The ink jobs on the visible parts of his body pointed to lengthy terms spent behind bars.

My phone chimed, and I checked my messages quickly, without really taking my eyes off the man. "Devon 'Tiny' Burch," the message from Fletcher read, in response to the photo I'd sent. "Ten years for manslaughter, three for B&E." Fletcher's FBI friend was worth her salt; I'd never before seen a facial recognition ID come back so quickly.

The door opened, and Huber invited me in. I followed him through a corridor shrouded in darkness, lit only by a yellowish bulb hanging from the ceiling by its twisted wires. He stopped halfway and patted me down carefully, enjoying it a little too much, especially in the lower parts of my body.

As he was crouched down, running his hands down my legs, I grabbed his chin between my index and thumb as if he were a child. "Are you having fun there, Mr. Huber? Or just a plain old death wish?"

He stood abruptly, glaring at me. "How the hell do you know my name?"

"I like to know who I'm dealing with."

He removed the gun on my belt and the one in my ankle holster, but completely missed the Sig hanging from my bra. Then he beckoned me to follow him to the storage area.

My heart thumped loudly as I entered through the flexible, rubber, swing doors, recognizing the images I'd seen earlier when Holt had been dragged down the same hallway. Then, after passing through those doors, I saw Snowman sitting in his armchair just like I'd seen him before, in the grainy video feed captured by Holt's camera. To my right, about fifteen feet in front of Snowman, I saw Holt, tied to a metallic chair with power cords attached, bleeding from his nose, but very much alive. I contained a sigh of relief and refrained from giving him too much attention; instead, I walked straight to Snowman.

The goon by his side wolf-whistled, and I stared him down with all the contempt I could muster.

"Do that again, and you're dead," I whispered, my voice casual, factual as if I were telling him the cash register had run out of paper.

His whistle died on his lips and his jaw slacked. He looked at Snowman for guidance, but his boss's eyes were riveted on me.

"I don't like the way you treat my people," Snowman said.

"And I don't care," I replied calmly. "I'm here to speak with you, not entertain your lap dogs."

He shifted in his seat, leaning forward. Then he snapped his fingers and Huber brought him a cold beer from the fridge.

I could feel Holt's eyes on my back, but I couldn't turn to look at him. Not yet. Before I could say what I was there to say, Snowman had to trust me, at least in part.

"You threw a big name to walk through that door," Snowman said. "Would you mind if we check your story?"

"Suit yourself," I replied.

Huber appeared with a digital fingerprint scanner, and I offered him my index finger. He disappeared after that, somewhere further in the back, probably to pull up my background.

I walked casually, looking at the merchandise stacked up on the heavy-duty, gray shelving.

"Plumbing," I commented. "Out of all things, plumbing." Then I laughed quietly.

Snowman didn't take the bait. He stared at me intensely, his jaws clenched, his eyebrows ruffled, ready to pounce.

Huber walked back in and stopped behind Snowman's chair, then whispered something in his ear. Snowman slouched an inch lower; I'd passed, at least for now.

"Who are you?" Snowman asked quietly, shooting Holt a quick glance, based on the direction of his look.

"Supply," I replied. "You're distribution, which makes the two of us a match made in heaven."

"Yeah, right," he reacted, stiffening his upper body. I'd pushed it too far.

"I bring you northeast metro, if you want it. If not, Dry Bones will jump on the opportunity. He's already made a move on that sector."

"Whoa," he reacted. "Any cop could set up a background, and I ain't falling for it." Huber stepped closer, his hand on his piece and a menacing smirk on his face. "Who can vouch that you're who you say you are?"

"Dry Bones himself," I replied calmly. "I'm willing to bet you and he are frenemies, and his phone number's stored somewhere handy."

"I got him on speed dial," Snowman announced with a smug grin.

I made an inviting gesture with my hand. "Go ahead, call him. While you do that, have one of your lackeys bring me a chair. We've got lots to talk about."

He snapped his fingers again, and Huber brought an office chair on wheels. The dark gray fabric was stained with something that had left a powdery, off-white residue. I crinkled my nose and remained standing.

"Who sent you?" Snowman asked.

"The Don," I replied. "Want to call him too? It's still early in Bogota, you'll probably wake him, but he won't mind. He likes low risk in his business," I offered boldly, while silently praying that Fletcher had finished his homework, and that Nieblas wouldn't pick that day to screw something up.

Snowman started to dial a number on his phone, while I casually paced the space, this time approaching Holt. I stopped in front of him, observing every detail. The size of the blood pool at his feet. The pallor of his skin, where it wasn't bruised or bloodied. The anguish in his eyes as he looked at me.

I leaned forward, bringing our eyes on the same level, only inches apart. Then I winked quickly, and his jaw slacked.

When I heard Snowman end his call, I turned and walked quickly until I was less than two feet away from him.

"Hey, smartass," I said quietly, "did you know that's a cop you got there? He works Homicide on the Strip. What the hell are you people doing?"

Snowman laughed, his cackles echoing loudly against the corrugated metal walls. "What, you thought I didn't know?"

I shook my head disapprovingly. "You touch a cop, and this place will be swarming with them in no time. I'm out of here." I turned to leave and took a few brisk steps before he grabbed my elbow.

I glared at his hand where it touched my arm, and he let it go as if it burned his skin.

"There's no rush," Snowman said. "No one's coming after this cop, trust me."

I stood my ground, clenched in a silent fight of wills with Snowman, staring him down despite his imposing stature.

"I thought Dry Bones had that region already," he eventually said, breaking eye contact. He returned to his armchair and let himself fall against the leather cushions with a satisfied groan.

"Don's not happy with his performance," I replied coldly. "He believes you can do better. But with this…" I added, my words trailing as I pointed toward Holt.

"Don't worry about him," Snowman replied, aggravation tingeing his voice.

I walked toward Holt, studying him carefully, as the real Olivia would've done with a captive cop. I propped the tip of my shoe against his groin and pretended to lean on it with all my weight but I had leveraged my heel along the edge of the chair, barely touching him. I leaned toward him, letting my long hair fall around my face in a convenient curtain, and whispered, "Don't say a word, just go with it. Scream, damn it."

Before I could pull back, Holt whispered, "Jeez, woman, you're insane."

I removed my foot just as Holt was finally starting to groan and pull against his restraints, then I circled him a couple of times, a pretend predator pacing around its helpless prey, anticipating the thrill, calculating the right moment to strike.

His hands were tied with wire, wrapped around his wrists multiple times. Cutting through that would take a while. Snowman was surrounded by three armed men, and another one stood guard outside, ready to barge in at the slightest sound of trouble. I only had one weapon left, loaded with ten, nine-millimeter rounds. Not early enough.

"What are you going to do with this bucket of manure?" I asked, throwing Holt a look filled with disdain for Snowman's benefit.

"That's none of your business," Snowman reacted.

"Oh, is that true?" I replied slowly, one word at a time, leaving an unspoken threat lingering in the air. "He's seen our faces; there's no turning back now. You have to kill him."

36

Raid

Fifty hours missing

Captain Morales couldn't remember the last time he'd strapped on a bulletproof vest. Once it was firmly in place, he stretched his arms to get used to the way it felt, the heaviness, the way it restricted his movements. Then he put on his tactical jacket with the initials LVMPD in bold, yellow lettering on the back, and joined the SWAT team leader by the armored truck.

One bothersome question gnawed at the corner of his mind: if this was the address where Holt's daughter was taken, how come Holt wasn't already there, guns blazing? Fletcher would've shared his findings with the detective, no doubt.

He shrugged the question away and focused on the mission at hand.

The SWAT team had blocked the streets leading to the residence where they suspected Samuel Klug had taken Meredith Holt. It was an isolated property on the far end of Eveningside Avenue, built on at least two acres of land. The property backed against a hill, under Amargosa Trail, but that was far enough away to give the occupant the privacy required in the kidnapping business.

Morales saw one of the SWAT officers approaching quickly.

"We're done, sir," he announced, "ready to go."

That meant all the neighboring houses had been evacuated and all traffic contained; in the off chance that a shootout would ensue, Morales didn't want any stray bullets claiming the lives of innocent people.

He caught the eye of the SWAT team leader and nodded when the young man signaled everything was good to go. Snipers were in place, holding the target property in their unobstructed line of fire from multiple vantage points. All team members were ready to proceed, lined up behind the point man, weapons drawn. Satisfied, he gave the order.

"You have a go."

The single-file formation set in motion and followed the masonry fence approaching the targeted property, watching for signals coming from the point man, the one at the front of the line they called a snake. They passed in front of the three-car garage and approached the door. Two team members took positions left and right of the massive, wooden door, while two more rushed forward with a battering ram.

"Breach, breach, breach," the team leader ordered, and the battering ram busted the door open, sending wood splinters flying through the air.

They entered the house and spread out quickly, taking immediate control of their respective areas of responsibility. They started to clear the rooms one by one, their voices confirming by radio one after another.

Then a gunshot was heard, followed by an immediate burst of rapid fire.

"Clear," the officer announced, kicking the weapon away from the fallen man.

He recognized the fallen perp whose blood pooled rapidly around his body; Morales had recently seen his photo on the BOLO released by Fletcher. He was one of the kidnappers, Jeremiah Foley, aka Greer. That meant they were on the right track to finding Meredith. He crouched with difficulty, the bulletproof vest making it hard to bend his spine, and checked for the man's pulse, out of habit mainly, because Foley had been shot center mass at least five times.

That was unfortunate, and Morales threw the shooting officer a disappointed look. The order was to capture the perps alive, a standing order for all kidnapping cases, until the victim was located.

"Over here!" a man shouted, and the urgency in the officer's voice had Morales scramble toward him. He rushed past the kitchen and the dining room and through the adjacent hallway leading to the garage.

The first thing he noticed was the smell, a nauseating mix of blood, bleach, and gasoline. He saw the cages against the walls, most of them empty and with their doors open, but one of them was still locked. A half-naked girl lay on the stained cement floor, apparently unconscious; she hadn't reacted when they'd entered the garage, hadn't raised her head to look their way.

"Get an ambo here, now!" he called, then rushed to the cage trying to pry the door open. A SWAT team member approached with a bolt cutter and severed the padlock shackle, then opened the door. Morales stepped inside and kneeled next to the girl, his fingers desperately searching for a pulse.

"She's still alive," he shouted. "Where's the damn bus?"

"Two minutes out," an officer replied.

It was freezing in the garage. He picked her up gently and took her inside and laid her on the couch. "Someone, get me some blankets," he called, as he started rubbing her hands between his to restore blood flow. The girl moaned but didn't open her eyes.

"Coming through," he heard an unfamiliar voice, and saw the EMTs approaching with a gurney loaded with two large medical kits. He stood and moved to the side, making room for the EMTs. They worked quietly and effectively, barely saying a word among themselves. Within moments, they had the girl loaded on the gurney, an IV in her arm, strapped in, and ready to leave.

"Will she live?" he asked, looking at the fragile shape under the heated blanket. She seemed so frail, so damaged.

"Most likely, yeah," one of the EMTs replied, a sturdy, freckled woman.

"We're listing her as critical for now."

"When can I speak to her?" he asked, although he feared he knew the answer.

"Not now, that's for sure," the woman replied. "Do you know her name?"

Morales shook his head. That girl wasn't Meredith Holt.

"We'll find out and let you know," he replied. Crime scene technicians were already on site and always carried a mobile fingerprint scanner.

The technician scanned the girl's index finger, then pressed a button and waited. A few moments later, a chime announced he'd found a match. "Krista Hatfield, fifteen years old," he revealed, reading off the small display. "She was reported missing on January ninth. She vanished on her way home from school."

The EMTs loaded the gurney into the ambulance and took off with the siren blaring, leaving that place of horrors in its rearview mirror.

Morales joined the SWAT team outside the house; their job there was done, while his was just beginning. He hadn't found Meredith yet.

He approached the SWAT team leader and extended his hand. "Thank you," he said and shook the officer's hand. "You guys did good today, you saved a life."

The officer smiled widely, showing two rows of perfect teeth. "Three," he said, his voice boasting, upbeat.

"Which three?" Morales asked, frowning.

"We found those two upstairs," the officer replied, gesturing toward an Interceptor SUV.

Morales rushed to the SUV and opened the back door. He looked at their faces hoping to see Meredith's long, dark hair and black eyes, but the two girls were strangers he'd never seen before.

"What's your name?" he asked one of the girls, feeling a rush of adrenaline. Maybe he still had a chance to find out what happened to Holt's daughter.

"Nadine," one of them replied, sniffling quietly. She had auburn hair falling in rich waves over her thin shoulders.

He looked at the other one. "Jean," she replied, shooting him an angry glare. "You have no right to hold us, we didn't do anything."

He scratched his head, realizing things weren't always what they seemed. Jean might've been just as young as Krista, but she behaved more like a jailer than a prisoner. "Where is Meredith Holt?"

"I don't know," Jean replied coldly, crossing her arms at her chest.

"They took her—" Nadine started to say, but Jean cut her off.

"Not another word, bitch," Jean hissed.

Nadine clammed up and started to cry softly. She wasn't going to cooperate while the other one was present, intimidating her into silence. Morales repressed a sigh of frustration and grabbed Jean's arm. "Let's go," he said, then handed her to one of the officers. "Load her in a radio car, will you?"

Morales climbed in the back of the SUV, careful not to touch Nadine or come too close to her. Sexual abuse victims always reacted badly to the close proximity of a stranger, especially a male.

"Do you know where Meredith Holt is?" he asked gently.

"He came and took her," she said, pulling at the sleeves of her sweatshirt to shield her frozen fingers from the biting cold, despite the strong flow of warm air coming from the SUV's vents.

"Who took her, Nadine?"

"S—Snowman did," she stuttered, looking left and right as if expecting to find him there, within earshot, ready to pounce on her for her betrayal.

"Where did he take her? Do you know?"

She shook her head, looking at him with pleading eyes. "Uh-uh, no, I don't. They took Mindy right after that, but Homeboy took Mindy, not Snowman. I think he took Mindy to work, but Meredith, I don't know. She wasn't trained."

He frowned. "Trained to do what?" he asked, running his hand over his forehead.

She shot him a sideways look filled with embarrassment. "You know, to make money, um, with men."

He gritted his teeth, looking at Nadine, noticing her pale skin, her sickly thin arms, her bony shoulders poking through the fabric of her sweatshirt.

"How long have you stayed here, Nadine?" he asked gently.

"Since December seventh," she replied, starting to sob quietly. "That's when they…"

Her words trailed off, swallowed by a wave of sorrow.

"We'll take you home to your family, Nadine. It will be all right, I promise."

His kind words had the opposite effect. Instead of soothing her pain and giving her reassurance, it made things worse. Nadine's sobs intensified, her shoulders heaving spasmodically.

"No, please," she said, grabbing his forearm with both her hands. "I can't look them in the eye, not after this. Promise me you won't tell them where I've been all this time… please."

He watched the girl crying, thinking of things he could say to give her the comfort she needed, but at a loss for words. As a parent, he knew what she needed to hear, but thinking of his own kids only made things worse, because he couldn't bring himself to articulate any of those soothing reassurances. In his mind, only one phrase kept repeating, playing like a broken record, over and over, and that phrase he couldn't say out loud.

When I find the bastard who did this, I'll kill him on the spot.

37

Ransom

Fifty-one hours missing

"You don't get to tell me what to do," Snowman shouted, jumping off his armchair with unexpected agility and towering over me in an attempt to intimidate me. I hated to admit it, but I felt a little uneasy about the progress of our negotiations.

He'd obviously called Don, and Nieblas had managed a reasonable job convincing him I was representing the Sinaloa Cartel in Las Vegas, but I wasn't sure how far I could stretch that mile of good luck.

I didn't budge, didn't lower my eyes. "You assume this cop will walk out of here and just forgive you? Is that what you think?" I saw a flicker of movement in his eyes as his pupils dilated, a sign of fear or angst. "I don't know if Don will consider this good business practice for someone handling his product."

The muscles around his mouth tensed. "Why would he care? He's in Colombia, we're here in Vegas. We pay good money for the product he sends. It's not like we're doing each other any favors; this is business. And we're choppin' like none other."

"Why would he care?" I repeated the question slowly, pacing myself to make a point. "Because if you piss off the local five-oh, then you'll become high risk to Don's organization, and he'll spit you out faster than you can say sorry. You could be infiltrated, and that could bring things tumbling down overnight. Don doesn't like unmanaged risk."

"I'm managing the damn risk, aren't I?" he raised his voice again, gesturing toward Holt.

"No, you're not. You're creating risk for the overall organization, Snowman. It's got to stop and never happen again."

He stared at me angrily, the tension in his jaw increasing with the levels of his bursting rage.

"You're part of a family, one that takes care of you if you get in trouble," I offered a soothing piece of bait.

He nodded reluctantly, finally lowering his eyes for a brief moment. "Yeah,

I guess."

"Don't go federal for no reason, Snowman," I insisted calmly, resisting the urge to cross my arms at my chest. "I don't know what your plan is, but did you think of calling Don to ask his advice? You're obviously in some bind here, or else you wouldn't risk someone dropping a dime on you over this piece-of-shite cop."

His eyes flared a little when I suggested calling Don, another microexpression of fear. I was on the right track; I just needed to take it slowly.

"My men are one hundred percent loyal," he replied coldly, eyeing them one at a time. He'd sent them to wait by the door, giving us the needed privacy for our conversation. "They know what I do to snitches, you feel me? They've seen it with their own eyes."

I followed his glance and looked at the three men waiting by the door, doing a poor job at hiding their frustration. Like in any organized crime, the boss's lieutenants had a sense of entitlement and being forced out of a critical conversation was insulting to all of them. Each of them would've killed me in a heartbeat, even if that meant bringing down the wrath of the almighty Don Cardenas; it was that personal, their hatred that palpable.

I found myself wondering how long my legend was going to last. Would it be good for another hour? A day? A month? What would I be able to do from inside Snowman's organization?

But first things first: I needed to find Meredith and walk out of there in one piece with the girl and her dad. I still didn't know how I was going to pull that off.

I rolled the office chair next to his armchair and repressed my urge to investigate what that powdery, off-white substance was, staining the fabric of the seat cushion. Instead, I sat, conveying the message that I was there to stay. He soon followed suit and sat in his armchair.

It was interesting to observe the scene as a whole. The armchair was entirely out of place in the middle of a poorly lit, chemical-smelling, plumbing supply warehouse. Snowman sat in it all spread out, slouched and with his legs widely opened, elbows leaning on the high armrests, a veritable king on his throne. The image he projected was a powerful one, although it made me think of an overly engorged cockroach in its nest.

I leaned forward with genuine interest and asked quietly, "How can I help?"

He chewed on his lower lip, probably still doubting if it was a good idea to share his thoughts.

"That cop will do me a favor today, if he wants his kid to live," he eventually said.

"You got his kid?" I reacted, feigning surprise and playing Olivia's part masterfully. "Jeez, Snowman, you must be crazy." He frowned, unhappy with the continued criticism of his actions. Of course, he was a narcissist; no one climbed to his level in an organized crime structure without being one. "Or desperate," I added, trying to soften the blow.

"Yeah, right on," he replied. "My brother's been busted."

I waited patiently for more details, afraid to break the thin veil of trust that I'd established.

"He'll be arraigned today; they're moving him from lockup to the courthouse in about three hours," he added, after checking the time on an oversized gold Rolex watch encrusted with diamonds. "This loser will break him out."

"You need the cop to break out your brother from jail?" I asked incredulously, not even acting in that moment. He *was* crazy, completely unaware of how prisoner transport was conducted, precisely to avoid situations such as that. "Then, what do you think is going to happen?" I asked, forcing my voice to sound supportive.

"Then he'll know the moment any cop looks in my direction, that I'll slice his kid's throat like it's butter," he replied coldly, his eyes sending flickers of excitement as he spoke. "I'll set this dog free to keep the other dogs at bay. He's my slave for as long as I have his kid."

Holt started shouting oaths and threats in a slew of mixed words that made little sense. Within moments, one of the men shut him up with a punch to his face.

"I meant, what's going to happen after he breaks your brother free from jail?" I asked candidly. "They'll hunt him forever; there's not a single corner of this earth where they won't look for him, especially if a cop, one of their own, was involved. You're looking at a lifetime of heat brought upon your organization."

"He'll go to Argentina," Snowman replied. "Our money's like gold over there, and they won't extradite. He'll be free."

"Argentina will extradite him; there's a treaty," I clarified.

"They won't give him heat, and he'll keep his head on the DL for a while. The Argentina cops won't care."

I wondered what made the narcissistic sociopath installed on his leather throne care about his brother that much. Brotherly love? I seriously doubted it. I still wasn't getting the entire picture.

"You bloody fool," I laughed, "it's not such a bad plan, I'll give you that, but it's got holes in it."

He grinned, full of himself after my compliment.

"How did your brother get nabbed?"

"Bringing in last month's shipment," he admitted, lowering his gaze to the floor for the first time since we'd started talking. It must've been big.

"The whole thing?" I reacted, raising my voice just a little bit. "You lost an entire load of product?"

"Tyson stashed it before they took him in," he replied. His voice conveyed mixed emotions, frustration and pride at the same time. "He knew the heat was onto him, and he managed to park the skid somewhere safe."

"Oh, so you still have the product," I replied, starting to understand his crisis.

"Not unless I put Tyson's ass on a private jet to Argentina, I don't," he admitted, letting a pained breath of air escape his lungs. "The little bitch's got me by my short ones."

I felt like laughing. The hostage taker was being held hostage himself; well, his precious product was. I refrained from smiling and started working the escape plan in my mind. It was a game of dominoes; if all pieces fell into place the right way, we could hope to survive. A long shot.

"Ah, you got yourself in one hell of a bind," I said casually. "You know, Don can't advance you any replacement product just because you misplaced a load."

"I'll get it back, all right?" he reacted. "The moment that jet takes off, Tyson will give me the location of the dope."

"And you're sure the cops don't have it yet?"

"He swore to me, and that's good enough," he replied, wringing his hands nervously. He probably wanted to believe his brother more than he actually did.

I turned toward Holt and locked eyes with him for a brief moment, then faced Snowman.

"How's this cop going to get your brother on a private jet?" I asked. "I can see how he's going to flash his badge and get the armored transport to pull over and make up some shite excuse to grab your brother and leave with him, but then what?"

Snowman looked at me angrily. "We were sortin' through that when you came in."

I laughed, a quick, calm chuckle. "Come on, Snowman, this dude hasn't seen a private jet in his entire sorry life, man."

"What are you sayin', huh?"

I smiled like he and I were best friends. "I'm saying it's all good, man, you can use mine."

"You have a jet?" Snowman reacted, standing and pacing excitedly around my chair. "Fo' real?"

"How do you think I travel back and forth from Colombia? By Uber?"

His excitement quickly cooled to arctic levels. "How do I know I can trust you?"

"Really?" I laughed again. "I'll stay behind with you," I replied. "I have no intention of leaving today; your brother can leave with my pilot." He relaxed a little, but I wanted him punished for his lingering distrust. "I have to run this by Don, you know. Before we do anything."

His pupils dilated.

"He's going to frown a little; he doesn't like people losing entire shipments, especially those that can be tracked to his family. It means you're not on top of your game." I paused for a moment, letting him squirm.

He licked his lips and clasped his hands together but didn't say a word.

"Why don't you let the kid go?"

He shook his head violently. "Nah… no way. She's leverage."

"She's a liability, Snowman. Every moment she's not home doing homework, her mother's running her big mouth to other cops she's probably shagged. Is that what you want?"

"No, man, I ain't doing it," he replied, then sat on his throne again, his body language saying the conversation was now over. "Kid's not even here, anyway. She's tucked away nicely until the cop does his part."

I breathed, having difficulty hiding my frustration. "I'm leaving," I announced, standing and arranging my jacket. "I'm going to call Don because this bungler risks blowing up the entire local distribution." I stopped talking and glared down at Snowman for added effect. "Contain this mess, Snowman, or else lose the supplier. I'm willing to help you out of this bind, but don't take Don Cardenas or me for granted." Then I turned to leave.

He stood abruptly, catching up with me. "It's two hundred kilos," he blurted, "what was I supposed to do? Tell Don it won't happen again. I've been good for my word all these years, always paid on time."

I did a bit of quick math in my head. The street rate for a brick of cocaine was twenty-five thousand dollars. That times two hundred equaled a nice, round five mil. I grinned.

"I'll try, but when you misplace five million dollars' worth of product, I can't promise you anything. I'll explain, and if he agrees to let me help you, I'll be back within the hour and make sure the jet is fueled." Then I got close to him and grabbed his cross pendant, pulling him even closer. He stank of sweat and grime and metabolized beer. "You'll owe me a big one, Snowman."

38

Help

Fifty-two hours missing

I was reunited with my guns and escorted to the door. The first thing I did when I stepped out of the plumbing store was to enjoy the direct sunlight on my face. It scared away the shadows, the unspoken fears, the doubts lingering in my mind about what I was planning to do. I walked as quickly as I could, rushed to get to the car and out of there as soon as possible. One of Snowman's muscle, Tiny Burch, followed me with his squinty eyes, probably looking to see where I'd gone, or if I was with someone else they didn't know about. I chose to ignore him, but then flaunted my wheels in his face, driving slowly toward the parking lot exit.

As soon as I was out of sight, I breathed a sigh of relief.

There was good news: Holt was alive and in no immediate danger, because Snowman needed him to bust his brother out of jail.

There was bad news too. I had no idea where Meredith Holt was being held. That Henderson address Fletcher had been talking about might've been our best shot at finding her.

Finally, there was a bit of annoyance with my own performance as a cop. As soon as I'd heard of Snowman, I should've pulled everything that had to do with that man from the system, including his brother's arrest. How come I didn't think to do that?

Another thought crossed my mind, equally annoying. None of Snowman's muscle had given me the serial killer vibe. Holt was right; Snowman was not serial killer material. I didn't think of myself as the ultimate authority in such matters; no one could claim 100 percent accuracy in their gut assessment of criminal potential, but still, I wondered, if not any of them, then who? Who was the man who raped and tortured Alyssa and Elizabeth, took them to the Mojave, buried them alive, and left them to die?

I pushed that bothersome thought to the side; I had other, more stringent priorities, like calling Fletcher with an update and a long list of requests. He picked up immediately.

"Hey, B, isn't that car just awesome or what?" he asked, speaking excitedly. "If you finish early, mind if I take it for a spin?"

"Sure, why not?" I replied. "The day is far from over, Fletch. I need your help big time."

"Go for it, what can I do for you?"

"For starters, I need you to get me a private jet. Fueled, prepped, lined up on the tarmac at McCarran International."

There was a brief silence, then a sarcastic burst of laughter. "You have got to be kidding me," he said. "You lied and got caught, and now you have to make it happen? Is that it?"

"Close enough," I replied, taking the Interstate ramp heading north. "It doesn't have to take off; just start the engines, show off a bit, pretend it's Olivia's plane. The LVMPD must know someone who's willing to lend us a jet for a thirty-minute sting operation, huh? What do you say?"

Another brief silence. "This one's for the sheriff. When do you need it?" he asked, his voice professional, committed.

"In thirty minutes to an hour, tops."

He laughed again, just a quick chortle of disbelief. "Fabulous. What else?"

"Meredith Holt wasn't there, Fletch. She must be in Henderson, at that address you found."

"No, they raided that two hours ago. She'd been there, but Snowman apparently took her elsewhere, no one knows the location. They shot a perp, freed three other girls, but no Meredith."

"Great, just bloody great," I muttered, unreasonably angry at the Benz for not being equipped with sirens and flashers. "One more thing, where can I find that fed who's been working on Meredith's case?"

"Which fed? There's more than one. The place is crawling with them."

"The lead agent."

"Oh, that's Special Agent Glover. He's holed up at Meredith's house. Let me give you the address."

"No need, I got it," I replied, groaning from the bottom of my heart, anticipating how welcoming the former Mrs. Holt was going to be.

"Nieblas said he got the call," Fletcher said. "Was everything okay?"

"Yes, it was, but it's not over yet. He's on standby; he might get another call."

I briefed him about what the call could be, and what he should say, if Snowman was asking for advice about the kidnapped cop and his kid, about the missing dope, about Snowman's recklessness and the associated heat that the organization had drawn upon itself.

"I'll take care of it," Fletcher said. "He's right here; the captain had him wait for your instructions."

"What?" I reacted. "What does Morales know about all this, Fletch?"

"A few things," he replied, his voice strangled. "He asked me, and I couldn't just keep on lying. I'm so sorry, Baxter, I really am."

I breathed. Yes, that was bound to happen, regardless of what I did or didn't do. "Nothing to be sorry about, Fletch. You were, and still are, bloody fantastic, and we couldn't do what we're doing without you." I swallowed hard, thinking what to do, how to contain the wild card that was my boss. Then I remembered that they might've already tapped Fletcher's phone, so I spoke from the heart. "Tell Morales we're close to getting Meredith back, but Holt is in a precarious situation and any intervention would cost him his life. Please ask him to trust us and wait for our signal."

"You got it," Fletcher replied, a trace of hesitation in his voice telling me he wasn't over yet. "Hey, you might want to know that the locations your ornithologist shared with us panned out. In all but one we found more victims."

"Four more girls?" I said, feeling a wave of anger and sadness rushing through my entire being.

"Yeah, about the same age. Crime Scene is still on site, processing. I'll keep you posted." He paused for a moment, but I didn't hang up. "Could I ask for a favor?" he eventually said.

"Shoot."

"Please make sure I don't have to change assignments when this is over, okay?"

I let out a nervous chuckle after the three tones marked the end of the call. That was the young analyst's way to ask us to come back in one piece. I could make no promises, and he knew it; that's why he'd hung up already, not waiting for an answer.

A few moments later, I pulled the black Benz up at the curb in front of former Mrs. Holt's house. I checked the time; twenty minutes had already passed, wasted on the drive between Henderson and southwest Vegas through dense traffic.

I pushed the doorbell button but heard nothing. I didn't have time to wait, so I knocked loudly. Within moments, Meredith's mother opened the door. She was disheveled, her eyes red, puffy, and hollow, her skin devoid of color. She recognized me on the spot and managed to summon a lot of rage, considering how frail she appeared.

"How dare you show your face here?" she shouted, unconcerned with the neighbors who might've heard her.

"I'm looking for Special Agent Glover," I replied calmly, making sure I kept my distance from the door. "I apologize for disturbing you; this is police business."

A woman wearing an FBI badge clipped to her suit jacket lapel appeared, and, speaking softly, managed to talk the enraged Jennifer back inside the house. Immediately after they disappeared from the hallway, a middle-aged man wearing a dark suit and a wrinkled, white shirt showed up, extending his hand.

"SA Glover," he said. "Let's talk out here if you don't mind."

I nodded. That seemed like a great idea. "I'm Detective—"

"Laura Baxter. Yes, I know."

My eyebrows shot up. "You do? How come?"

He shrugged, but the gesture was friendly, relaxed. "Just diligence." Then he offered a tiny smile and made a movement with his eyes toward the house. "What was that all about?"

My face heated with embarrassment. "No clue. I met Holt a month ago, and only met her yesterday. I gave her no reason to—"

He raised his hand in a pacifying manner. I'd said enough. "What can I do for you, Detective?"

That was the five-million-dollar question. I forced some air into my lungs, feeling how cold it was, despite the bright sun shining above our heads.

"We're on the same team, right?" I asked, a lame opener but I couldn't think of anything else to say.

"Sure, absolutely," he said, looking at me with scrutinizing eyes. "Just tell me what you need."

"I don't trust people easily," I confessed, "but I'll take a leap of faith here."

He nodded, while I searched his face for signs of deception, of a hidden agenda. There were none.

"We're close to finding Meredith, but we need something to happen before we can pull that off. I'll tell you what that is, but if you budge ahead of time, if you do anything other than what we agree here, you're going to be responsible for that girl's death, possibly Holt's too. Do we understand each other?"

"Yes," he replied, his forehead just a little bit tense. "You have my word, Detective."

"I need you to help Holt break a perp out of lockup. You have to make sure this escape happens, but then is contained nicely and the perp doesn't walk."

"So, that's the ransom for his daughter's life," he said plainly.

"Precisely. This perp knows the location of two hundred kilos of dope, and he will share that information when he's on a jet taking off to Argentina. We're securing the jet as we speak, but we need your help in getting all the game pieces together."

"My job is to find Meredith," SA Glover replied. "That's why—"

"That's exactly what you'd be doing, finding Meredith," I cut him off, afraid he was going to refuse to help me.

He nodded with a tiny, tight-lipped smile. "I was about to say the same thing. My mandate is to do whatever it takes to find that girl, to bring her home safely. You'll have my team's full cooperation."

I looked at him, feeling choked with gratitude and a bit embarrassed for assuming he'd brush me off. Maybe later down the road there would be hell to pay, but today I needed all the help I could get.

"Holt will intercept the convoy and will radio to instruct them to stop and surrender the prisoner because he's needed for something else. I don't know what Holt will claim the reason is; we couldn't speak freely."

"Where is Detective Holt?"

I looked away for a moment, then sighed, a pained breath filled with frustration.

"He's traded his life for his daughter's, but the kidnapper broke the deal and captured Holt too. He's holding them both hostage now."

"Do you know where?"

"Yes, for Holt, no, for Meredith; not yet. Please, Agent Glover, do not intervene in any way until I give the signal."

"Yes, understood. I gave you my word."

I felt a bit ashamed of my distrust and my own insecurities, but, under the circumstances, I could never be too sure. I cleared my throat quietly and continued.

"After Holt takes over the prisoner, Tyson Klug, he'll transport him to McCarran International, where the jet should be fueled and ready on the tarmac. Do you think you can help me with this? It's supposed to go down in two hours."

"Yes, we can make this happen, Detective. What else?"

I smiled, a touch of sadness fluttering on my lips. It was time I started making someone pay for my husband's senseless death, the real villains, not that piece of street scum murderer, Reyes. It was time I took my game to a whole new level. I wasn't scared; the thrill of the hunt, the adrenaline rush fueled my energy, my courage, and my desire to prevail.

"Out of the two hundred kilos, I'll need to hold on to twenty," I announced, then waited for a reaction, but there was none. Glover was quietly taking notes, not a trace of judgment or surprise on his face. "You can take possession of the rest. Oh, and please pass on a message to IAB Lieutenant Steenstra for me."

That sounded weird, in the age of mobile phones, but he didn't show any concern in his supportive eyes; only surprise. "Go ahead, what should I say?"

"Please tell her I'm going deep undercover. I have the possibility to infiltrate Snowman's organization at the top level, and bring it carefully down, without soaking the city streets in blood. I can find and sever the pipelines used by the cartels to bring the product through Mexico straight to the Strip. I can gain intel about the drug lords behind the supply and lure them into our traps. Please let her know she needs to set it up."

He looked at me as if I were completely insane. Maybe I was; I sure acted as if I were, but it made so much sense to me. I'd found a new purpose in life, the purpose I'd been searching for while roaming the streets of my city at night, looking for my husband's killer, driven to bring justice where during the day I couldn't.

"Detective, this is an operation that requires months of preparation time," he reacted.

"I'm going in now, in less than twenty minutes."

"Why ask IAB for that kind of support setting this up? That's not what IAB normally does."

I laughed, a quiet, slightly bitter laugh at my own past, my screwed-up personnel file, at yesterday's fears for my future and my career, that through some twist of fate had stopped being relevant overnight.

"That's because she knows better than anyone else what I can and cannot do."

"Okay," he said, nodding twice as if forcing himself to accept the information against his better judgment. "Who will you work with?"

"Holt, and only Holt. I don't trust anyone else. Tell Steenstra I'll be in touch."

"Will do," he replied, giving me a long stare. I didn't read contempt or ridicule in his eyes; only encouragement and a hint of admiration. "Good luck, Detective."

I waved and rushed back to the car, then sped out of there. I had less than twenty minutes left before I had to be back at the plumbing store.

Behind the white sheers lining the living room window, Lieutenant Steenstra stared at the vacant driveway, slack-jawed, silent, preoccupied.

39

Games

Fifty-three hours missing

The traffic was lighter on the way back to Henderson, without an apparent reason. Many times, traffic behaved like a swarm of sentient beings; in fact, it was a swarm. Multiple entities coordinated their movements in precise ways to achieve a goal, not unlike bees or sparrows. Sometimes, the swarm moved fluidly, making good use of the speed limit tolerance, other times it just slowed without any reason.

I was already on I-15 when the phone rang. It was Fletcher.

"Do I have a private jet yet?" I asked.

"Unbelievably, yes, but that's not why I called," he replied. "Patching through a call from Anne."

I waited until I heard her voice. "Anne?"

"Yes, Anne, who'd kick your ass Marine-style if she could get her hands on you. What the hell are you thinking, Laura? I can't lose you too."

"You won't lose me, I promise," I said, knowing I had no basis for that statement, knowing she knew that too.

"You can't just show up at a drug boss's den and… Jeez, woman, you're crazy."

I weighed that statement for a moment. "Yeah, I am, but you already knew that, didn't you?" I asked, trying to bring a bit of optimism into the conversation.

"You're right," she replied. "No point in trying to talk you out of it, is there?"

"No," I said calmly. "Seven more minutes of driving time, and I'm there. Fingers crossed, my dear friend, I'll need it."

"Toes too," she replied, a hint of sadness in her voice. "But that's not why I called. I ran the Henderson perp's DNA against the serial killer's, and it's not a match."

"Bollocks," I reacted. I needed a break and wasn't getting one. "I don't think any of the guys at the plumbing store will be a match either."

"But I found a TV remote control at the scene, as dirty and as gross as only

TV remotes can be, chock-full of epithelials, saliva, even semen."

"Eww," I reacted.

"One of the samples on the remote was a match to the Mojave Desert killer. At some point in recent history, that man was in the Henderson house, watching TV."

I took a moment to let that sink in. We were getting close to that sick son of a bitch. What if my gut was off, and one of Snowman's goons was the killer?

"That's good news, Anne. We'll find the bastard. I'll get some DNA samples from the plumbing store crew. What did you find at the new scenes in the desert?" I asked, and held my breath, bracing for more horror.

"The same MO, same signatures. Young girls, violently and repeatedly raped, chemically paralyzed, and left to die a slow death in the desert. The killer showed no concern whatsoever with leaving his DNA all over the victims, which made me think of something."

"What?"

"Mandatory collection of DNA for convicted felons was implemented in 2009. I'm thinking it's impossible that someone with his behavior doesn't have a record, but he must've done his time before that year, or his DNA would be in the system. We could look at rapists who were convicted and released prior to that date and see if a particularly sick bastard pops up."

"What would you be looking for? Other than the obvious, sexual assault of young girls?"

"I'd look for chemical restraining. One doesn't *start* with modified tetrodotoxin; one grows into that, learns, experiments, evolves. He might've tried Rohypnol first, maybe other agents. Or he might've been busted for necrophilia."

"That's excellent thinking, Anne," I reacted. "Please ask Fletch to run that search for you, then cross it against Snowman's known associates. I'm almost at the store; got to go."

She wished me good luck again and made me promise I'd be careful. I ended the call, the sound of her voice still reverberating in the silence inside my car as I pulled into a parking spot at the store.

Snowman's muscle, Huber, didn't bother with the pat-down this time; he grunted at me, then opened the door. I walked down the dark hallway quickly, clacking my heels, a way to give Holt the heads-up I was coming.

I found Snowman shouting at Holt, my partner still tied up to the same chair but showing his usual stamina and contrarian attitude. What was it with men that fueled their urge to defy their captors, the only thing resulting being more beatings, more pain?

When I approached, Snowman stopped his shouting mid-phrase and turned my way.

"Well, ain't that our newest friend, Don's personal envoy to Sin City," he reacted, the sarcasm in his voice unmistakable. It made me worry, wondering what could've happened to make him change his attitude. It could've been the influence of his frustrated lieutenants, who saw a threat in my presence. Or it could've been the real Don, calling him for whatever reason. That thought sent chills down my spine.

As I always do when I'm cornered, I bluffed. "If you figured things out already and no longer need my help, I'll be on my way," I said calmly. "Take today to sort through this, and if you're still alive and out of jail tomorrow, call me to discuss northeast metro."

"Why the rush, sweetheart?" he said, grinning widely and giving me a lewd, head-to-toe look.

I glared at him with a searing expression on my face, then I lowered my voice as I spoke, pacing my words for a more menacing effect. The real Olivia would've shot him in the groin; I didn't have that option, at least not yet, but it wasn't completely off the table.

"Be careful, Snowman, this is one of those defining moments in your life. You could be reflecting back on this moment and all the bad decisions you made today, from your deathbed or from jail. I'll give you that choice."

He held my eyes without blinking for a few moments, then looked away. "What did Don say?"

"He said it's up to me if I help you or not, but if this happens again, or if you don't fix the mess you've made with the cops, he'll cut you off and bring on someone new."

He turned to me and closed the distance between us in two huge steps. I refrained from reaching for the gun I was carrying in my holster.

"That simple, huh?" he hissed, so close to my face I could smell his sour breath.

"That simple, Snowman. It's your call. Do this right or do this wrong, it's entirely up to you."

He broke eye contact and started pacing the stained cement in front of Holt's chair, angry and rushed at first, then slower and slower, as the voice of reason sunk in and won the match in his interiorized battles.

"Will you let me use your jet to get that no-good piece of shit off to Argentina?"

I looked at him for a long moment, as if weighing my options. "Okay, I will. But you owe me big. Keep that in mind, because I'll come calling."

"Yeah, yeah, I get it; I ain't stupid," he replied, looking at his watch nervously.

"The hell you ain't," I replied coldly. "You're a bloody tosser, that's what you are. A wanker and a twat."

"What the hell language is that?" he reacted. "Got something to say, say it so I can understand it."

I scoffed, but then walked over to Holt. "Look at what you've done to this cop's face. You want him to go out there and make those other cops release your brother in his custody, when he looks like that? Anyone could see he'd been beaten all night. Your macho bullshit jeopardized your own plan. Beat him afterwards if you have to, but right now, let him wash himself, eat something, drink some coffee. Get him some clean clothes."

"This ain't a damn hotel," he reacted. "Where the hell can I get him clothes and stuff?"

"Hint, wiseass: you're in a mall," I replied. "Send one of your boys shopping."

He hesitated, looking at his watch again, then at Holt, then at me. Holt's clothes were stained with blood and soiled from the times he'd been kicked to the floor. His face was swollen and covered in cuts and bruises.

"No one's going to release a prisoner to a cop who looks like this, Snowman. Use whatever brain you have and do this right."

I beckoned one of his goons, a man whose name I still didn't know, and asked for pen and paper.

"What for?" he asked, and in response, I scowled at him. Olivia would never justify herself.

He scrambled and returned with half a pencil and a stretch of cash register receipt paper. I scribbled a short shopping list. "You'll get these items from a cosmetics store."

He looked at me, confused. "What's all this stuff?"

"Makeup, to cover the cuts and bruises that you boneheads thought he'd need to get the job done. Now, move it."

He looked at Snowman for approval, and his boss shrugged and made an indifference gesture with his hand, and he left in a hurry.

We spent the next fifteen minutes in a tense silence mixed with brief dialogue. I kept asking him details about the escape plan, he kept avoiding giving me any straight answers. It was as if he felt something was off, and I kept wondering why. Was I not playing Olivia that well? What if my acting career hadn't picked up in the London of my youth because I wasn't that good of an actress to begin with?

I replayed the earlier scenes in my mind and found no fault in my acting. The only thing I'd let slip was my burning hatred for the man pacing the floor in front of me. He was a sex trafficker of underage girls, a rapist, a torturer, and a drug dealer. He was the scum of the earth, and my gut ached for the release of putting a few holes in his chest. He was a predator.

Like all predators, he had instinct, and that instinct probably rang all sorts of alarm bells in his head whenever I drew near, sensing my intentions to end his life. I pretended to examine a shelf with pipe fittings and used the time to center myself, to purge all that emotion out of my body. Yes, when the time came, I'd put the bastard down, but until then, no emotions were to cloud my judgment. Olivia would've been cold as a snake, a killer and a predator just like him.

With that commitment made to myself, I walked over to him and touched his elbow. He flinched almost imperceptibly.

"Let's grab us a coffee and walk through the details one more time," I said calmly, in a friendly tone.

He looked at me as if he'd just noticed my hair color had changed, and then snapped his fingers. Within one minute, Huber delivered a cup of coffee for me and a cold beer for him.

I ignored the layered grime on the cup and sipped a tiny bit. "How much time until you leave?" I asked.

"Thirty minutes," he replied, "but I ain't going nowhere. My man's taking the cop over to the place where they're going to grab Tyson. I'll wait here for the call, then I'll get my dope back."

"Let the cop drive his own car over there, for authenticity," I suggested, knowing Holt always kept a loaded Glock Velcroed under his seat. "He won't do anything funny; you've still got his kid."

Snowman frowned and checked the time again. "Yeah... Then they need to leave in thirty minutes. His car ain't here."

He walked over to Holt and cut his ties. Holt stood and rubbed his wrists to restore the blood flow, then stomped in place; he was probably numb from being tied to a chair for so long.

When the reluctant shopper returned, he had everything I'd asked for, including a new suit and shirt for Holt. He took my partner in the back restroom and stayed with him until they both came out.

He looked better, the dried blood now gone from his face and hands, but his face still needed work.

"That's an improvement," I said. "Does anyone here know how to apply makeup?"

No one said anything; Huber grinned and muttered something I didn't understand.

"All right, then, I need light, lots of it, and a mirror."

Huber and the other man looked at their boss, who pointed them toward the restroom. "Set up in there but make it quick. You got two minutes."

I had Holt sit on the office chair, in front of the mirror, and I started applying concealer, then rubbing it in gently with the tips of my fingers, careful not to cause him any pain. Huber watched me anxiously from the door, and that was going to pose a problem. The entire plan was going to fall apart if I couldn't be alone with Holt for one brief moment.

"Get him something to eat," I ordered, while focusing on covering a nasty cut across his brow, "a candy bar or something. He looks hungrier than a pound dog."

The moment Huber stepped away, I plunged my hand inside my cleavage and extracted the backup Sig holstered under my bra, then I slid it quickly into Holt's right pocket.

He grabbed my hand and stared at me with burning intensity, his pupils large, dark. "Why?" he whispered.

I looked into his eyes and couldn't find the words, a storm of emotions threatening to bring down my act. A tiny smile tugged at the corner of my lips. "You know why," I replied, just as Huber returned with two candy bars.

Within minutes, Holt and the third, still unidentified goon left the building, leaving Snowman and Huber in the back with me, and Tiny Burch guarding the door from the outside. It was a moment as good as any other.

I walked aimlessly for a while, giving Snowman the time to cool off and take his usual seat on his throne, then strolled behind him casually. When Huber turned his head for a moment, I pulled out my weapon and shoved the barrel into the back of Snowman's head.

"Greetings from Don Cardenas," I said. "Not a move, wanker," I ordered, then beckoned Huber over. "You, drop your weapon. Call Burch in here, disarm him and tie him up."

"I told you she was bad news," Huber said, looking at Snowman.

"Do it," Snowman yelled. Like most predators who preyed on young, defenseless women, Snowman was a coward, and I was counting on that.

Huber did as he was told, disarmed Burch and secured his hands behind his back with cable ties taken off a shelf in the back. I disarmed Snowman and, while keeping my gun aimed at his chest, tied Huber's hands together, pulling the zip tie snug.

Snowman must've thought it was a good moment to make a run for it, because he lunged from his chair, coming at me incredibly fast. I pulled the trigger twice in rapid fire, then once more, after he'd hit the ground.

40

Jailbreak

Fifty-four hours missing

They waited in Holt's unmarked SUV by the Washington Avenue ramp on I-15, ready to start pursuit the moment the prison transport showed up. It was delayed by a few minutes, but Holt wasn't worried; the transport could still make it on time. The first court appearance for one of the perps listed on that transport was at three in the afternoon, almost an hour away.

Under the watchful eye of Snowman's trusted muscle, he contacted Dispatch and informed them he was picking up Tyson Klug; he was needed as a material witness in a matter that could not be delayed until after the perps' court hearing.

The dispatcher let a moment of silence pass, then said, "I'll need approval for that, Detective, please hold."

The man sitting on the passenger seat of Holt's vehicle prodded him with the barrel of his gun, shoving it against his bruised ribs.

"Don't try anything funny," he whispered, "or the boss will gut your kid wide open."

Holt didn't bother to reply; just shot the man a quick glance loaded with promise. If only he could get his hands on these people, after Meredith was home safely, there'd be no stopping him.

But it wasn't a matter of if, he realized; it was a matter of when. And he counted the minutes 'til that was going to happen.

"Detective," the dispatcher said, after the line crackled to life when she released the mute button, "the captain needs more detail about Klug."

He'd feared that, so he had a story prepared. "Tyson Klug could be instrumental in identifying Alyssa Conway's killer. We have reason to believe he was associated with him, that he was one of his many drug-dealing cohorts in his brother's organization. We hope he'll be willing to talk in exchange for a deal."

Another moment of silence ensued, but this time Holt didn't let it run its course.

"Dispatch, there are lives at stake; this killer could be torturing another girl right at this moment, while you're concerned with the perp's court dates. Could we just use some common sense here?"

Nothing, not a sound. Then, another crackle, and the dispatcher's voice said, "You have approval to proceed, Detective. The prison transport has been notified to release Klug in your custody."

"Copy that, Dispatch," he replied, then ended the call. "There, happy?" he asked the thug sitting next to him, but all he got in response was a grunt and ridges on the tattooed forehead.

After a few minutes, he saw the prison bus speeding by and he engaged in pursuit with his siren and flashers on. The bus pulled over to the side of the road, and he stopped in front of it.

"Stay here," he said to his passenger. "Don't move."

Holt climbed out of his vehicle and approached the prison transport. Only a few detainees were taking the benches, and one of the officers was already removing Tyson Klug's restraints, leaving his handcuffs on.

"Detective," he greeted him with two fingers at his cap, "here's your scumbag."

Holt grabbed the man's arm and turned to leave.

"What the hell happened to you?" the guard asked, frowning a little and scratching his chin, seemingly suspicious.

Last thing Holt needed was the curiosity of a prison transport officer to get in the way of his already flimsy strategy. He grinned awkwardly, pointing at his shiner. "What, this? Just another day at the office."

The officer laughed. "I hate to think how the other guy looks. Not that good, I guess, huh?"

Holt laughed wholeheartedly, escorting Tyson down the steps toward his SUV. Then he opened the back door and shoved him inside, keeping his hand on the perp's head, regulation style. Then he uncuffed him, reluctantly, under pressures from both men.

He climbed behind the wheel and peeled off at high speed, heading straight for the airport.

"Hey, homie," Tyson said, happy to recognize the passenger. "I thought you were some piece-of-shit cop, man. You here to bust a brother out of jail?"

"What else I'd be here for, huh? Sure as hell ain't for the company," he added, looking derisively at Holt.

They both burst into laughter.

"Where you taking me, brah?"

"Airport, like you said. Snowman made it happen."

"Cool," he replied, moving his head and arms to a rhythm only he could hear, a happy dance for his freedom. "Got any music in this fancy ride, man?"

Holt didn't reply.

"Hey, this brother asked you a damn question, bitch," he shouted, speaking of himself in the third person.

"I've been told to break you out of jail, take you to the airport, and put you on a jet to Argentina. If you're not happy with the agenda, I can always catch up with the prison bus and tell them I changed my mind."

The barrel of a gun shoved forcefully into his ribs reminded him who was really in charge.

"Play some damn music," his passenger requested. "Ain't gonna kill you."

He pressed his lips together, deciding it was wiser to keep his comments to himself, then turned on the radio. The knucklehead in the passenger seat played with the knobs until he found something they both liked and turned up the volume to the point where Holt felt like smashing the whole media center to bits.

Two endless songs later, he pulled in front of the gates at McCarran, parked, and escorted the two men to the VIP terminal.

"Do I need to go through there?" the muscle asked, pointing at the security check gates. "They'll take my piece."

"VIPs don't do security checks," Holt replied. "We go straight to the tarmac."

He didn't really know what he was doing; he'd never been to the VIP terminal before, nor had a private aircraft ever pulled up at the gate just for him. He followed the signs and asked a TSA agent for directions, but eventually he found it.

There was a lounge with large windows and glass sliding doors overseeing the tarmac, and a Phenom 300 was sitting in front of it, with the engines running. He had no idea if that was the right plane, and there wasn't anyone he could ask.

"Let me see if this is your plane," he said, but the two men were understandably distrusting.

"We're coming with you," Tyson said.

An airport security officer stopped them before they could approach the exit. "Name and destination?" he asked.

Baxter had set things up, had somehow managed to make a private jet happen, and she knew what he'd ask, what he'd say, what he'd think, what issues he could run into. He needed to trust she'd done everything in her power to make things work without a glitch.

"Tyson Klug on a flight to Argentina," he replied, hoping it was the right thing to say.

The man checked the list affixed to his clipboard. "I have you right here, sir. Please proceed," he invited them, gesturing at the Phenom.

The muscle prodded Holt to be the first one to climb on board, and he obliged. The plane was empty, except for the pilot. Tyson and his homie climbed on board right behind Holt, grinning widely.

"Your ass is flying south in style," the muscle commented. "Wish I was you."

"Gentlemen, welcome aboard," the pilot said, as he rose off his seat and came to greet them.

Holt nearly choked but managed to maintain a straight face. The pilot was none other than SA Glover, dressed as an aviation captain with four gold stripes on his sleeves.

"Miss Gaines has me flying you straight to Argentina," the pilot added.

"This aircraft has a maximum range of two thousand miles, which means we will stop twice to refuel along the way, first in Guatemala, then in Ecuador. Total flight duration will be sixteen hours, not including the layovers." He smiled professionally. "Will all of you gentlemen be flying today?"

"No, just me," Tyson replied. "Let's get those wheels up in the air, man."

"You're welcome to hang out on board until we're cleared for takeoff," the pilot said, then took his seat and buckled his seatbelt. Tyson looked at him, wondering what the hell he was waiting for.

Glover pressed a button on the throttle. "Las Vegas ground, Phenom Whiskey-Alpha-Two-Four-Niner, Phenom 300 uniform, at the Centurion Lounge, requesting taxi for departure to Buenos Aires, with Tango."

The radio crackled, then a voice said, "Phenom Whiskey-Alpha-Two-Four-Niner, taxi twenty-five, at or below two thousand."

"Copy that."

Glover turned toward Tyson and smiled. "I was instructed to proceed after we have confirmed the location of a particular item. I'm supposed to call with the item's location, then wait for confirmation before takeoff."

Tyson lunged at the pilot and grabbed him by the throat, choking him. Glover didn't fight back, just sat there, taking it.

"That's not what was supposed to happen, you hear me? I'm not sayin' shit until we're up in the air," Tyson shouted, his voice raspy, choked with fear.

"Only an idiot would strangle his pilot before flying out of the country," Holt said calmly.

Tyson let go of Glover's throat and turned to the muscle. "That wasn't the deal, homie. And where's my brother?"

"He couldn't come," he replied. "Just tell this dawg what he wants to hear and get the hell out of here, all right? Don't screw this up."

Tyson pressed his lips together, looking around like a trapped animal. He had no idea how trapped he really was, but maybe he was starting to sense something was off.

"I can make you take off," Tyson said. "I'll get Chuck's piece and shove it down your throat until you do as I tell you."

So, the muscle's name was Chuck, Holt reflected. Good to know. He smiled, and his grin got Chuck angry as hell.

"Chuck ain't giving you his piece, you moron," Glover replied, "'cause you're too stupid to walk this earth with one. Give that location already, or the deal's off, and I'll let this cop throw your ass back in the slammer."

"That's what my brother said?"

"Yeah, dumbass, that's exactly what your brother said. He ain't exactly sweet on you these days."

"All right," Tyson reacted, his rage visible in the way he paced the tiny space between the flight deck and the front row of seats, more like twirling in place, restless, colorful oaths spilling endlessly out of his mouth. "If you screw me, Chuck, I swear to you, you're going to wish your momma never got laid."

Glover smiled again, calmly, inviting Tyson to talk. The man stood silent, as if stuck in a daze of undecided angst. Holt understood his dilemma; he was about to trade his only bargaining chip before he felt safe enough to do so. He actually deserved some credit for realizing the implications of his decisions. But with every passing moment, Holt feared something terrible could happen to Meredith and would've gladly tortured the perp for that piece of information.

The radio crackled. "Phenom Whiskey-Alpha-Two-Four-Niner, what's the delay?"

"Las Vegas ground, we will be proceeding shortly. We have a passenger issue we're working on."

"Copy, Phenom. Request new clearance when ready."

"Understood," Glover replied, then looked sheepishly at Tyson.

Glover said, "We can sit here all day," he added, "or we can leave as soon as Miss Gaines approves the departure."

Tyson grunted, slamming both his fists against his legs. "All right, it's at CubeSmart Self Storage on Maryland Parkway, unit 223."

Glover pulled out his phone and sent a text message.

"Now what?" Tyson asked.

"Now we wait," he replied. "Miss Gaines said it shouldn't take more than ten minutes."

"Got any booze in here?" Chuck asked, taking a seat in the back. He ran his hand against the soft leather of the seat in front of him, then the lacquered surface of the table. "I want to feel like a VIP today."

"There is liquor and wine in here," Glover said, opening a small storage cupboard. "How many glasses?"

Holt refused with a hand gesture, and Glover poured whiskey generously in two, cut crystal glasses, adding ice from a small bucket.

Tyson and Chuck started chatting casually while the minutes dragged on, painfully slow, leaving Holt to mull over his many thoughts. What was going to happen next? Snowman would never release his daughter, not without a fight. Maybe Baxter could find out where he was keeping her. Baxter... he couldn't believe the nerve of that woman, the recklessness she'd proven by waltzing into Snowman's lair on her high heels like she owned the place. That wasn't how undercover work was done. Baxter's actions were brash and desperate, and she risked a bullet in the head with every minute that passed. How long did she think she could keep up that ruse? He'd been undercover himself; it took months to gain the trust of a drug dealer, not... minutes. She should've stayed out of it, working Alyssa's murder case, going home in one piece at night, and leaving him to worry only about Meredith, not Baxter too.

A chime alerted Glover, and he checked the message on his phone.

"Gentlemen, we're ready to proceed," he announced, but didn't take his seat. Instead, he stood smiling. "As soon as you two non-passengers disembark, I will close the aircraft door and take off." He locked eyes with Holt for a brief moment, nodding almost imperceptibly.

Holt got the message and stepped out of the plane, climbing down the ladder, plunging his hand in his pocket to find the gun Baxter had put in there.

Four more officers took positions around the plane's door, waiting for Chuck to step out.

When he appeared at the top of the stairs and saw all those weapons trained on him, he instantly put his hands up.

"Ain't done nothing, just took a friend to the airport. Is that a crime?" he asked, his pitch higher and higher as he was being handcuffed. "Tell me, is it?"

Two officers held him to the side, while Holt climbed back inside the plane to see about Tyson, but Glover already had him cuffed and ready to ship out. The scumbag was crying, begging the pilot to take off.

"Yeah, we'll take off in just a minute," Glover replied, pulling the zip ties tightly around his wrists. "And we'll land you in jail, nonstop flight, courtesy of the Federal Bureau of Investigation."

"Was that Baxter on the phone?" Holt asked Glover.

"No, it was my partner, SA Rosales."

Holt rushed back outside and ran over to Chuck, then slammed his fist in the man's face. "Where is she?" he shouted. "Where the hell is my daughter?"

41

Incentives

Fifty-five hours missing

Huber and Tiny Burch sat on the floor, their hands tied behind their backs, leaning against a shelf loaded with shop vacs in big, cardboard boxes. I'd secured their handcuffs against the bottom railing of the shelves with loops of cable ties, leaving them with little room to move. If they struggled against the restraints, they risked bringing down a twenty-foot tall shelf loaded with heavy materials.

They grunted and gave me an endless barrage of oaths and dirty looks, while I paced slowly in front of them, thinking what to do. How could I get them to tell me Meredith's location? They seemed more likely to die than cooperate with me.

There was no time to do things by the book; taking them in, reading their rights, then taking a stab at them in an interrogation room would've meant hours that Meredith didn't have. They've both been inside; they knew not to say anything to the police without a lawyer present, and that would've killed all my chances.

I could've tried torture; the thought had crossed my mind and, in my current state, I wasn't unwilling; I was tired and angry as hell, still reeling from what I'd witnessed out there, in the Mojave, from the death of that poor girl who jumped off the balcony of the Scala out of fear of those guys who sat, cursing and uttering threats at my feet. Yeah, torture was tempting, but it could take too long.

I couldn't recall the last time I had a warm meal or a couple of hours of rest. I'd mainlined caffeine for the past two days, and the slight tremor I felt in the tips of my fingers was warning me I was about to reach the end of my wick. Whatever I was planning to do, I had to do fast.

Unfortunately, the man who knew where Meredith was being held lay dead at my feet, in a half-congealed pool of blood, his lips forever sealed in silence. But two others knew where Meredith was, they were still alive, and they would tell me if I played my cards right.

Holt's daughter had been missing for a long time, and that thought kindled waves of anxiety unfurling in my gut. She was stashed somewhere with at least one of Snowman's trusted lieutenants, who, if they happened to watch TV and see how the bodies were starting to pile up in familiar places, could get creative and slash the girl's throat just to cover their tracks.

I looked at the two pieces of scum in front of me, this time critically, weighing my chances of success. Caucasian males in their late thirties or early forties, covered in prison gang tats, their forearms thicker than my thighs, the hatred in their eyes palpable, searing. No… torture wouldn't do anything for these men; they'd been through years of prison hell and survived it unscathed.

But greed had a chance of working.

I stopped in front of them and smiled, ignoring their spiteful reactions.

"Gentlemen, we can handle this situation one of two ways."

Burch spat near my feet, probably missing his intended target, while Huber spouted a slew of oaths in a mix of Spanish and English, then said, "Don't care about anything you have to say, bitch. Go the fuck back to where you came from."

I shrugged and looked each of them in the eye firmly, coldly, just as Olivia would've done. Well, maybe she would've shot both pieces of shite right where they sat, but I was still a cop, and, most of all, I needed to find Meredith before it was too late.

"I could kill you with one shot to the head, quickly, painlessly, not that you deserve any of that humane treatment," I said, and my statement shut them up for a brief moment, right after I kicked Snowman's foot out of the way, making a point. "Or I can make you rich."

That got their attention. The hatred carved on their faces turned to interest, and they exchanged a quick glance between themselves.

"News flash," I continued, "Don Cardenas is coming to Vegas to help me sort through this mess. Until he shakes hands with someone new, I'll be running Snowman's organization, but it won't be forever; I have no interest in doing that. However, even if it's for a short period of time, I can't do this alone."

I leaned forward and looked at them closely, first at Huber, then at Burch. No blobs of spittle or renewed oaths flew my way.

"I need someone I can trust," I said, "and I'm willing to buy that trust right here, right now." I straightened my back and propped my hands on my hips. "Are you in? Or out?"

"Big words," Burch scoffed. "Show me the money."

"How about I show you the product?" I said. "Two bricks of dope for each of you. Today. Yours to do with as you please," I added, cringing inside as I realized where that product was going to end up. On the streets, poisoning people, killing children. I forced myself to remember the 180 kilos we recovered, that would never hit the streets, and the future shipments that we could intercept, if I played my cards right.

"Hell, I'm in," Huber replied with a full, obnoxious grin.

I focused my intense gaze on him and said, "Be very careful. If you think you're taking the dope today, then turning on me tomorrow, you're sadly mistaken. Remember that offer to kill you quickly and painlessly? The moment I suspect the tiniest sliver of foul play, that offer is forgotten. You'll beg me to kill you quickly, and I won't. I'll take my time and make it last." I smiled crookedly, injecting enough arrogance into my grin to sell it well. "Ask Don Cardenas what I do to people who betray me."

As the two thugs were voicing their versions of reassurances mixed with expletives, I heard a noise toward the door and looked up. At the far end of the dark hallway, I saw Holt approaching quickly, and behind him, SA Glover, both with their weapons drawn. I raised my hand toward them in the universal gesture to stop. The two thugs couldn't see them yet, and, based on their behavior, had no idea they were there.

"Well, if you want to stay in this family, accept that there's a new sheriff in town," I said, pushing Snowman's body out of the way with the tip of my shoe and taking a seat in his leather armchair. As I sat, the cushions released his stench and I curled my upper lip, although I felt grateful for being able to take a load off my heels.

There was a flicker of hatred still glinting in Burch's eyes, and that could mean trouble. He wasn't entirely sold yet; he probably needed to see the goods. But I didn't have the coke yet, not the entire twenty kilos, only the kilo taken from Holt's wall.

"When we walk out of here in a few minutes, I'll give you the first installment: one kilo, top grade, uncut product."

"You said two each," Burch reacted. "Now it's half a kilo a head?"

"I don't carry a truckload in my car with me, but you'll have it by tonight. This is just a down payment, to give you a taste of what it means to work for me."

Huber grinned, and eventually, Burch nodded. They weren't the sharpest plumbing tools in the store, but they understood the international language of greed.

"What do you need from us?" Burch asked.

"We're going to run this as a real business, not some shady, street-corner scam of all trades. Manage your people effectively and keep risk down. Don't do stupid shite for a buck or two more. Want to make more money? Come to me, and we'll discuss it. There's always more business to be had, other markets to penetrate, other cities to conquer. When you have the supply that I bring to the table, everything is possible. But we have a serious problem," I added, looking at them as if they were to blame.

Huber shifted in place, while Burch scowled.

"Your former boss put this organization at war with the police, and we can't afford this war," I said, adding so much contempt for Snowman, I almost expected him to rise from the dead and start calling me names. "We need to make peace with this city's law enforcement. To do that, we're going to offer them a head, dead or alive, on a silver platter." I smiled calmly as if I were talking about cookies for Thanksgiving dinner. "Would you like that head to be yours?"

They shook their heads, but Burch's forehead wrinkled, deep ridges running across it. He was not as easy to manipulate as Huber; he was a dangerous piece of human refuse. My threatening question had refueled his hate.

I looked briefly toward Holt; he gestured his impatience with a roll of his hand, telling me to make it faster.

"There's a pervert among you who's done nothing but jeopardize your lives, this family, our business. And his life ends today. You know who he is, don't you?"

They looked at each other, then both started talking at the same time.

"Homeboy," Huber said. "It's that sadistic son of a bitch—"

"Ernie Marsh, he's a sick perv. He and I did time together back in the day. He's got something unscrewed up here," Burch said, waggling his head.

"Good. He won't live to see the light of tomorrow; I'll take care of it," I said with a tinge of deep hatred in my voice. I didn't have to fake that; the thought of Alyssa and his other victims fueled my rage to levels I could barely contain.

I crossed my legs and started bouncing my left foot up and down impatiently.

"I've taken the first step to make peace with the cop whose daughter you wiseasses kidnapped. He's willing to put everything behind him, if we return his daughter safely and give him half a million dollars in cash. I took care of the money," I added, looking at them with an unspoken question.

Burch fidgeted. "I think it's time you cut us loose."

"Make me believe you're worthy of that, and not a bullet in your head."

I picked up the gun I'd left on the wide armrest of Snowman's throne, and played with it casually, checked the mag, made sure it had a slug on the spout.

Burch mumbled another oath, then said, "She's two blocks from here, on Wigwam Parkway, by the ballpark."

Satisfied, I stood and holstered my weapon under my belt, then rushed to catch up with Holt and Glover, who'd run out the moment Burch had spoken the address.

"Hey," Burch shouted, "what about us? Hey! Cut us loose!"

"I'll be back with your dope, if your story checks out," I shouted from the hallway. "I better find you where I left you."

I meant that; I still had plans for the two pieces of scum.

42

Meredith

Fifty-six hours missing

"SWAT will be here in ten minutes," Glover insisted from the back seat of Holt's SUV. "Just wait for them, Holt. You don't know what you're walking into."

He'd argued that point for the last few minutes of screeching tires and turns taken at sixty miles per hour, and Holt hadn't budged a single bit. He wasn't going to wait. Baxter seemed to agree with her partner; after all, ten minutes could mean the difference between life and death.

Holt reduced speed as he approached the address, while Baxter rummaged through the glove box looking for spare ammo. She found a couple of Glock mags and handed them to him the moment he pulled up at the curb in front of the neighboring house. He grabbed the spare he had tucked under his seat, and said, "You take the back, I'll take the front."

"Let me take the front," Glover said. "No one knows my face, but they might know either of you."

He had a point; Holt let him take the lead on approaching the main door and hid from view behind the corner of the garage, while Baxter tiptoed alongside the six-foot tall masonry wall, careful not to clack her heels and give the perps a warning.

Glover rang the doorbell and waited a moment. They heard heavy footfalls approaching, then a man's hoarse voice said, "Yeah?" as he opened the door.

"Hi," Glover said, smiling and speaking in a friendly voice. "I'm your neighbor across the street," he added, making a gesture toward one of the houses behind him. "I found a wallet with a lot of cash in it, right here, on the sidewalk in front of your house. Is it yours?"

The man stepped outside on the porch, his face lit with interest. He wore a dirty, sleeveless shirt and a pair of shorts that had seen better days. He seemed to have come from the same place that had forged Burch and Huber; same tribal tats, same muscle, same attitude, even the same shaved scalp.

"Where is it?"

"Right there, at the curb," Glover replied, pointing toward the gutter.

He barely took two steps toward the curb, when Holt jumped him from behind and grabbed him in a chokehold, while Glover stuck the muzzle of his gun against the man's cheek.

"Don't breathe; don't make a sound," Holt said, then cuffed his hands behind his back. "How many more inside?"

"Go fuck yourself, asshole," he hissed, and then tried to headbutt Holt. He was quick to react and got out of the way, then hauled the perp to the SUV and locked him in the back.

Glover entered the house first, followed by Holt, while Baxter kept an eye on the outside perimeter, in case anyone wanted to take the back exit, jump the fence, and run. They checked the living room and the kitchen, but found no one, no sign that Meredith was there.

Holt noticed something on the small table by the door and pointed it out to Glover. Five playing cards, fanned out face down, as if the player had left them there after being interrupted during a game.

Somewhere inside the house, the man's card-playing partners were waiting for him to come back.

They looked at each other, agreeing without words to change their strategy. From that moment, they'd both enter a room, training two guns on the potential targets waiting behind closed doors.

They took positions left and right of the first room, guns in hand, their nerves taut, ready to pull the trigger at the first sign of danger. Holt turned the knob gently, quietly, then pushed the door open when it had cleared the latch bolt. No one was there; it was a bedroom that stank of sweat and dirty feet, the bed slept in and the sheets dirty. They pulled out, closing the door quietly, and approached the next room.

That's when Holt heard her scream. He recognized Meredith's voice, and it gutted him. He wanted to bolt toward the source of the sound, but Glover had already grabbed his hand. "No," he mouthed. "Do this right, one room at a time."

They took positions left and right of the next door, Holt's face scrunched with rage. Glover opened the door, then cleared the room in one quick sweep. That left only one other room on that floor, then the three upstairs, where Meredith's screams were coming from.

They quickly cleared the remaining room and headed upstairs, carefully climbing the carpeted steps, aware that a squeak might give them away. Holt had a few more steps to go, when another shriek came from the farthest bedroom, followed by the sound of a slap that ended her wails. A roar of laughter erupted from the second bedroom, and a man's lewd voice, commenting, "That cop's little bitch is getting it good." Then he joined the others in their roaring cackles.

"Three voices," Holt mouthed toward Glover. The fed raised his thumb, then took position in front of the door.

Holt was about to turn the knob when the door opened, and a black man came out yelling, "Yo, Jimmy!" Then he froze when he found himself staring at two guns, but only for a moment. "Cops," he yelled before Holt could shove him against the wall and silence him.

Then all hell broke loose.

The two other men who'd been drinking beer and playing cards had their pieces within reach and went for them lightning fast. Glover shot one in the leg as he lunged toward the door, but then had to withdraw to avoid the spewing bullets coming from the other one. The perp he'd shot in the leg started firing too, and Holt couldn't do much other than take the occasional blind shot, keeping his body shielded behind the wall and sneaking his armed hand in the door opening, then quickly pulling back.

Holt pistol-whipped the first man who'd come out of the room; the massive individual fell to the ground as if someone had cut his knees, completely inert. He rushed to the last bedroom, where he'd heard Meredith's screams coming from. He kicked the door open, then froze.

He recognized the Latino man holding a gun to Meredith's head; he'd put him in jail a few years back, for a felony assault charge against a minor. He was a rough, cruel brute who hadn't been charged with aggravated sexual assault because the victim had recanted, afraid she'd be forced to testify in open court. His belt was loose and his zipper halfway down. The man, standing close behind her, had one hand around Meredith's shoulders, and the other held a gun against her temple.

"Daddy," Meredith whimpered, "I knew you'd find me."

"Yeah, Daddy, remember me?" the man said, grinning widely and licking his lips nervously.

"Sure, I remember you, Marco," he replied. "I'd never forget a piece of scum like you. Now let my kid go, and we'll talk this through."

He tightened his grip on Meredith, who yelped. "Put your gun down, or I'll paint these walls with your daughter's brains," he replied, his grin now a snarl, showing a few missing teeth.

"Shoot him, Daddy," Meredith cried, "shoot him!"

Marco laughed. "Yeah, shoot me, but it will be too damn late. What's it going to be, Daddy?" Then his snarly grin disappeared, turning suddenly to a scowl. "Drop that fucking gun, or I'll shoot her, I swear."

Holt listened to the gunfire still carrying on behind him and understood Glover wasn't going to help him anytime soon. The rash of firing bullets had thinned, but there was at least one active shooter down the hall, keeping Glover busy.

He looked at Meredith's tearful eyes and saw a fierce determination. Whatever they'd done to his little girl since she'd been taken, her spirit had not been broken.

"Yeah, I'll drop the gun, but what guarantees do I have that you won't shoot my kid anyway?" he asked Marco, stalling for time. Marco mumbled something, but Holt didn't pay any attention. He looked at Meredith again and said gently, "Everything will be all right, Mer. Remember what I taught you?"

She nodded vigorously, then started mouthing words he could lip-read, but

Marco couldn't see from his vantage point.

"One, two, three," she mouthed, then let herself fall inert, as if she'd fainted, a trick her dad had taught her a few years back. Her unexpectedly limp body created enough confusion and put enough distance between her head and Marco's gun for Holt to take the shot.

He squeezed the trigger once but heard two shots, two bullets ripping through Marco's skull. With her smoking gun still reeling from the recoil, Baxter stood by his side, like she'd been there for him every moment since he'd met her.

Holt rushed and picked Meredith up in his arms, "Mer, baby, it's over now," he said, burying his face in her hair. "The other shooters?" he asked Baxter.

"All down, permanently," she replied. "Glover's been shot in the shoulder, but he'll live." She dug through the closet and pulled out a blanket, wrapping it around Meredith's shivering body. "Glover called it in already, it won't be much longer until EMS gets here."

Holt carried his daughter in his arms, afraid to ask how badly she'd been hurt, afraid to know. The street had been filled with law enforcement vehicles' flashing lights, and two ambulances were pulling in. The medics pulled out their medical kits and a gurney.

He set her down gently on the gurney, still holding on to her hand, thankful he'd arrived in time, grateful she was still alive. She refused to lie down and remained sitting, tightening the blanket around her body and looking straight at him through a thinning veil of tears. He didn't see anything but courage in her eyes, a courage he never knew she had in her.

Driven by SA Rosales, a black sedan with grille-embedded flashers pulled right behind the ambulance, and his ex-wife climbed out before it had come to a complete stop. She rushed to the gurney and grabbed her daughter's hand, then hugged her tightly, rocking her back and forth as if she were an infant.

"Meredith, my baby," she said between tears.

Then she looked at Holt and said, "Thank you," still pressing Meredith's head against her chest.

The medics loaded the gurney onto the bus, and it was soon set in motion. Holt looked around, feeling the immense exhaustion of the past two days hitting him with a crushing wave of numbness, now that his daughter had been found and the adrenaline was wearing off. He checked on Glover, who was being patched up in the back of the second ambo, then looked for Baxter.

She stood to the side, leaning against a car and checking her phone. She looked at him with an unmistakable urgency in her eyes and handed Holt her phone to see for himself. There was a message from Fletcher that froze the blood in his veins.

The birdman had sent new coordinates; his precious vultures were circling again.

43

Death's Playground

Mindy shook violently in the cold, January wind blowing across the Mojave expanse, the gusts lifting and carrying dust and dry yucca leaves in small, localized whirlwinds. Her bare legs were as cold as ice and starting to turn blue, and she could barely feel her toes. She crouched to the ground, hugging her knees, unable to take her eyes off Homeboy.

She knew she'd die today; she'd heard Snowman give the order himself, showing immense contempt for her and calling her a waste of time and a good-for-nothing piece of trash. She welcomed death, the bringer of peace and the end of her suffering, and, in the face of the Grim Reaper, she felt serene and liberated, ready to receive the forgiving bullet.

But she'd never imagined this.

The drive in the back of Homeboy's SUV, a few miles southwest of the city, then another few miles across the uneven, rocky terrain of the Mojave. The threats he made, making her realize her hell wasn't over yet. It was just beginning, out there, in the desert, where no one could ever hear her scream.

She'd been at Homeboy's mercy before and knew what he could do. Back then, she'd hoped he'd grow tired of her, maybe he'd choose someone else to satisfy his urges, maybe Snowman or his other men would stop him. Nothing like that had happened, and her tormentor had returned to her again and again, each time more violent, more sadistic, making her wish she'd be dead already.

But death doesn't come when it's summoned. No, it sits back and laughs in the face of those invoking its mercy, because it has none.

She'd cried until she ran out of tears, her pleading sobs ridiculed, her wails nothing but an aphrodisiac for her captor. Then she'd fallen silent, watching in horror Homeboy's preparation for what he'd called, "a night to remember."

He took a couple of gulps from a flask, then resumed work on what seemed to be the digging of a shallow grave. If it was that shallow, maybe she could dig herself out after he'd gone. He wasn't going to kill her now; he'd already shattered that hope. No, he was going to play with her for days, if she were to believe him.

That thought sent new shivers down her spine and the urge to scream and scream. She'd done that before and no one had heard her; no one heard Homeboy's roars of laughter either.

But she wouldn't last that long, not in the cold, barefoot and almost naked, wearing only a short-sleeved T-shirt and panties. She remembered a scene from a movie she'd seen recently, about people who fight for survival in arctic conditions; they mustn't fall asleep or death will come sooner.

That's what she needed to do... fall asleep and never wake up again.

The shadows grew longer, then vanished, the desert twilight a quick and purple-hued transition from day to night. In the falling darkness, the grave he was digging terrified her, fear clasping its claw around her throat, squeezing until she couldn't breathe anymore.

He dropped the shovel and walked to the car, grinning at her and licking his lips with a lewd glint in his eyes. He returned with a piece of tarp he laid on the ground, a black shroud for her untimely burial.

Then he came for her.

"No, no," she whimpered, feeling tears burning her eyes and blurring her vision. "Please, no."

He grabbed her arm and forced her to stand, pressing her body between his groin and the hood of his vehicle. He pulled a small bottle from his pocket and, with an eyedropper, extracted a few drops of liquid, and then he grabbed her face and forced her lips open. She fought him as best she could, but she was no match for him. Her mouth was forced open and the liquid dripped into the back of her throat. He forced her head upward, and her mouth closed until she swallowed a few times, and then he let her go.

He took a step back, and, in the darkening crepuscule, he looked at her with avid eyes, while slowly undoing his belt. When she whimpered quietly, his grin widened, and his hand plunged to free himself.

Numbness took over Mindy's body and she screamed, knowing it was useless and no one would hear, stunned that all the effort she made to scream didn't even produce the tiniest sound. The paralysis spread through her entire body, leaving her mind intact, her fears exacerbated. Her knees gave way and she fell, willing her hands to reach for support, to grab onto the SUV's front bumper, but failing, feeling herself falling as if she were watching a strange movie in slow motion.

She fell hard onto the ground, sharp-edged rocks cutting her flesh, her head bouncing as if she were a rag doll. Then her fallen body finally settled; all she could hear was the howling wind and Homeboy's satisfied groan.

And something else, distant, barely intelligible. Perhaps it was her weary mind, playing tricks on her. Possibly she was dreaming, an attempt to escape her brutal reality.

"Step away from that girl," a man's voice commanded. "Put your hands up and step away, now."

Homeboy hesitated a little, looking at her, then at something in the distance, and then reached for the gun he carried in his shoulder holster. She heard two, distant, popping sounds and bullets shearing through the air, then Homeboy's body landed hard on the ground next to her, his eyes wide open, looking into hers, his blood sprayed on her face.

Now she could sleep.

44

Terms

"All right, thanks, Jennifer," Holt said and ended the call with a long sigh of relief and, for a moment, he kept his eyes closed. He sat on the boulder by my side and patted my knee. "She's okay," he said, his voice breaking, barely above a whisper. "Meredith's okay."

"She wasn't…" I asked, not able to fully articulate the question.

"No," he replied quickly, letting another breath of air leave his lungs. "She was roughed up though, and the doctor said she's dehydrated and malnourished, but thankfully, they didn't touch her. We got to her just in time."

I listened to the howling winds rushing across the desert, focused on the stars that were coming out, barely visible against the powerful lights deployed in a circle by the Crime Scene Unit. The rescue helicopter had just taken off, raising a cloud of dust that was yet to settle. When she woke, Mindy would be surrounded by family and friends, starting her journey to healing. It wasn't going to be an easy road, but she was going to live; she was strong, a fighter, a survivor.

All in all, an excellent end to the day.

I was so tired, I couldn't move. I just sat there on the cold boulder by Holt's side, knowing that at some point I'd have to haul it back home and get into bed. I still had a few loose ends to worry about.

The fifteen girls who worked the Strip, carrying embedded microchips in their arms, were Snowman's sex slaves. I was aware that cops were locating them and picking them up one by one, the moment they stepped away from the Strip hotels, as their tracker chips showed motion. Many families would be reunited with their missing children tonight.

Then there were the two thugs I'd left bound to a shelf in the plumbing store warehouse. Their fate was still up in the air.

Holt dissipated those thoughts when he grabbed my hand, seeping heat into my frozen fingers.

"Can you live with what I've done?" he asked, his voice calm, accepting.

I looked at him for a moment, his eyes, dark and intense, having the same effect as always, sending a rush of mixed emotions in a rampage through my brain. Everything I'd been so worked up about before seemed like ages ago, inconsequential, trivial, almost forgotten.

I nodded a few times before speaking. "Yeah... Can you?"

He looked at the desert soil for a moment, then back into my eyes. "Yes, I can."

One question swirled through my mind, now that we were safe, that his daughter was safe. My partner knew all my secrets, and I had no idea what he felt about that. Did he feel betrayed? Was our vicious circle of distrust finally broken?

I had to ask, although I feared the answer and the loneliness it could bring. "Can we still be partners, after—"

"Ah, there you are," Anne interrupted, rushing toward us with her medical kit.

"Yes, we can," I heard Holt reply to my unfinished question, and I smiled.

She crouched in front of us and shone a flashlight into my eyes, one at a time. "Any concussions, broken bones, anything I should know about?"

I squinted, the ray of light piercing and inflicting physical pain, sharp needles of burning ache in my skull. "I'm fine," I replied, "just tired, hungry, and my feet are killing me. Why are you here?"

"I heard the Dispatch call and wanted to check on you," she replied, then gave me a quick smooch on my cheek. "All right. You're good to go."

She moved over to Holt, and did her flashlight torture, taking more time with him, focused on his left eye, the one that was still black and blue and swollen. She examined the bruises on his forehead, then turned toward me with amusement in her eyes.

"Makeup?" she asked, rubbing the tips of her fingers together.

I sighed. "Long story."

"Share it sometime, all right? Should be one for the books."

She asked Holt about broken bones and painful parts of his body, and he lied like the brave son of a bitch he was. I needed to catch my breath a little, and then I'd get him to the hospital to get checked out, even if I had to use a couple of drops of modified tetrodotoxin to get that done. A crime scene tech was carefully packing the bottle, only a few yards away. It wouldn't be too hard to swipe.

Anne rose to her feet, the medical kit in her hand, ready to leave. I reached out and squeezed her other hand, suddenly tearful without cause. I turned away to hide my tears from Holt, from her, knowing I was probably too bloody tired to hold myself together. Keen on my state of mind as always, Anne gave me another clinically scrutinizing gaze and reluctantly walked away, just as the two people I really didn't want to see that night approached at high speed in a UTV.

The vehicle came to a stop a few feet away. Captain Morales was the first to climb out, followed by Lieutenant Steenstra, visibly infuriated to find herself in the desert that late at night.

"Baxter, Holt," Morales said, "we knew we'd find you here."

"Yeah, before you disappeared again," Steenstra said coldly. "You broke so many rules I don't even know where to start."

"Special circumstances, Lieutenant," Morales said, raising his hands in a pacifying gesture.

She pressed her lips together and gave us a stare as if we were in tenth grade, caught smoking behind the gym. "I expect a full report on my desk from both of you by Monday morning. Start with why you had to abandon your phones and use burners and continue with how you coerced an analyst to break protocol and help you off the record."

I looked at Holt, and both of us smiled. That nuisance was nothing, compared to what we'd been through.

Steenstra looked at Morales, infuriated probably because he wasn't siding with her.

"What's this I'm hearing, you went undercover in an unsanctioned deployment, then had the nerve to send word to me to make it ongoing? Since when am I working for you, taking orders from you, Detective Baxter? This is unbelievable."

She was the usual bitch I knew so well, but I had no energy to argue. "It was a kind request from one distressed cop to a ranking officer, nothing else," I clarified, then stopped short of saying anything else. Instead, I stood with a groan, my feet unhappy to be put to work again, and looked her in the eye. "Yes, I've gone undercover, taking a huge risk, because I saw an opening to catch a serial killer and find Holt's daughter."

She didn't flinch, but my gaze didn't falter either. "And I'm going back," I announced.

Everyone started talking at the same time.

"What? No," Morales reacted. "You're not going anywhere but home, to bed."

"In your dreams, Baxter," Steenstra replied coldly. "I could always fire you, so don't push it."

"Baxter, no," Holt whispered, his fingers touching mine in passing.

My partner's plea was the hardest to ignore.

"Yesterday about this time, a girl jumped off the terrace of my hotel room because she was too terrified of what would happen to the other girls if she talked. Do you think I've stopped thinking of her? I don't think I'll ever be able to forget her."

"And we're on it, Baxter," Morales said. "Your three-day adventure left us with a pile of cases to work, all excellent leads, great police work."

"Like what?" Holt asked, still frowning.

"Like those predators who meet with underage girls and pay for sex in West Flamingo Park," he replied. "Forgot about them? Because we didn't; we're casting a net so wide the pervs will wish they were never anywhere near Las Vegas."

Holt looked at me visibly confused; he wasn't there for the conversation I'd had with Heidi, and I hadn't had the chance to bring him up to speed. I just shook my head quickly and whispered, "Never mind, it's all good." Then I turned toward Steenstra. "I have the unique opportunity to infiltrate this organization at the top level—"

"Yeah, yeah," Steenstra cut me off, "I heard you the first time."

"What?" I reacted.

"I was there when you told Glover to pass me the message," she said, staring at me firmly, not condemning, but not encouraging either. "Yes, I know exactly what you can and cannot do."

"And?" I asked, propping my hands on my thighs, ready to argue with her some more. A new flush of adrenaline had dissipated some of my weariness, leaving me ready for a deathmatch with my IAB nemesis.

"And I believe your idea has potential, but it needs prep. You can't just show up in the middle of a drug-dealing, sex trafficking organization and announce candidly, 'Hey, I'm your new boss.' You're going to get killed, and fast."

"Baxter, this is not how undercover work is done," Holt added. "I've been there—"

I grabbed Holt's arm. "Haven't you seen me in action? Huh? Wasn't I getting them to eat from the palm of my hand?"

He rubbed his forehead with his fingers as if willing a headache to go away. "Yeah, maybe. But there are issues you need to sort through. Your background. The people you'd work with—"

"Only you," I said quickly, then looked at Steenstra and Morales. "I'd only work with Holt. I don't trust anyone else."

"Okay," Morales said, taking one step closer to me in our tiny circle. "Let's say we embrace this crazy idea of yours for a moment."

"Thanks, Captain," I said quickly.

"Hypothetically," he underlined, glaring at me for a brief moment. "How long would you stay under? What kind of support will you need? Because we're not going about this in any traditional way, I'm assuming you have a plan."

I nodded, then swallowed with difficulty. I was thirsty, my throat dry from desert winds carrying the fine dust from which there was no escape.

"I'd start with the two perps I left tied up at the plumbing store. I'd buy their loyalty, then have them tell the rest of the organization. I'd bring in a couple of my people, straight from Colombia, so to speak, whatever Spanish-speaking officers would be interested in this assignment. Under the ruse of preparing for Don's visit and the naming of a successor for Snowman, I'd be speaking with the lieutenants, finding every one of them, and learning how they move product."

The three of them stared at me as if I'd just broken loose from the loony bin.

"Listen, guys, we cleaned Snowman's organization tonight. The top levels are gone, except those two losers I left tied up at the plumbing store. The worst is done, over. All I need is a little more information about how they move the product and how they sell the girls. Then I'm back."

Silence ensued, the only sounds were the howling wind and the distant noises of the Crime Scene unit going about their business, getting ready to wrap up and leave. I didn't insist further; I let them mull it over for a while, too tired to speak.

"We'll need time to think about this," Steenstra said. "For now, you'll go—"

"How about those two at the store?" I asked. "They're critical assets for my plan."

Steenstra groaned and threw her arms in the air. "How's this? We arrest them tonight, then, if you're approved, you'll post their bail and look like a superhero. If not, they'll rot in jail where they belong."

"That means you're considering it?"

Steenstra looked at Morales before speaking. "Only for forty-eight hours, then we pull you out with whatever intel you get."

"Keep one convict, Pedro Reyes, in solitary with no phone access until I'm back, okay?" I said to Holt, and he nodded.

"Isn't that your husband's—" he started to ask.

"Yeah, him."

I looked at Steenstra; she was shaking her head, her gaze cold, unforgiving. I couldn't tell what she was thinking, and I was surprised to realize how little I cared.

Because I knew who I was, what made me tick.

I'm Laura Baxter, an American who swears like a Brit. This morning I was a Las Vegas homicide cop. Tomorrow, I might become Olivia Gaines, the interim boss of all Las Vegas crime.

Whatever may be, I'll be ready for it.

I smiled and looked at Holt, whose dark eyes burned, loaded with an emotion that stirred me in ways I didn't think my body could handle after the past few days. I was ready to go home.

"What next, Lieutenant?" I asked, eager to get going.

"We'll clean up your mess, arrest the store thugs, put Reyes in solitary, collect all the bodies you scattered across town," Morales replied. "Tomorrow we'll talk about this some more. But for now, get out of here and go home, straight to bed."

I bit my lip to contain a highly inappropriate smile. "You got it, Cap."

A few moments later, we were gone, leaving them in a cloud of fine desert dust. When the highway lights became visible in the distance, Holt slowed a little and looked at me with a mischievous grin.

"I hate it when the brass gives unclear orders," he said, his sultry voice sending heatwaves through my blood.

"What's unclear?" I asked.

"Your place or mine?"

~~ The End ~~

Read on for previews from:

Dawn Girl:
A short-fused FBI Agent who hides a terrible secret. A serial killer you won't see coming. A heart-stopping race to catch him.

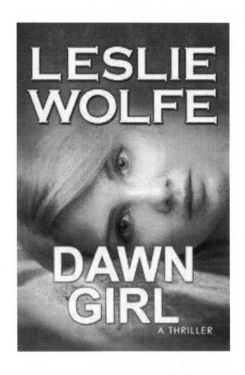

~~~~~~~~

Thank You!

A big, heartfelt thank you for choosing to read my book. If you enjoyed it, please take a moment to leave me a four or five-star review; I would be very grateful. It doesn't need to be more than a couple of words, and it makes a huge difference. This is your link: http://bit.ly/LVCThrill.

Join my mailing list to receive special offers, exclusive bonus content, and news about upcoming new releases. Log on to www.WolfeNovels.com to sign up, or email me at LW@WolfeNovels.com.

Did you enjoy Baxter and Holt? Would you like to see them again in another Las Vegas crime story? Your thoughts and feedback are very valuable to me. Please contact me directly through one of the channels listed below. Email works best: LW@WolfeNovels.com or use the button below:

Connect with Me

Email: LW@WolfeNovels.com
Facebook: https://www.facebook.com/wolfenovels
Web: www.WolfeNovels.com
Leslie's Amazon Web Store: http://bit.ly/WolfeAll

Books by Leslie Wolfe

BAXTER & HOLT SERIES

Las Vegas Girl
Casino Girl
Las Vegas Crime

TESS WINNETT SERIES

Dawn Girl
The Watson Girl
Glimpse of Death
Taker of Lives

STANDALONE NOVELS

Stories Untold

ALEX HOFFMANN SERIES

Executive
Devil's Move
The Backup Asset
The Ghost Pattern
Operation Sunset

For the complete list of Leslie Wolfe's novels, visit:
Wolfenovels.com/order

Preview: *Dawn Girl*

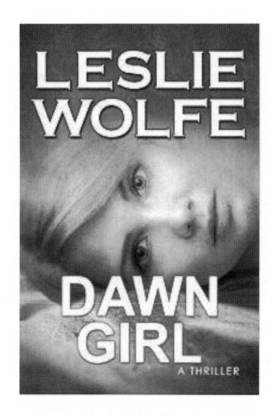

1

Ready

She made an effort to open her eyes, compelling her heavy eyelids to obey. She swallowed hard, her throat raw and dry, as she urged the wave of nausea to subside. Dizzy and confused, she struggled to gain awareness. Where was she? She felt numb and shaky, unable to move, as if awakening from a deep sleep or a coma. She tried to move her arms, but couldn't. Something kept her immobilized, but didn't hurt her. Or maybe she couldn't feel the pain, not anymore.

Her eyes started to adjust to the darkness, enough to distinguish the man moving quietly in the room. His silhouette flooded her foggy brain with a wave of memories. She gasped, feeling her throat constrict and burning tears rolling down her swollen cheeks.

Her increased awareness sent waves of adrenaline through her body, and she tried desperately to free herself from her restraints. With each useless effort, she panted harder, gasping for air, forcing it into her lungs. Fear put a strong chokehold on her throat and was gaining ground, as she rattled her restraints helplessly, growing weaker with every second. She felt a wave of darkness engulf her, this time the darkness coming from within her weary brain. She fought against that darkness, and battled her own betraying body.

The noises she made got the man's attention.

"I see you're awake. Excellent," the man said, without turning.

She watched him place a syringe on a small, metallic tray. Its handle clinked, followed by another sound, this time the raspy, telling sound of a file cutting through the neck of a glass vial. Then a pop when the man opened the vial. He grabbed the syringe and loaded the liquid from the vial, then carefully removed any air, pushing the piston until several droplets of fluid came out.

Dizziness overtook her, and she closed her eyes for a second.

"Shit," the man mumbled, then opened a drawer and went through it in a hurry.

She felt the needle poke deeply in her thigh, like it was happening to another person. She felt it, but distantly. She perceived a subdued burning sensation where he pushed the fluid into her muscle, then that went away when he pulled the needle out. She closed her weary eyes again, listless against her restraints.

The man cracked open ammonia salts under her nose, and she bounced back into reality at the speed of a lightning strike, aware, alert, and angry. For a second she fought to free herself, but froze when her eyes focused on the man in front of her.

He held a scalpel, close to her face. In itself, the small, shiny, silver object was capable of bringing formidable healing, as well as immense pain. The difference stood in the hand wielding it. She knew no healing was coming her way; only pain.

"No, no, please…" she pleaded, tears falling freely from her puffy eyes, burning as they rolled down her cheeks. "Please, no. I… I'll do anything."

"I am ready," the man said. He seemed calm, composed, and dispassionate. "Are you ready?"

"No, no, please…" she whimpered.

"Yeah," he said softly, almost whispering, inches away from her face. "Please say no to me. I love that."

She fell quiet, scared out of her mind. This time was different. *He* was different.

2

Dawn

"What if we get caught?" the girl whispered, trailing behind the boy.

They walked briskly on the small residential street engulfed in darkness, keeping to the middle of the road. There were no sidewalks. High-end homes lined up both sides, most likely equipped with sensor floodlights they didn't want to trip.

She tugged at his hand, but he didn't stop. "You never care about these things, Carl, but I do. If we get caught, I'll be grounded, like, forever!"

The boy kept going, his hand firmly clasping hers.

"Carl!" she raised the pitch in her whisper, letting her anxiety show more.

He stopped and turned, facing her. He frowned a little, seeing her anguish, but then smiled and caressed a loose strand of hair rebelling from under her sweatshirt's hood.

"There's no one, Kris. No one's going to see us. See? No lights are on, nothing. Everyone's asleep. Zee-zee-zee. It's five in the morning."

"I know," she sighed, "but—"

He kissed her pouted lips gently, a little boyish hesitation and awkwardness in his move.

"We'll be okay, I promise," he said, then grabbed her hand again. "We're almost there, come on. You'll love it."

A few more steps and the small street ended into the paved parking lot of what was going to be a future development of sorts, maybe a shopping center. From there, they had to cross Highway 1. They crouched down near the road, waiting for the light traffic to be completely clear. They couldn't afford to be seen, not even from a distance. At the right moment, they crossed the highway, hand in hand, and cut across the field toward the beach. Crossing Ocean Drive was next, then cutting through a few yards of shrubbery and trees to get to the sandy beach.

"Jeez, Carl," Kris protested, stopping in her tracks at the tree line. "Who knows what creatures live here? There could be snakes. Lizards. Gah…"

"There could be, but there aren't," Carl replied, seemingly sure of himself. "Trust me."

She held her breath and lowered her head, then clasped Carl's hand tightly. He turned on the flashlight on his phone and led the way without hesitation. A few seconds later, they reached the beach, and Kris let out a tense, long breath.

The light of the waning gibbous Moon reflected against the calm ocean waves, sending flickers of light everywhere and covering the beach in silver shadows. They were completely alone. The only creatures keeping them company were pale crabs that took bellicose stances when Kris and Carl stomped the sand around them, giggling.

"See? Told you," Carl said, "no one's going to see us out here. We can do whatever we want," he said playfully.

Kris squealed and ran toward the lifeguard tower. In daylight, the tower showed its bright yellow and orange, a splash of joyful colors on the tourist-abundant stretch of sand. At night, the structure appeared gloomy, resembling a menacing creature on tall, insect-like legs.

"It looks like one of those aliens from *War of the Worlds*," Kris said, then promptly started running, waving her arms up in the air, pretending she was flying.

Carl chased Kris, laughing and squealing with her, running in circles around the tower, and weaving footstep patterns between the solid wood posts.

"Phew," Carl said, stopping his chase and taking some distance. "Stinks of piss. Let's get out of here."

"Eww…" Kris replied, following him. "Why do men do that?"

"What? Pee?"

"Everybody pees, genius," Kris replied, still panting from the run. "Peeing where it stinks and bothers people, that's what I meant. Women pee in the bushes. Men should pee in the water if they don't like the bushes."

"Really? That's gross."

"Where do you think fish pee? At least the waves would wash away the pee and it wouldn't stink, to mess up our sunrise."

"Fish pee?" Carl pushed back, incredulous.

"They don't?"

They walked holding hands, putting a few more yards of distance between them and the tower. Then Carl suddenly dropped to the ground, dragging Kris with him. She squealed again, and laughed.

"Let's sit here," he said. "The show's on. Let's see if we get a good one."

The sky was starting to light up toward the east. They watched silently, hand in hand, as the dark shades of blue and gray gradually turned ablaze, mixing in dark reds and orange hues. The horizon line was clear, a sharp edge marking where ocean met sky.

"It's going to be great," Carl said. "No clouds, no haze." He kissed her lips quickly, and then turned his attention back to the celestial light show.

"You're a strange boy, Carl."

"Yeah? Why?"

"Other boys would have asked me to sneak out in the middle of the night to make out. With you, it's a sunrise, period. Should I worry?"

Carl smiled widely, then tickled Kris until she begged for mercy between gasps of air and bouts of uncontrollable laughter.

"Stop! Stop it already. I can't breathe!"

"I might want to get on with that make out, you know," Carl laughed.

"Nah, it's getting light. Someone could see us," Kris pushed back, unconvinced. "Someone could come by."

Carl shrugged and turned his attention to the sunrise. He grabbed her hand and held it gently, playing with her fingers.

Almost half the sky had caught fire, challenging the moonlight, and obliterating most of its reflected light against the blissful, serene, ocean waves.

Carl checked the time on his phone.

"A few more minutes until it comes out," he announced, sounding serious, as if predicting a rare and significant event. He took a few pictures of the sky, then suddenly snapped one of Kris.

"Ah… no," she reacted, "give that to me right this second, Carl." She grabbed the phone from his hand and looked at the picture he'd taken. The image showed a young girl with messy, golden brown hair, partially covering a scrunched, tense face with deep ridges on her brow. The snapshot revealed Kris biting her index fingernail, totally absorbed by the process, slobbering her sleeve cuff while at it.

"God-awful," she reacted, then pressed the option to delete.

"No!" Carl said, pulling the phone from her hands. "I like it!"

"There's nothing to like. There," she said, relaxing a little, and arranging her hair briefly with her long, thin fingers. "I'll pose for you." She smiled.

Carl took a few pictures. She looked gorgeous, against the backdrop of fiery skies, pink sand, and turquoise water. He took image after image, as she got into it and made faces, danced, and swirled in front of him, laughing.

The sun's first piercing ray shot out of the sea, just as Kris shrieked, a blood-curdling scream that got Carl to spring to his feet and run to her.

Speechless, Kris pointed a trembling hand at the lifeguard tower. Underneath the tower, between the wooden posts supporting the elevated structure, was the naked body of a young woman. She appeared to be kneeling, as if praying to the rising sun. Her hands were clasped together in front of her in the universal, unmistakable gesture of silent pleading.

Holding their breaths, they approached carefully, curious and yet afraid of what they stood to discover. The growing light of the new morning revealed more details with each step they took. Her back, covered in bruises and small cuts, stained in smudged, dried blood. Her blue eyes wide open, glossed over. A few specks of sand clung to her long, dark lashes. Her beautiful face, immobile, covered in sparkling flecks of sand. Her lips slightly parted, as if to let a last breath escape. Long, blonde hair, wet from sea spray, almost managed to disguise the deep cut in her neck.

No blood dripped from the wound; her heart had stopped beating for some time. Yet she held upright, unyielding in her praying posture, her knees stuck firmly in the sand covered in their footprints, and her eyes fixed on the beautiful sunrise they came to enjoy.

~~~End Preview~~~

Like *Dawn Girl?*

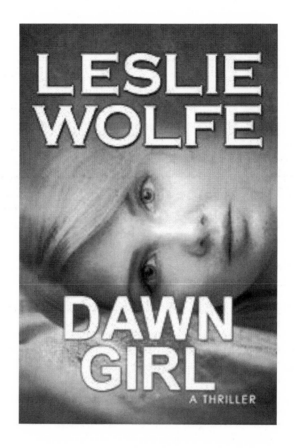

Read it now!

About the Author

Leslie Wolfe is a bestselling author whose novels break the mold of traditional thrillers. She creates unforgettable, brilliant, strong women heroes who deliver fast-paced, satisfying suspense, backed up by extensive background research in technology and psychology.

Leslie released the first novel, *Executive*, in October 2011. It was very well received, including inquiries from Hollywood. Since then, Leslie published numerous novels and enjoyed growing success and recognition in the marketplace. Among Leslie's most notable works, *The Watson Girl* (2017) was recognized for offering a unique insight into the mind of a serial killer and a rarely seen first person account of his actions, in a dramatic and intense procedural thriller.

A complete list of Leslie's titles is available at https://wolfenovels.com/order.

Leslie enjoys engaging with readers every day and would love to hear from you.

Become an insider: gain early access to previews of Leslie's new novels.

- **Email: LW@WolfeNovels.com**
- Like Leslie's Facebook page: https://www.facebook.com/wolfenovels
- Visit Leslie's website for the latest news: www.WolfeNovels.com
- Visit Leslie's Amazon Web Store: http://bit.ly/WolfeAll

Contents

Acknowledgments 3
Silent Screams 5
Gone 8
The Call 12
The Ex 16
School...20
Casey 25
Vultures 31
Visit 34
Request 39
Crime Scene 43
News...47
Warehouse 51
Feds 55
Autopsy 60
Bad News 64
Lies 69
Heidi 73
Snitch..79
Captive..84
Immersion...88
Two Cases 93
Another...97
Lessons 102
Cocaine...105
Resources..111
Gear 116
Fear Factor..122
Lust...127

Exchange 130
Collaboration 134
Territories 137
Internal 140
Inmate 145
Building Olivia 150
The Meet 155
Raid 160
Ransom 164
Help 169
Games 175
Jailbreak 181
Incentives 187
Meredith 191
Death's Playground 195
Terms 198
Thank You! 204
Connect with Me 204
Books by Leslie Wolfe 205
Preview: *Dawn Girl* 206
About the Author 213

Made in the USA
Columbia, SC
17 January 2019